GABRIEL HUNT

HUNT THROUGH THE CRADLE OF FEAR

D0037369

CHARLES ARDAI

A GABRIEL HUNT NOVEL

HUNT
THROUGH THE
CRADLE OF
FEAR

TITAN BOOKS

Hunt Through the Cradle of Fear
Print edition ISBN: 9781781169902
E-book edition ISBN: 9781781169919

Published by Titan Books
A division of Titan Publishing Group Ltd
144 Southwark Street, London SE1 0UP

First edition: April 2014
1 2 3 4 5 6 7 8 9 10

A CIP catalogue record for this title is available from the British Library.

Printed and bound in the United States.

www.huntforadventure.com

Did you enjoy this book?
We love to hear from our readers. Please email us at readerfeedback@
titanemail.com or write to us at Reader Feedback at the above address.

To receive advance information, news, competitions, and exclusive
offers online, please sign up for the Titan newsletter on our website
www.titanbooks.com

A GABRIEL HUNT NOVEL

HUNT
THROUGH THE
CRADLE OF
FEAR

1

"GO," GABRIEL SHOUTED, AND HE FIRED ONCE MORE INTO the pack of men racing toward them. It was his last bullet and it found its mark, dropping a burly Magyar in a fringed vest before the man could take Gabriel's head off with a two-handed swing of his sword. The curved blade fell from the man's hand as he spun and collapsed; it slid along the stone floor until Gabriel stopped it with his foot. A scimitar, three feet from hilt to point if it was an inch, the steel tarnished but still deadly enough. Gabriel transferred his Colt to his left hand and scooped the sword up with his right. Unless they'd kept count, they didn't know the gun was out of bullets, so keeping it in view might still do some good.

"Go," he said again, shooting a glance over his shoulder toward the stone wall where Sheba crouched, clutching the shreds of her dress to her chest. "Now!"

"I can't just leave you—"

"I'll be right behind you."

"There are too many for you to fight alone!"

There were. But having to keep an eye on Sheba didn't make things any easier. Gabriel feinted with the sword, then smashed it broadside against the face of a squat, muscular man who'd stepped forward in an aikido stance. He planted a boot in the man's midsection and shoved, toppling him backwards into one of his cohorts.

Gabriel took two rapid steps back, felt the stone of the low wall against his legs. Sheba was beside him. She'd made the mistake of glancing down and now looked terrified.

"Just grab hold and keep your eyes closed," Gabriel said.

With trembling hands she reached up for the shuttle locked onto the metal cable overhead. The inch-wide metal strand descended at a steep angle from the turret above them to the treeline far below. She slid one wrist through each of the padded loops and took hold of the handgrips, releasing the lock. "Please," she whispered, "be care—"

Gabriel shoved her off the wall. Her screams echoed as gravity pulled her down along the cable, loud at first, then quieter and quieter still. In the distance they heard branches crack and foliage cushion a fall.

He smiled at the two men in front of him and the three more behind them. "All right now, boys, no one else needs to die. She's gone. You can't bring her back."

"On the contrary," came a voice from behind the pack of men, and then Gabriel heard the uneven triplets of Lajos DeGroet's step: slap, slap, click; slap, slap, click. The men parted to either side as the point of DeGroet's iron walking stick appeared between them. "We can and we will. This is no more than a temporary setback."

Gabriel leveled the Colt at DeGroet as the man limped forward. "You might as well put that away, Hunt, unless you plan to throw it at me. I know it's empty."

"How do you know that?" Gabriel said.

"Because you haven't shot me with it yet."

Gabriel considered that for a moment, then returned the gun to his holster, snapped it shut. He kept the scimitar raised and ready to strike—but he didn't swing it. He had some skill with a blade, could even wield an unfamiliar one like this one with some hope of success, but only a fool would try to attack Lajos DeGroet with a sword. A suicidal fool.

"And how, Mr. Hunt, were you proposing to follow your young friend? I do not see a second shuttle on the line anywhere, and if you tried it bare-handed, your palms would be shredded within ten yards."

Without looking behind him, Gabriel climbed up onto the wall, edged over to where the cable ran. His feet were steady, but he was conscious of being only one accidental step away from a three hundred foot plunge. The wind whipped teasingly at his clothes, as though eager to sweep him over the edge.

With his free hand, he unlatched his belt buckle and yanked the belt free. He slung it over the cable, caught the free end as it dropped toward his hand.

"I see," DeGroet said. "Yes. Well. That might work, Mr. Hunt, I suppose, depending on what that belt of yours is made out of. But before you attempt it, you might want to look up."

"Why?" Gabriel said, looking up. He saw a man run up to the edge of the turret, holding in each hand one arm of a gigantic pair of diagonal cutters. He positioned its open blades on either side of the cable.

"*Akarja hogy most csináljam uram?*" the man called, and DeGroet nodded. The blades came together with a snap like the closing of an alligator's jaws. Gabriel let go of his belt just before the end of the cable came snaking past and whipped out into the distance. They could all hear it whistling as it fell and ringing each time it struck the rock face on the way down.

"Now," DeGroet said, "you will put down that weapon and get off the wall and turn yourself over to Mr. Molnar's custody." A bald, round-faced man stared viciously at him and cracked the knuckles on one hand with his other. "I don't promise that he'll treat you gently; you did just kill his brother, after all. But I promise you'll live. You're no use to me dead."

"What makes you think I'll be useful to you alive?" Gabriel said.

"You really don't have a choice, do you?" DeGroet said. He pointed to either side of him with his stick. The five men around him came in closer. Gabriel looked from man to man, from face to face. Molnar's showed the fiercest emotion, but all of them looked as though they'd be glad to tear him limb from limb.

"That's where you're wrong, Lajos," Gabriel said. "There's always another choice." He let the scimitar drop, turned, and hurled himself into space.

2

"WAIT A SECOND," MICHAEL HUNT SAID, HOLDING UP a hand to halt the story of Gabriel's escape from the castle in Hungary. "You jumped off the wall?"

Gabriel shrugged. He was leaning against one of the floor-to-ceiling bookcases in the second-story library of the Hunt Foundation building on Sutton Place. His younger brother's desk was in one corner of the room with an elaborate computer set-up on it and a fancy speakerphone the size of a dinner plate, and both pieces of equipment had lights blinking urgently, no doubt announcing the arrival of messages from all over the world, but Michael was ignoring them. "Explain that to me," he said.

"I jumped," Gabriel said. "Off the wall. What's there to explain?"

"How you survived," Michael said. "You didn't have a parachute on under your jacket, did you?"

Gabriel shook his head. "Come on, Michael. A

parachute? You've watched too many James Bond movies."

"So then how…?"

"Please," Gabriel said. "Do I ask you how you make your arrangements with museums and universities and what-have-you? To transfer objects from one to another, or whatever it is you do all day?"

"You could ask," Michael said. "I'd be glad to tell you."

"Well, I don't. Professional courtesy. A man needs to have a trade secret or two."

"But, Gabriel, a three hundred foot drop—"

"Yes, that is quite a lot, isn't it?" Gabriel grinned. He knew it was driving Michael crazy and wasn't about to let him off the hook a moment sooner than he had to.

"You said the castle overlooked Lake Balaton," Michael said. "Is that it? You dropped three hundred feet into the lake, then swam away?"

"That would have been handy," Gabriel said. "But no. The castle overlooks Lake Balaton from half a mile away. And before you ask, there was no donkey cart passing by at the foot of the mountain either, piled high with mattresses to cushion my fall."

"Gabriel, please, you're making a joke of it, and I'm quite serious. You know I don't like your risking your life on these missions of yours—"

"I do, Michael. I do know that. I'm sorry."

"Bad enough we lost Lucy," he said. "I don't want to lose you, too."

Lucy was their younger sister; she wasn't dead, as far as either of them knew, but neither of them had seen her since she'd struck off for parts unknown at the age of seventeen amid the chaos surrounding what had happened to their parents. Today she'd be twenty-six.

"You won't lose me," Gabriel said.

"So, then, tell me," Michael said, "how did you do it?"

"I'll make you a deal," Gabriel said. "You can keep guessing, and if you guess right, I'll tell you that you did. In the meantime," he said, glancing at his dented Bulova A-11 wristwatch (and fingering the dent gently—it had stopped a bullet once), "I have an appointment with a young lady."

"Sheba?"

"Who else?" Gabriel reached into his pocket and dropped a crumpled wad of receipts on Michael's desk. "You can reach me on the cell phone—but I'd really prefer you didn't. At least for an hour or two."

Michael followed him out into the hall and down the curving grand staircase to the first floor. "Did someone fly underneath you, with a plane or a glider or something of that sort, and catch you as you fell?"

"That's very creative," Gabriel said. "Extremely creative. I'll have to try that next time."

Michael thought for a bit. Finally he said, "You had a second cable, attached to the side of the mountain lower down. One you could grab hold of as you fell past it. A backup in case the first one got cut. That's it, isn't it?"

Gabriel stretched out one hand, took hold of the back of Michael's neck and pulled him forward, planted a kiss on the top of the younger man's head, where his sandy blond hair was starting to thin. "You see, Michael? I'm always careful."

"If you call betting on being able to catch a narrow filament of wire as you fall past it at thirty-two feet per second squared being careful!"

"I do," Gabriel said, and shut the door behind him.

* * *

WALKING WEST ON 55TH STREET AND THEN UPTOWN
on Park Avenue, Gabriel thought about his escape
from Hungary—his and Sheba's, since they'd ridden
out together, first hidden briefly under blankets in the
bed of a truck, then stashed in the crew quarters on
the lower deck of a Romanian trawler on the Danube,
and then finally darting onto a commercial flight back
to the States just as the jetway was detaching from the
plane's fuselage.

As they'd taken their seats, Gabriel had seen,
through the closing door, two pursuers come
skidding to a halt at the ticket counter. They were
pointing furiously toward the jetway and for a
moment he'd worried they might succeed in holding
the flight back. But the door had slammed shut and
the plane had pulled away from the terminal on
schedule, taxied down the runway, and lifted off
without incident. They'd landed without incident,
too, though Gabriel had kept his eyes out for trouble
all the way back to Manhattan. After all, it wasn't
as though DeGroet's men couldn't find out exactly
when and where they'd be landing.

Rather than bring Sheba back to the Hunt
Foundation building, he'd stashed her in his rooms
on the top floor of the Discovers League, a century-old
gentlemen's club devoted to exploration, cartography,
mountaineering, and similar pursuits. It was widely
known that Gabriel was a member—Michael was, too,
and the Foundation had supplied part of the League's
funding for years—but only a handful of people knew
he kept an apartment there. It would hardly be fair to
call it his home since Gabriel spent so little time there,

but he didn't have any *other* home in New York, try as Michael might to convince him to leave at least a toothbrush and some pajamas at the ancestral manse, and it seemed the safest place to keep Sheba hidden from prying eyes.

And whose eyes, exactly, might be prying? Well, DeGroet hadn't given up—that much was clear. The real question was what he'd wanted with her in the first place. Gabriel had questioned Sheba in an attempt to figure this out, but she claimed to have no clue. They'd grabbed her out of the lobby of Goldsmith Hall in Dublin, chloroformed her when she'd fought them, and when she'd woken up she'd been in the cell in Hungary where Gabriel had found her. It was just good luck that Jim Kellen had seen it happen from his office window and had thought first to write down the license number of the van they'd bundled her into and then to phone Gabriel.

But what had DeGroet wanted? Sheba shrugged. He hadn't said.

Had he asked her to *do* anything? No—nothing. He'd asked her a few questions about her thesis—but for heaven's sake, Gabriel (Sheba had demanded, fists on her hips and outrage in her expression), did it really make sense to kidnap a girl if you wanted to ask her about her thesis? Christ's sake, buy her a drink, you won't be able to shut her up.

Gabriel turned onto East 70th Street and returned the wave he got from Hank, the elderly doorman who'd been manning the League's front entrance since well before Gabriel had been born. Hank handed him a cardboard shipping box as he entered and Gabriel recognized his own handwriting on the label. It was the cost of flying commercial. They made you take off your shoes, stow your liquids, pass through metal detectors—no way they'd have let him on board with this baby. He worked a thumbnail through the packing tape as he waited for the League's creaky two-person elevator to descend. An elevator hadn't been part of the building's original design and when the time came to add it later, in the 1920s, the only space they could use for it was a dumbwaiter shaft—which meant riding in a space originally meant for stacks of dishes.

He finally got through the tape as the indicator above the elevator door rotated from '3' to '2' and he removed a crumpled ball of packing paper from the box as it went from '2' to '1.' A bell pinged then and the door slid open.

Inside the narrow elevator, a man with a gun was holding Sheba with one arm around her throat and the other around her waist. She was struggling, wrenching against him. They both noticed Gabriel at the same time.

"Step back or she gets it," the man said, angling his gun to point at the underside of Sheba's chin.

Gabriel reached into the box, pulled out his Colt, thumbed back the hammer, and shot the man in the forehead.

Sheba screamed as the man's grip first tightened, then slackened. He slumped backwards, though in the confined space there was no room for him to fall.

"Mr. Hunt," Hank said, coming up from behind as fast as his ancient legs would carry him, "Mr. Hunt, is there trouble?"

"No, Hank. No trouble. Just need a mop." The man's blood had gone everywhere.

Hank looked inside the elevator. "Here, young lady, let's get you out of there." He directed an angry look Gabriel's way. "Shootin' up my elevator again. I thought I told you..."

"You did, Hank. You told me." Gabriel took Sheba's hand, led her out of the elevator. She was trembling. He could hardly blame her. "We'll take the stairs, Hank."

"You do that, Mr. Hunt. You take those stairs." He headed off to the back, muttering something about what was he going to tell the police.

Gabriel led Sheba to the staircase.

"We should get out of here, Gabriel. They'll come back. He'll send more men."

"You're right," he said, "but we need to clean you up first."

"Clean...?" She reached a hand up to touch the back of her head and it came away sticky. Sticky and red.

"Come on," he said. "Quick shower, it'll come right out."

"What do they want from me, Gabriel? Why are they after me?"

"We're going to find that out." He led her up the steps two at a time till they got to the fifth floor. The door to his suite was standing open and the entry foyer showed the signs of the fight Sheba had put up: a wooden stairstep cabinet knocked over onto the floor, dozens of its tiny drawers lying beside it, their contents spilled; a full-height wall mirror hanging at a crooked angle; the throw rug kicked into a tangle in the corner. Inside, Gabriel saw more destruction. His coffee table was listing, one of its legs having been neatly snapped off. Books were scattered across the floor.

"Well, at least you didn't go quietly," Gabriel said.

But Sheba wasn't listening. She was already halfway to the bathroom, her coral blouse pulled open. She let it fall to the floor behind her and Gabriel left it lying there. The bloodstains wouldn't come out, not from silk. She could find something else to wear in the closet.

"Did this guy say anything when he broke in?"

"Yeah," Sheba said, unhooking her bra, stripping it off her shoulders and flinging it at Gabriel's chest. "He said come quietly or I'll blow your brains out." Furiously, she stepped out of her slacks and turned to get the water running in the shower.

"Anything about where he was taking you?"

"He didn't seem to feel the need to share that much information with me." She stood facing him, thumbs hooked under the waistband of her panties, naked otherwise, blood smeared in the long cascade of her auburn hair, and Gabriel thought back to his conversation with Michael. He'd had hopes of getting Sheba out of her clothing, but this wasn't the way he'd had in mind.

"Why don't you take your shower, I'll wait for you outside—"

"Like hell you will," she said. "You and that gun of yours will stay right here with me." She stripped off the last bit of clothing she had on and stepped under the steaming spray.

MINUTES LATER, SHEBA EMERGED DRIPPING BUT NO longer trembling, angry but no longer scared. She wrapped a towel turban-style around her head and made a beeline for the closet. Gabriel kept very little clothing for himself there, just a few linen shirts in various shades of cream and tan, a few pairs of khaki pants—items pretty much indistinguishable from the outfit he had on. But there was a good-sized selection of women's clothes, things various guests had left behind optimistically after stays of a night or two. Sheba flipped through the hangers like a shopper at a sale, discarding one option after another. "Jesus, Gabriel, why are all your women so goddamn flatchested?"

"Only by your standards," Gabriel said. He'd met Sheba's family, and nature had been generous to all the McCoy women.

She found a dress, finally, a red satin number with a long slit up the side and no sleeves, but at least it fit when she pulled it down over her head. It had once held the ample charms of a woman named Cierra Almanzar; she'd left it here when she'd returned to her post as director of the Museum of the Americas in Mexico City. She wouldn't mind sharing it with a fellow academic, Gabriel decided.

Gabriel strapped on a hip holster for his Colt, put a leather jacket on over it. He checked the gun's cylinder—just two shots left. And naturally he didn't have any more ammunition here in the apartment. Who would have thought he'd need any?

Sheba stepped back into the shoes she'd kicked off earlier, gaining three inches in the process, and Gabriel led her to the front door. They'd been in here barely ten minutes, but he knew she was right: for safety's sake, they couldn't leave soon enough.

He swung the door open.

Then he swung it shut again, spun, and, grabbing Sheba around the waist, took her down like a lineman making a tackle. They hit the floor an instant before the wood of the door splintered inwards and a cloud of shotgun pellets sped through the air inches above their heads.

3

A SECOND BLAST FOLLOWED THE FIRST, TEARING great gouts out of the wall opposite the door.

Gabriel put a finger to his lips, then gestured in the direction of the bedroom. Sheba nodded and began crawling that way on her hands and knees. Gabriel unholstered his Colt, armed it, waited one second... two seconds... three—and then popped up when he saw a shadow on the ruined surface of the door inch closer.

In a glimpse he saw the shotgun wielder, a big bear of a man in a black windbreaker, and behind him a pair of skinnier whippet types, hawk nosed, their severe hairlines shaved down to stubble. All three were holding handguns, though only the two in back had them pointed at Gabriel.

Gabriel fired twice and dodged away, not waiting to see who he'd hit. Return fire sounded loudly and bullet holes blossomed in the wall behind where Gabriel had been standing. A ricochet zinged into the mirror, which shattered, shards of glass pouring onto the floor with a sound like rain. This was the first bit of damage that really pissed Gabriel off—that mirror had been an antique. But there'd be time to mourn it later. If he was lucky.

The Colt was empty; he jammed it back in its holster and cast about for another weapon he could use.

Hanging from a pair of hooks on the wall was an aboriginal boomerang he'd been given by the chief of a tribe in New Guinea. Gabriel had learned to throw it while he was there, and if he were in one of the wide open spaces for which it had been designed he might have pulled off a slick maneuver, taking out multiple assailants with one flick of his wrist. But he was in a Manhattan apartment, where the best thing you could say for a boomerang was that it was a pretty good-sized stick. When he saw one of the gunmen's hands come into view, pistol extended, Gabriel swung the boomerang down, smashing the man's wrist. The gun fell to the ground and Gabriel kicked it out of sight under a couch.

The second of the two skinny gunmen elbowed his fellow aside and thrust his pistol in Gabriel's face, but Gabriel caught it backhanded with an upswing of the boomerang as the man squeezed off a shot. The bullet flew over Gabriel's shoulder, into a window, and out over 70th Street. Gabriel swung once more, striking the man in the temple with a blow that split the wooden boomerang in half. The man crumpled. But behind him the other gunman had recovered sufficiently to leap forward, the squat blade of a boot knife shining in his left hand.

Dropping the remnants of the boomerang, Gabriel threw up an arm to block a jab that would otherwise have given him an impromptu tracheotomy. Then he swung his other fist into the man's gut. But the man didn't fold up in pain; on the contrary, he took the punch without reacting at all, not surprising given the rock-hard solidity of the abdomen that had met Gabriel's knuckles.

Pressing with a forearm that had none of the showy bulk of a weightlifter's but all the strength, the man forced his knife closer and closer to Gabriel's face, millimeter by millimeter. With his free hand, Gabriel grabbed the man's injured wrist. The man squealed in pain and Gabriel took the opportunity to lunge in and deliver a headbutt to his forehead.

If the man's abdomen had been hard, that was nothing compared to his skull—Gabriel's vision swam for a moment and his ears rang with the sound of the impact. But the strength went out of the other man's arms, and he dropped to his knees amid the shards of the mirror. Gabriel lifted one of his own knees into the man's chin and the guy slumped to one side, unconscious.

"Not so fast," a voice said.

Gabriel looked up into the twin barrels of the shotgun.

"I reloaded it," the man in the black windbreaker said, looking less like a bear now than a wolf, his eyes narrowed to slits, a vicious, hungry expression on his face. "In case you had the idea that maybe I hadn't."

Gabriel put his hands up, annoyed. Had his own shots hit no one at all?

"I always assume," Gabriel said, "that any gun that's pointed at me is loaded."

"That's smart," the man said. "Now step back— over there by the couch will be fine."

Gabriel stepped backwards toward the couch

where he'd kicked the gun earlier. Looking over, he could just make out the shape of the barrel in the shadow by one leg. If the guy allowed him to sit down at that end—

An enormous clang sounded, like the ringing of a churchbell, and looking back Gabriel saw the man go down, shotgun and all. Sheba was standing above him with a newly dented brass coal scuttle clutched between her hands.

"Thank you," Gabriel said.

"No problem," Sheba said, tossing the scuttle aside. It clanged again when it landed. "I owed you one."

"You owed me two," Gabriel said, "but who's counting. Come on."

He led her back to the stairs. Before they made it one flight down, though, they heard a clatter of footsteps racing up toward them.

"Other way," Gabriel said. They turned around and pounded back up, past the fifth floor, to the heavy metal door that led out onto the building's roof. Even with the door shut behind them they could hear the footsteps and shouts of the men coming closer.

"Fire escape," Gabriel said and pulled Sheba along.

At the edge of the roof they both leaned over the side, looked down at the topmost fire escape balcony some dozen feet below. Some old buildings in New York had metal ladders connecting the fire escape to the roof, but this wasn't one of them. Some also had wide, modern fire escapes with protective railings to keep you from slipping off, but this wasn't one of those either. The only way down from here was to climb over the edge of the roof, dangle, and let go—and if you slipped, you slipped five stories to the pavement.

"Oh, Jesus," Sheba said. Her face had gone pale,

much the same as it had in Hungary; sixty feet wasn't three hundred, but a fall would be just as fatal. "Gabriel, I don't know if I can—"

"Of course you can," he said. "Here, I'll lower you." He wedged himself up against the stone wall at the edge of the roof and held tightly to her forearms as she carefully climbed onto the ledge. She extended one leg over the edge, then moved the other off, and as he suddenly found himself bearing her entire weight, Gabriel lost hold of one of her arms.

"*Gabriel!*"

"It's okay, I've got you." And he did, if only by one arm. He bent at the waist and carefully lowered her as far as he could. Her feet were still some distance from the platform. "Ready? I'm going to let go."

"One second," she said, and kicked off her heels again. One landed on the fire escape—the other slipped between the widely spaced metal laths and plummeted to the concrete below.

"Ready?" Gabriel said again.

"Wait—"

The door banged open behind him then, and Gabriel let go. He heard Sheba's scream and a clatter as she landed, but he couldn't spare a glance to see how she was doing. Not with three men pouring through the doorway onto the roof, three men who all matched Gabriel's six-foot height but topped him in breadth and whose revolvers were probably not as lacking in bullets. That's what he had to assume, anyway.

He quickly ran through some options in his head. There wasn't any place he could run—it was a small roof. There wasn't much for him to take shelter behind, just a single roof fan in a metal housing, and if he tried that they could split up and pin him down from both sides. Maybe if he could somehow make it past them to the stairs—

Gabriel turned and vaulted over the side of the building.

There was no second cable waiting for him this time. No first cable, for that matter. Just a narrow fire escape and a five-story drop.

For an instant, as he fell through the air, Gabriel found himself thinking about how much of his adult life he'd spent jumping from high places with people who wanted to kill him close behind. It was a topic, he decided, that might reward reflection sometime, when he could think about it at his leisure. But as his feet hit the fire escape and his legs buckled under him and he slid toward the edge, his mind was drawn sharply back to more pressing matters.

Scrabbling with one arm, he caught hold of the last of the laths just as he plunged over the side. He held on tight and found himself swinging from it in a great arc, back and forth, like a kid on a jungle gym. At the inner end of one swing he let go, dropping onto the next balcony down.

Glancing between the laths at his feet, he saw Sheba two flights below him, a shoe in one hand, descending as quickly as she could manage. Glancing up, he saw the men on the roof looking back down and then the barrels of their guns as they extended them toward him.

Three triggers were pulled simultaneously, and three bullets went spanging off various bits of metal between them and him.

Gabriel got his legs under him and, staying low, hurried down the metal steps. From overhead he heard the sound of first one, then another, of the men landing on the fire escape. The third attempted it but missed.

A moment later he fell past Gabriel, arms windmilling desperately; their eyes locked for an instant and then he was gone. The sound when he hit the ground was wet and terrible.

Gabriel chanced another look down and was briefly concerned when he didn't see Sheba below him. Then he realized it was because she'd already reached the bottom. He caught sight of her running along the sidewalk toward Park Avenue, both shoes in her hands now, bare feet pounding against the pavement.

Another bullet flew past him, this one within inches of his face. He saw Sheba stop and look back. "Go!" he shouted. "Don't wait for me. Just go!"

She turned again—and ran head-on into the arms of a man who'd stepped around the corner into her path.

He was at least a foot taller than her and quite a bit heavier; despite the warm weather he wore a heavy overcoat and black leather gloves. And when she tried to back away, he wrapped his long arms around her and lifted her entirely off her feet.

The shoes fell from her hands.

Gabriel hurried to get to the bottom of the fire escape, but by the time he made it, leaping over the side of the lowest balcony and landing in a crouch, Sheba had already been bundled, screaming, into a black car that peeled away from the curb in a cloud of exhaust.

He ran after the car, chasing it out into the street as more gunshots exploded behind him. The car swung around the corner onto Park, where for once—this being a weekend morning in New York City in the middle of August—traffic was practically nonexistent. There'd be no catching it on foot. Gabriel looked back the other way, saw a yellow cab speeding downtown, and stepped into its path. The car screeched to a stop just inches from his legs.

The cabbie, a turbaned and bearded Sikh, stuck his head out the driver-side window and shouted, "You wish to be killed? Is this what you desire?"

Gabriel threw open the door to the back seat, piled inside. "You see that car," he said to the driver in Punjabi, "the black one, there? Follow it. Don't let it out of your sight. A woman's life depends on it."

Through the rear window, Gabriel saw the men from the roof round the corner. One of them kicked Sheba's shoes into the gutter as he ran. The other raised his gun.

"Now!" Gabriel said, ducking.

The cabbie glanced in the rear view mirror just in time to see the rear windshield of his car shatter. He put the gas pedal to the floor and, swerving around a double-parked delivery van, roared off.

4

THEY MADE IT THREE BLOCKS BEFORE A SEDAN
pulled in behind them, a silver Audi with smoked-
glass windows and a dent the size of a melon in the
hood. The four silver circles across the car's grill made
Gabriel think of the ring in the nose of a bull, particularly
when the driver revved the engine angrily and the car
surged forward. The Audi came within a few feet of
the cab's rear bumper before the taxi driver—Rajiv
Narindra, according to the ID displayed on the back of
his seat—swerved again, nearly sideswiping a street-
corner hotdog cart in his haste to change lanes.

Above the next intersection, the traffic light changed
from green to yellow. Narindra sped through it. It turned
red before the Audi reached it, but they sped through as
well. A chorus of honking erupted behind them.

"Who are these men?" Narindra shouted back at
Gabriel.

"They are hired killers, abductors," Gabriel said,

testing the limits of his Punjabi vocabulary. "They have taken a friend of mine and… mean to…" Damn it, what was the word? "Harm her."

"Why?"

"If I could tell you that," Gabriel muttered, in English this time, "I wouldn't be here in the first place." He bent forward over the front seat, thankful to have gotten into one of the minority of cabs in New York that didn't have a wall of bulletproof Plexiglas between the driver and the passengers. He rifled through the pile of odds and ends cluttering the passenger seat: a thick, spiral-bound book of maps, a handful of ballpoint pens, half a sandwich, an unopened bottle of Snapple. Narindra turned the wheel sharply to the left, throwing Gabriel against his shoulder, and then swung it back to the right.

"Do you have anything we could use as…" Gabriel's language skills petered out again. Desperately he resorted to English. "A weapon—a gun… a, a, a *jack*, something heavy—anything you could use as a weapon?"

Narindra shook his head. "A weapon? This I do not have."

Up ahead, Gabriel saw the black car speeding up, pulling away. A glance at their own speedometer showed they were doing close to fifty themselves.

From behind, meanwhile, came the *crack-crack-crack* of gunfire. Narindra cut across two lanes and then back.

Beggars can't be choosers. Gabriel grabbed the Snapple bottle and, turning in one swift movement, cocked his arm and launched the bottle through the open space where the rear windshield had been. The driver of the Audi pulled to one side to avoid it, but the bottle struck, leaving a spiderweb of cracks in the glass.

That was something—but hardly enough. And now

he was out of projectiles completely.

An arm holding a gun emerged from the Audi's passenger-side window and fire erupted from the barrel. Gabriel dropped to his knees in the cab's footwell. A line of bullet holes stitched across the back of the front seat, throwing puffs of padding into the air. That it was only shreds of foam rubber raining down on him and not blood was just dumb luck, Gabriel knew—two feet to the left and he'd have been hurtling down Park Avenue in a cab with a corpse at the wheel.

He peeked over the front seat again, looked at the dashboard. There had to be *something*—

The meter.

Mounted on a metal bar, tallying up his fare in 40-cent increments, a curl of cash register tape trailing from the receipt slot at the top—it was a compact unit but looked heavy, the perfect combination. It also looked firmly attached, but what had once been mounted had to be removable. It would be easier with the proper tools, of course, but—

Gabriel lunged forward, took hold of the meter with one hand on either side, and wrenched it violently.

"What are you doing?" Narindra cried. "I am responsible for that!"

"I'll—" Gabriel wrenched at it again. "I'll pay—" One more time. *Come on.* "I'll pay for it," he shouted, pulling and twisting till with a snap of breaking plastic and metal the unit came free. It made a sad little grinding noise as it lost power. "And the windshield," Gabriel said breathlessly. "I'll cover it all, just keep driving."

"Crazy, you are crazy," Narindra said, and Gabriel didn't bother to argue. Instead, he turned back, crawled halfway out onto the trunk of the cab and, anchoring his feet against the back of the rear seat, rose up on his knees, hefted the taxi meter in both hands, took aim, and hurled it directly at the Audi's windshield.

A direct hit would smash the glass this time—it was already cracked. And whatever smashed the glass would continue on through the glass into the driver's face at a relative velocity of somewhere north of fifty miles per hour. Realizing this, the driver pulled the wheel violently to the right, and this time he succeeded in avoiding the missile, though only by inches. What he didn't succeed in avoiding was the curb, which vanished under his right front tire as the Audi leapt onto the sidewalk; or the fire hydrant by the curb, which crumpled the front of the car like it was made of tinfoil. The driver and his passenger were both hurled forward and would have collided painfully—maybe fatally—with the steering wheel in one case and the windshield in the other, had it not been for the car's airbags, which deployed with showroom precision.

Safe cars, Audis.

Gabriel carefully crawled backwards, ducking back into the cab and collapsing in the back seat. He saw Narindra eyeing him in the mirror.

This was the moment of truth—would he stop the car and insist that Gabriel get out, which in practice would mean losing the other car, and Sheba, possibly permanently? Or would Narindra keep going, to help save a young woman's life?

"You say you will pay?" Narindra said.

"Anything," Gabriel said. "Name your price."

"A thousand dollars?"

"Five thousand," Gabriel said.

"You are crazy," Narindra said. But he kept driving.

* * *

THE BLACK CAR WAS HALF A MILE AHEAD BY THEN, but they made up some distance when it turned crosstown and began plowing through the slightly denser traffic on the way to the Lincoln Tunnel. They reached the tunnel entrance just a few hundred yards behind the other car and spotted it again the instant they emerged.

They were on the highway now, barreling through the wilds of northern New Jersey, and could really put on some speed, but at Gabriel's request Narindra hung back, leaving several car lengths and at least one lane between them and the black car at all times. From the rear they presented an unusual sight, with the missing windshield and the trunk riddled with bullet holes, but from the front there was nothing out of the ordinary—just a New York cab taking someone on a short hop outside the city—and Gabriel was counting on their being able to go unnoticed, as long as they didn't get too close.

It was the only choice. Gabriel couldn't see trying to run the other car off the road or bring them to a stop in some other way, not with Sheba's life at stake and Narindra at risk, too—especially not when the occupants of the other car were almost certainly better armed than he was. The thing to do was to find out where they were taking her; he could regroup then, return with the proper equipment and help, maybe even involve the police. Or maybe he'd mount a solo rescue the way he had in Hungary. There were all sorts of options. But first he needed to know where they were planning to stash her.

It was with a sinking feeling that Gabriel saw the

airfields and hangars of Teterboro Airport loom at the horizon.

Narindra said, "They seem to be headed for the—"

"Yeah," Gabriel said, "I see it."

Stashing didn't look like it was in the cards.

He fingered the cell phone in his pocket. He hated the things, but even he had to concede there were times when they were indispensable. He speed-dialed Michael's number and, while it rang, dug a handful of hundred-dollar bills out of his pocket. He passed three to Narindra across the tattered back of the front seat. "A down payment," he said. Then, to Michael: "Two things, Michael, and I don't have much time to talk. First: I need you to take care of someone for me... a cab driver, his name is Rajiv Narindra, he'll be calling you... five thousand dollars... he can tell you that himself. Just make sure he gets what he needs—it's got to be enough to repair his taxi plus some extra. That's right, on the Foundation's tab." Gabriel paused while Michael peppered him with questions, most of which he couldn't have answered if he'd wanted to and the remainder of which he didn't want to. When his brother fell silent again, Gabriel said, "Second thing: I may not be home for a little while. I've got a feeling there's some plane travel in my future."

Michael's tinny voice sounded weary through the phone's speaker. "When has there ever not been?"

"Well, this is a little different than usual. I don't have a ticket, I don't have a passport, and I don't know where I'm headed."

"Getting away from it all?"

"I wish," Gabriel said. "Now, listen. I'm going to leave my phone turned on and I want you to track it—to track me. You understand? I may need your help when I get wherever it is that I'm going."

"My help?" Michael sounded anxious suddenly. He was only thirty-two, six years younger than Gabriel, but he worried like an old man. "What's going on, Gabriel? Are you in trouble?"

"We'll see," Gabriel said. "Maybe not. But just in case, I want you to know where I am."

Michael didn't say anything for a bit. "You're stringing a second cable here, aren't you? In case the first one gets cut."

"So to speak," Gabriel said.

"All right. Consider yourself tracked. But, Gabriel—your cell battery won't last forever. You know how plane travel drains it. If the flight's more than ten hours…"

"Then let's hope it isn't," Gabriel said, and ended the call before Michael could protest further. Up ahead, the black car had just driven off the main highway onto an unlabeled side road. Gabriel returned the phone to his jacket pocket. He didn't turn it off.

They drove past the road the black car had used. Teterboro catered to private jets and chartered flights, with accommodations of varying degrees of exclusivity. Ordinary businessmen drove in through the main entrance and underwent a check-in process similar to what they'd have gone through at LaGuardia or JFK; the wealthier sort drove on unlabeled roads up to private hangars and took off without once getting patted down or wanded or asked for I.D. They could carry all the Colts on board they wanted.

Narindra pulled the cab to a stop in a small cul-de-sac that was screened from view by a thick copse of trees. Gabriel got out and, using one of the pens from the front seat, dashed off Michael's private office number on a scrap torn from the sandwich wrapper. Then he shook Narindra's hand.

"Michael will take care of you," Gabriel said. "I promise."

Narindra said nothing. He was looking over the wreckage of his taxi.

"These men," he said finally, "who kidnapped this friend of yours, this woman. Who shot up my car. You will see they get what they deserve, yes?"

"I'll do my best," Gabriel said.

ON THE FAR SIDE OF THE TREES A FENCE WITH COILS of barbed wire at the top bore a sign warning that trespassers would be prosecuted to the fullest extent of the law. Gabriel pulled the sign off, carried it under his chin as he scaled the fence, and used it to press the strands of barbed wire out of his way. Once he'd bent enough strands down to make room, he climbed over the top and down the other side.

There were no more trees here, but there was plenty of underbrush, none of it recently trimmed, and by moving in a low crouch Gabriel was able to keep out of sight. The first hangar he passed was, as you might expect on a Sunday morning, empty, and the second seemed occupied only by a mechanic who was up to his elbows in a disassembled engine. But the third hangar was bustling. Two trucks and several cars were parked outside, including the one he'd followed here from New York. The black car's door opened as he watched. The big man came out first, walking backwards, and Sheba came with him, still clutched in his arms, her kicking feet swinging some distance off the ground. "Let me go!" she shouted, and Gabriel ached to race forward and make him do just that, pull the big ape's paws off her, teach him a schoolyard lesson about picking on someone his size. But there were too many other people around, easily a dozen or more, most of them this guy's size or close to it, and most wearing holsters on their hips or under their arms. Some were unloading long, low crates from the back of a truck, others were wheeling the crates over to the hangar building. Gabriel might have been able to take any one of them, maybe two—but all at once? With nothing but his bare hands? There was bravery and then there was idiocy.

But he had to do something. He watched Sheba's captor carry her into the hangar, and through the open bay doors Gabriel saw him drag her up the rear ramp of a cargo plane—the same place all the crates were being loaded. He tried to get a glimpse of the plane's registration, but no luck—there were numbers on the tail, but nothing to indicate what country it might have come from or been heading to.

He crept closer, keeping the body of the larger of the two trucks between him and the workers still busily unloading and moving the cargo. Through the hangar doors, he heard a pair of voices in conversation, one nasal and high-pitched, the other a lifelong smoker's rasp. Both had an accent, one he'd heard plenty of in recent weeks.

"You did well, Andras," the smoker said, pronouncing the name the Hungarian way, with a soft 's': AHN-drahsh. "Mr. DeGroet will be pleased to get her back."

"Someone should cut the bitch's nails," Andras said. His was the nasal whine. "You see this? You see what she did to me?"

"Poor baby," the smoker said. "A scratch."

"It's *three* scratches, and you wouldn't find it so funny if it was your face. She nearly took my eye out."

"What do you want for it, Andras, some iodine? Or maybe hazard pay?"

Andras grumbled. "And why *not* hazard pay? That's not a bad idea."

"Well, then," the smoker said, "you go ahead and bring it up with Mr. DeGroet when we land, why don't you? He'll probably be glad to entertain your request."

"He should be," Andras said.

"But do be prepared," the smoker said, "if I am incorrect and he is not glad—if, say, he is in a bad mood because his plans have been delayed this long—in that case you realize he will kill you just for suggesting such a thing. You do know that, don't you?"

"Ah, go to hell," Andras said, but his voice lacked conviction.

"Maybe he'll use you for practice, the way he did with Janos. Cut you to ribbons. With his saber, perhaps. It has always been his favorite."

Andras said nothing.

"Or," the smoker continued, "you could take the pay you were promised, go buy yourself a bottle and a girl, and keep your goddamn mouth shut. Mind you, it's up to you which you do—I'm just saying you *could* do that. It's your choice."

"You're a real bastard, Karoly, you know that?"

"Oh, yes," Karoly said. "I know that—and as long as you don't forget it, we'll get along fine."

Gabriel moved away from the wall of the hangar, where he'd been standing, his ear pressed to the metal. They were taking her back to DeGroet—back to Hungary, presumably, though probably not to the castle, not now that Gabriel had infiltrated it once.

Hungary wasn't a big country, relatively speaking, but it was big enough that one woman could quite easily be made to vanish. There was only one way to be sure that couldn't happen—and that was to stay with her. But how…?

He waited until the crew working on unloading the truck wheeled the next crate down the short metal ramp in back. There was one man still inside, Gabriel saw, seated on a folding chair; behind the wheel, in the truck's cab, there'd been one more. But that was all—temporarily the other men were all engaged in steering the bulky crates over to the hangar and onto the plane. That evened up the odds a bit, at least.

Gabriel walked casually up the ramp, gave a two-fingered wave to the seated man. There was only one crate left inside the truck. It was made of black plastic like the others he'd seen, with metal latches to keep the top down; the thing was at least six feet long and maybe two-and-a-half feet wide. It looked a little like a plastic coffin on wheels.

"Who are you?" the man said. He was paunchy and seemed to be thoroughly winded even though the extent of his physical labor appeared to have involved checking off items on a clipboard.

"I'm on Mr. DeGroet's personal staff," Gabriel said. "He wanted me to oversee this particular…" he waved at the crate "…container."

"Oh, yeah? What's your name?"

"Gabor," Gabriel said. "Gabor Nagy." It was the most common Hungarian surname he could think of; it meant 'big.'

The man flipped through a couple of pages on his clipboard and didn't find any Nagy listed. "You're not on here."

"I should be—he'd be mad as hell if he found out I wasn't. Let me see." He came up beside the man, who didn't bother standing, just held the clipboard out. "I'm right there," Gabriel said, pointing, and when the man took the clipboard back to peer at the page, Gabriel clocked him with a solid right cross. The man went down like a felled log.

Gabriel glanced outside. There was still no one in view, thankfully. With one hand under each armpit, he dragged the man down the ramp and around to the side of the truck. Once there, he rolled the man underneath, making sure to shove him far enough that he couldn't be seen. They'd find him there eventually, or he'd come to on his own; they were unlikely to drive over him. Just in case, though, Gabriel left him between the truck's wheels rather than in their path.

Then he went back up the ramp and unlatched the crate. It wasn't full. Inside, under a folded-up blanket being used for padding, were two wooden racks of rifles and, below them, box after cardboard box of ammunition.

Guns and ammo. For what? What private army was DeGroet equipping? His own, presumably—but to what end?

There was no time for speculation: from outside Gabriel could hear the steps of the men returning, still distant for now but getting louder.

He lifted the gun racks out, wrapped the blanket loosely around them, and laid them down where the man had been sitting. He set the folding chair on top for good measure. He then climbed into the crate. It was a tight fit—but it was a fit. He lowered the cover gently and heard the latches catch. Would he be able to open them again from the inside? He thought so. A swift kick should do it. If not, maybe he could blast the latches open—with the vast selection of cartridges he was lying on he figured he could probably find some .45 caliber rounds that would fit his Colt. Not that he relished the prospect of firing a gun in an enclosed container full of black powder.

Pressing up gently against the underside of the crate's lid with his palms opened the seal a crack, enough to let in a bit of air and a thread of light. The light was interrupted after a moment as two men climbed into the truck. One pair of legs sported khaki workpants, the other denim. Gabriel heard one of the men calling for someone named Stephen. Stephen didn't answer, presumably because he was otherwise occupied under the truck. A quiet conversation in Hungarian ensued. The men were trying to decide what to do. Wait for Stephen to return from taking a leak or having a smoke or whatever he'd decided he had to do right this moment? Or just take the last crate and the hell with him?

They seemed to settle on 'the hell with him' since Gabriel's view was cut off as the men stepped closer and then he could feel the crate being rolled down the ramp.

They rolled him across level ground for a minute and then up another ramp—longer, steeper—and shoved him against a bulkhead. Raising the cover again, Gabriel saw that the crate was conveniently facing a window, so that even if the activation of the plane's deafening jet engines minutes later hadn't been enough of a clue, the view of the land dropping out of sight would have told him they were on their way.

Gabriel did his best to get comfortable in the cramped space. He took his phone from his pocket and glanced at the display. New York to Hungary was a nine-hour flight with good tailwinds.

As he watched, the battery portion of the phone's readout silently dropped from four bars to three.

5

GABRIEL HADN'T INTENDED TO SLEEP, BUT HE FOUND himself waking with a start as the plane's landing gear touched down. They skipped once, twice, then settled on the tarmac, the big plane's momentum carrying them forward along the runway as the power to the engines cut out. Gabriel chanced a peek outside through the seam, but the window was dark—and so, when he tried it, was his phone. He pressed all the buttons. Nothing.

Had something kept them in the air longer than expected? Or had they landed somewhere farther away than Budapest?

Which led to the next question: For how long had Michael been able to track his location? Maybe only halfway there, maybe up until the moment before he tried turning on the phone. There was no way to know.

Gabriel heard the sound of seatbelts unbuckling, heavy footsteps moving around the cabin. He did not hear any lighter steps he could identify as Sheba's, and he didn't hear her voice, but that didn't mean anything—Andras could be carrying her, bound and gagged, or maybe she was being held in another part of the plane. They wouldn't have hurt her or killed her, he was confident of that; not as long as DeGroet wanted her for some purpose of his own.

Gabriel groped around beneath him, felt the cardboard boxes of varying sizes, slipped his fingers under one flap after another. He couldn't see a thing, of course, and though he had the Zippo lighter with him that he always carried, he could hardly light it here— even if the sudden appearance of a glow from inside the crate wouldn't give him away, the explosion it could easily set off would make the whole thing moot. But he'd handled enough guns in his day to be able to tell by feel a rifle cartridge from one for a semiautomatic pistol, a .32 from a .45. Telling a .44 Remington from a .45 Winchester was a bit harder, but not impossible. He ran the selection he found between his fingertips, comparing length and grooving. Wrong caliber was not so much of a worry—a cartridge too wide wouldn't chamber and one too narrow would announce the fact by the too-roomy fit. Too long, same thing. But slightly too short would be easy to miss, and could lead to a shot that either didn't go off when the time came or went off in a spectacularly bad way. So care was called for, and he exercised as much as he reasonably could, lying in the dark in a crate in the belly of a plane in the middle of god-only-knew-where.

He finished loading the cylinder just as the crate next to his was loudly pushed aside, smacking into the inner wall of the plane's hull with a jolt that made Gabriel hope it contained something less explosive than the one he was in. His was the next to move, and he lay still when it did, not wanting to draw any attention.

Once they were down the ramp, Gabriel gently raised the cover of the crate again, hoping for some glimpse that would tell him where they were, but beyond a blinding ring of magnesium vapor lights he could see nothing at all, just solid black. It was nighttime wherever they were, and except in your major cities, nighttime tended to look much the same from place to place—especially when you could only see a sliver of it.

Then a streak of red satin passed in front of him. He craned his neck to keep it in view as long as he could, but it was gone in an instant, followed close behind by the rougher folds of a long overcoat. "Keep moving," came Andras' voice, though whether he was talking to Sheba or the men loading the crates, Gabriel couldn't guess. In any event, both kept moving, and within minutes all the crates were on trucks and tearing along a road that seemed paved but just barely so—Gabriel felt every pit and gully in the surface as they passed over it.

But at least they were on their way. Gabriel settled back for the ride.

THEY UNLOADED HIM, ALONG WITH THE OTHER crates, a bit more than an hour later—Gabriel's cellphone may have died and its clock with it, but the luminous dial of his wristwatch, made in 1945 and only repaired once since, was still giving off its pale glow. Sometimes, he thought, the old technologies were better.

The texture of the ground under the wheels of his crate changed after a minute, from solid to… something less than solid, almost as though they'd left pavement for dirt, or not even dirt—it seemed looser, somehow. And the sound was different as they passed over it.

After a time, they came to a stop. All around him, Gabriel heard men walking rapidly, but barely any conversation, only the occasional order issued in a low bark. His crate was jostled once by another and then shifted to a new location a few yards away. A peek outside showed more crates around him, some stacked two or three high—he at least could be grateful that so far nothing had been stacked on top of his.

A car pulled up then, not in his sight, but in his hearing. The door opened and slammed shut, and a new set of footsteps approached. A set with three beats to it rather than two: slap, slap, click; slap, slap, click. Gabriel tensed at the sound.

"Well, well," Lajos DeGroet's voice came, from perhaps twenty feet away. "Well, well, well. My dear girl. So good to see you again."

"Who the hell do you think you are," Sheba said, sounding far more measured and reasonable than Gabriel thought he would in her place, "that you can kidnap a woman off the streets of New York City, fly her halfway around the world, and, and…"

"That's all right, my dear. Let it out. You are angry and I don't blame you."

"You don't *blame* me? *You don't blame me?*"

"No, don't hold her back," DeGroet said, apparently to one of his men, perhaps Andras, "let her go. She won't attack me. She knows better than that." Gabriel heard a click followed by the sound of metal sliding against metal, and he knew DeGroet had turned the grip of his iron walking stick and drawn from within the modified fencing saber it hid. "Don't you, my dear?"

Lajos DeGroet, son of a Dutch father and a Hungarian mother, both from artistocratic families with wealth and property to burn, had led the unproductive life his parentage entitled him to—with one exception. In his youth he'd gravitated toward the sport of fencing and at age twenty he'd competed for Hungary in the summer Olympics in Rome. He'd won a silver medal that year but famously refused to accept it; four years later, after intensive training under the great Hungarian fencing master Rudolf Kárpáti, himself a six-time gold medalist, DeGroet had returned from Tokyo with a gold.

After that, DeGroet had largely vanished from the public eye, returning to his family's customary pastimes of accumulating and squandering money in spectacular but private fashion. Gabriel had crossed paths with him more than once, since the man was an inveterate collector—the acquisitive sort who can't stop raising his paddle at an auction and, because of the resources at his command, never has to. Which was fine if you were on the selling end of a transaction, as Gabriel had been more than once— there'd been the gilt ceremonial bowl from Myanmar and the skull fragment from central Africa. But if you were competing with DeGroet to *buy* something, you might as well pack up and go home, and Gabriel had discovered that as well. The trust that underlay the Hunt Foundation was considerable, containing as it did all the many millions of dollars his parents' bestselling books had brought in over the years (a rich enough haul during their lives, but an absolute flood after their disappearance at sea in 2000 landed them on the front page of every newspaper in the world)— but there were fortunes and there were fortunes, and Gabriel could have bankrupted the Hunt family fortune twice over without making a dent in DeGroet's.

So: a collector, of gold medals and golden artifacts and gold itself, no doubt, as well as all the other forms in which wealth could be stored or expressed; also a fencer, one of the best Hungary had ever fielded, which was another way of saying one of the best the world had ever seen; and though the man was nearing seventy now and had lost some height and some hair over the years, he'd lost not a bit of his old quickness or his skill with a blade. Or his arrogance, or his bad temper. He didn't walk with a stick because, being old, he needed help with his balance. He did it to ensure he could always keep a sword close at hand.

"Now, my dear," DeGroet said, in a voice whose attempt at sounding friendly was as unctuous as it was unconvincing, "as I had been about to tell you when your meddlesome friend insisted on seizing you from my care back at Balaton, I am a great admirer of your work. I have read all your papers. Your work on the iconography of the ancient world is not just accomplished, in my opinion it is groundbreaking."

"You didn't bring me here at gunpoint," Sheba said, through what sounded like clenched teeth, "to compliment my scholarship."

"On the contrary. That is precisely what I did. Andras, please, show her over here." There was a brief flurry of footsteps and the voices, when they resumed, were further away. Gabriel thought this might be a good time to get out of the crate and quietly pressed upward with his knees until the latches popped. He climbed over the side, dropped lightly to the ground, looked around. But he was hemmed in by crates on all sides, so he couldn't see a thing.

"...you see, Miss McCoy," DeGroet was saying, "I have need of someone with your particular expertise. Some light, please, Andras. No, here." A faint orange glow lightened a portion of the dark sky in the direction the voices were coming from. "Can you read that, my dear?"

"I don't need to read it," Sheba said. "I know what it says."

"How foolish of me, of course you do. But just to humor me, could you perhaps tell *us* what it says."

"It's the story of the prince's dream," Sheba said. "How he came here and fell asleep at noon, with the sun overhead, and a voice spoke to him from heaven saying, 'I am your father and you are my son, I shall give you dominion over the land and all those who live within its borders, if you shall honor me and do my bidding.' Roughly speaking."

"Very good," DeGroet said. "But there is a specific instruction you omitted."

"What? The bit about unburying him?"

"Yes," DeGroet said. "That bit."

"'The sands in which I lie have covered me. Swear to me that you will do what I ask of you, my son, that I may know you as my source of help, and I may be joined with you in eternal sovereignty.'"

"'The sands in which I lie,'" DeGroet repeated. "The young prince had the best of intentions, but he never did manage to fulfill his promise. It took three millennia to do the job—longer, nearly three and a half. And then they stopped, because they thought they were done. The fools."

"What are you talking about?" Sheba said, and where he was crouching among the crates Gabriel thought the same thing. Three millennia? The

Hungarian countryside boasted any number of ruins dating back to the time of the Romans, but those were only two thousand years old, not three or four thousand. There was nothing in the country that old.

And sands? Hungary was landlocked, for heaven's sake.

Where the hell were they?

Gabriel glanced around, peered between the crates, saw no one facing in his direction. Reaching back into the crate he'd just exited, he dug under the boxes of ammunition till he uncovered the long barrel of a rifle—he'd felt it beneath him on the plane, but couldn't get at it while he was lying on top of it. Now he set it down on the ground, loaded it, and slung a bandolier of extra rifle shells over his head. Just in case the bullets he'd slipped into his Colt didn't fire after all. Or, hell, even if they did. DeGroet had at least a dozen men here, maybe more—it was impossible for Gabriel to be too heavily armed.

Gripping the rifle under one arm and unholstering the Colt, Gabriel crept cautiously out of his little enclosure and into the shadow of the truck that had brought him. Then he stood up for the first time in twelve hours. Once the pins and needles in his legs had subsided, he leaned around the rear corner of the truck to get his first good look at where he was—and his jaw fell open.

6

IT WAS THE DEAD OF NIGHT, TWO HOURS BEFORE THE dawn, and except for the movement of DeGroet's men, the Plateau of Giza was silent, still. In the distance, the Great Pyramid—Egypt's towering mausoleum for the Pharaoh Khufu, the last surviving Wonder of the Ancient World—loomed darkly against the deeper black of the sky. Around it, the smaller pyramids built to house Khufu's wives and mother, and further out the ones for Khafre and Menkaure, his successors, gave the plain a jagged skyline, like a giant jaw full of pointed teeth. The men, by comparison, looked tiny, insignificant, lost.

Immediately before them, facing them in its eternal crouch, blanketing them with its moon-cast shadow, was the Great Sphinx.

DeGroet and Sheba stood between the lion's paws, Andras shining his flashlight's paltry beam at the stone stele erected there by Thutmose IV. Other men bustled about, Hungarians in western clothing mixing with locals whose garb ranged from turban to fez to coarse burnoose, wrapped tight against the late-night desert chill. Camels stood beside cars, shivering and ducking their heads to nose at the sand. Tilting his own head back to look up, Gabriel saw the great beast towering above them all, its sculpted head as high in the air as the roof of the Discovers League building back in New York, its shoulders as broad as the building's facade, and its torso stretching into the distance behind it for the better part of a football field's length.

Its body, though eroded by thousands of years of exposure both to the elements and to mistreatment by men, still showed the muscular form of a prone lion, facing east to greet the rising sun as it ascended above the Nile. It had lain like that since before the pyramids themselves all were built. Two thousand years before the birth of Alexander the Great, one thousand years before the birth of Moses, the Sphinx had already been meeting each sunrise with its majestic stare for a century or more. Today the stare emerged from the face of a pharaoh, framed on either side by the traditional Egyptian headdress of state, his stone lips cracked and ruined, the better part of his great carved nose shattered off. But this pharaonic head looked strangely small compared to the size of the body and it was commonly thought that the statue had originally borne the head as well as the body of a lion—that it had begun its existence as a monumental statue of a cat, symbol of the sun god, and that only later, under the guidance of a despot mad with vanity, had the feline head been re-carved into a man's, making what had once been a gorgeous animal into a hybrid, a monster.

The Egyptians hadn't called the monster 'sphinx'— it had been the Greeks who'd given it this name when eventually they'd landed from across the northern seas, recognizing in its hybrid shape a resemblance to a local legend of their own, of a woman with a lion's torso, an eagle's wings, and a serpent's tail. The word meant "strangler" or "one who chokes" in Greek, a reminder of how the Greek sphinx killed unlucky travelers who failed to answer her famous riddle. But the Great Sphinx of Giza had no such reputation for limiting himself to a single method of slaughtering his prey, and in Arabic he was called simply Abul-Hôl, the Father of Fear.

"WHY HAVE YOU BROUGHT ME HERE?" SHEBA ASKED, when DeGroet's silence had stretched on uncomfortably long. "What do you want from me?"

"You see that, Karoly? I told you she would be cooperative once we got her here." Gabriel saw the man beside DeGroet, a short, broad fellow in black with a cigarette at his lips, nod impatiently. He looked around, intently scanning the area, and Gabriel ducked back behind the truck before Karoly's gaze made it to where Gabriel was standing. This was DeGroet's right hand, clearly—Andras was muscle, nothing more, dangerous only if you got within arm's reach, but this Karoly would be dangerous at any distance.

"I didn't say I would cooperate," Sheba said. "I just asked—"

"Enough," DeGroet said. "You will cooperate or I will cut that lovely dress off your body with three strokes of my sword and instruct every man here to take his pleasure with you. Do we understand each other?" He waited for a response. "Speak up, my dear. Do we understand each other?"

Sheba's voice shook. "Yes."

"Yes, what?"

"We understand each other."

"Do you believe I will do it or shall I give you a little taste to prove it?"

"No, I believe you."

"Good," DeGroet said, his voice softening again. "I regret the need to be so harsh with you, my dear, but we do have only a limited time here and there's no telling how long it might take."

"How long *what* might take?" Sheba said.

"Come here," DeGroet said, and as they walked around the left paw of the Sphinx, their voices became quieter once more—enough so that Gabriel could no longer make out what was being said. He glanced around, picked a moment when no one was looking his way, then darted out from behind the truck to where a local stood with a shovel against one shoulder. Gabriel took aim carefully, then slugged him two-handed on the back of the head, catching him and the shovel both before either could land noisily on the ground. He dragged the man back to the truck, stripped him of his burnoose, and rolled him between the wheels, much as he had Stephen at the other end of the journey. Gabriel threw the burnoose on, slipped its hood over his head and crossed the layers of fabric over his chest to conceal the bandolier. He hefted the shovel and the rifle together and hastened off toward the long, low paw around which DeGroet and Sheba had disappeared.

He almost stumbled over them. They were both squatting on the ground, looking at a cleared-off patch near the base of the paw. Gabriel stopped himself a step shy of kicking DeGroet in the side and spun swiftly to face the other way. As he turned, he saw an expression of annoyance on Karoly's face—the short man had seen how close a thing it had been, the near collision, and clearly saw no need to conceal his contempt for a worker so clumsy. Gabriel bent his head forward humbly, apologetically, trying to expose as little of his face as possible.

"When Thutmose found the Sphinx," DeGroet was saying to Sheba, "only its head was visible—the rest was all covered by sand. He undertook to unearth it—to unbury it, as you say. But he only got as far as uncovering the figure's chest and paws. The rest of the animal wasn't completely uncovered until 1925."

"And…?"

"And, my dear, once it was completely uncovered—that is, once the tons of sand had all been removed and the stone surface cleared—the men working at the restoration congratulated themselves on a job well done, took some photographs and went home. But the job was *not* done. There was more to be uncovered—below and within."

"What are you talking about, 'below'? 'Within'?"

"Over the past dozen years, analysis with ground-penetrating radar has revealed open spaces deep within the body of the Sphinx."

"In a figure this large," Sheba said, "carved from a single piece of stone, that's almost inevitable. There are open spaces in any hill or mountain, too—they're called caves. It doesn't mean anything."

"Well, that's your opinion," DeGroet said, "and you're in fine company, but your company is wrong and so are you. Most of the open spaces, it is true, are naturally occurring, irregular—but one is very clearly a man-made chamber. How do I know this? Simple: I was the one who commissioned the analysis, and I am the only one who possesses the full results."

"All right, you possess the results. What's the point?"

"The point, Miss McCoy, is that there's a way inside the Great Sphinx and a chamber in there that no one has entered in four thousand years. And the reason no one has found it until now is that the entrance was sealed up—buried, if you will. And two hundred generations of royal sons and archaeologists and treasure hunters and historians have failed to unbury it. Until now. I am going to unbury it—with, my dear girl, *your* help."

"Why do you need me?" Sheba said.

"Because you know how to read and interpret the instructions," DeGroet said. "Unlike the last eight people I sent in, all of whom are now dead."

7

DEGROET SNAPPED HIS FINGERS TWICE, POINTED TO the section of the paw they were next to, and then pulled Sheba away to one side. Two of the local workers—a hardy older man with wind-weathered cheeks and extravagant gray moustaches and a younger, beefier sort in a striped robe and fez, whose angular goatee and eyebrows made him look perpetually outraged—stepped forward and bent to the task of scraping out mortar around the edges of a block of stone that Gabriel hadn't realized was a separate block to begin with. Which was the point, of course—for this block to have remained in place undetected for all these centuries, the seam would have had to have been pretty damn well concealed.

They made short work of it, no doubt because they'd done it at least eight times before. Grunting and straining, they then levered the stone out of the way, moving it first just a millimeter at a time, then an inch, then a few inches, and then all the way. It slid smoothly, though ponderously, across the ground and the two workers left it where it lay, smacking their hands together to get rid of dust or restore circulation or both. A third local, wearing the same sort of striped turban as the older man (and looking similar enough facially, Gabriel thought, that he was likely related—a son, a nephew, something), brought a handful of torches and passed them around: one to each of the first two workers, one to Karoly. He also held onto one for himself, but that left one extra, and behind DeGroet's back, Gabriel stepped forward to take it. No way was he going to let Sheba go in there by herself.

The son/nephew went first, after lighting his torch with a flick of a lighter. The lighter went around from hand to hand and the torches all went alight quickly—they must have been doused in some sort of accelerant. Karoly followed the young man in, then DeGroet, pushing Sheba ahead of him, one of her bare and goose-pimpled arms in his left fist, his sword in his right. The two workers who'd moved the stone looked at Gabriel then, offering him the privilege of following directly behind the boss, but Gabriel had his own reasons for not wanting to get too close to DeGroet and waved the others on ahead. They grabbed some bags of supplies from the ground and went inside. Then Gabriel ducked to squeeze through the dark entrance himself. As soon as he did, he realized that this was not just a passageway—it was a crudely carved staircase, descending steeply into the rock below the statue.

The steps were about half a foot high and Gabriel counted fifty-three of them before the descent bottomed out. So they were some twenty-five feet below the statue's base. The passageway opened up, widening slightly, and the torchlight cast into relief a set of carved images on either side. Bordered with a double row of hieroglyphs above and below were long, narrow strips of art depicting seated deities with animal heads, men of various descriptions, what looked like scenes of court life on the left wall and of farming on the right. Sheba stopped at several points to examine a particular image or piece or writing, then continued on in silence.

Gabriel could only imagine what this was like for her—it was extraordinary enough for him, and he wasn't a linguist with a specialization in ancient languages. To someone in Sheba's field, this corridor by itself was a lifetime's work, handed to her on a platter. At the same time, she was twenty-five feet underground, in a claustrophobic stone corridor, breathing musty air and not enough of it, surrounded by men with torches and blades who'd already kidnapped her twice and threatened to do worse. Of course Gabriel was there, too—but she didn't know that, and there was no way he could tell her.

They came, eventually, to another staircase, this one leading up, and from the direction they'd been walking Gabriel concluded they were now ascending into the belly of the beast, literally: by his mental calculations he'd have said they were more or less at the geometric center of the Sphinx, equally far from the right and left sides, from front and back. The steps here were taller, and Gabriel only counted thirty of them before they had reached a chamber at the top. Gabriel hung back, pulled the fabric of the burnoose around to cover his nose and mouth and held his torch away from his face so that he remained in shadow.

"Rashidi," DeGroet said and gestured at the young man in the lead. "Show her."

Rashidi looked to his older relative for guidance, received a nod, and then cautiously brought his torch closer to the far wall.

Gabriel noticed two things immediately—three, really, if you counted the smell. The first was a rectangular panel on the wall, similar in size to the stele outside and filled with what to his eyes looked like similar writing. The second was a hole in the wall at waist height, circular and dark, just about wide enough for a trim man to fit inside.

Then there was the smell, which was the unwholesome odor of a morgue or a battlefield, the smell of bodies that had lain out too long and been neglected. Gabriel wondered if it was the remains of the unfortunate men DeGroet had sent in earlier that he was smelling. Even if they'd removed the bodies (and he didn't see them lying around anywhere), this was certainly not the sort of place you could air out afterwards.

The flickering torchlight played over the writing on the wall and Gabriel saw Sheba's face fixed in concentration. Her lips moved rapidly but without sound, as though she were talking to herself.

"You see what we are dealing with, Miss McCoy?" DeGroet said. "We've had the symbols translated as best we could—which was not very well, I'm afraid. But even if we knew accurately what each symbol meant, that wouldn't tell us anything by itself, would it?"

"No," Sheba said.

"So you tell us, please. What is on the other side of this wall, and how can we get to it?"

"It's a… a reliquary, a storage chamber for, for… well, it says here 'the remains of the gods,' but the word for 'remains' is ambiguous, it could also refer to artifacts—artifacts depicting the gods, ritual artifacts, that sort of thing." She paused. "There is a warning that says only priests shall enter. 'A priest of Sekhmet may cross the threshold'—you see the lioness figure, there, that's Sekhmet."

"Good, good," DeGroet said. "And how shall they enter?"

Sheba approached the wall, ran one index finger along the ancient images.

"'Through the portal'—that's this here, I've got to assume," she said, pointing to the circular hole, "'but,' it says, 'take heed the supplicant shall bear all right and proper offerings to... placate, mollify, something like that... the jealous heart of Hathor.'"

"And what does that mean?" DeGroet said.

Sheba shrugged. "There were many forms of ritual offering in ancient Egypt. Burnt offerings, bowls of grain, poured water, incantations."

"And which form does it say is called for here?"

"It doesn't."

"*It must,*" DeGroet shouted, and his voice echoed from the close stone walls. "It must. Read it again."

"I already—"

DeGroet whipped his sword up. The point of the blade danced an inch away from Sheba's throat. "Read it again, I said."

She stepped back, turned once more to face the inscription.

"'...all right and proper offerings... jealous heart...'" Sheba's voice took on a quality of despair as she ran her eyes along the rows of symbols again. Then her voice changed. "Wait, hold on. Here it talks about Hathor's role as guardian of the floods, ensurer of fertility... it says, 'Her heart is'... gladdened?... no, no, made light, 'her heart is made light by the vision of her holy ones loaded down with the river's wealth.' "

"The river's wealth," DeGroet said.

"It's an expression you see in inscriptions during the Early Dynastic Period," Sheba said. "They were a desert people and depended wholly on the Nile for survival. The river's wealth was its water—that and the red silt it left behind, the rich dirt in which they could cultivate crops."

"So what is it telling us," DeGroet said, a mocking tone in his voice, "that we must carry mud to enter?"

"I don't know," Sheba said unhappily. "All I can tell you is what it says."

DeGroet turned aside, surveyed his men.

Gabriel hung back, kept his chin tucked down.

"Zuka," DeGroet said, pointing with his sword at the the older man, who was loaded down with the pair of canvas rucksacks he'd picked up on the way in. "You have canteens in those bags of yours?" The man nodded. "Mix up some mud."

"Mud?" Zuka said. "With what?"

"You have a sandbag?" DeGroet said, and Zuka nodded again. "Use that."

"But—"

"Use it," DeGroet snapped. He turned to Rashidi. "You will carry it in."

The young man's face went pale, and Zuka's head snapped up. "Not my son, please, *effendi*," he said. "I will go. I will carry it."

"You?" DeGroet growled. "Do you think you could fit inside that hole, you fat ox? Or Hanif—" he waved at the man with the goatee "—or Karoly?"

Karoly frowned at this.

"Send the woman," Zuka said.

"I do not trust the woman," DeGroet said. "Your son will do it."

"But he will die, *effendi*."

"He most certainly will die if he doesn't go, since I will kill him, and you with him. Now make your mud." Zuka miserably returned to mixing water from one of his goatskin canteens with the contents of a heavy sandbag.

"You," DeGroet said, turning back to Sheba. "You will tell us what he is to do with this mud."

"I don't know!"

"Figure it out," DeGroet snapped. "You have one minute." He turned to Karoly. "It is like pulling teeth, sometimes. Getting anything done."

Sheba went back to the writing, searching it for any further indication of how the offering was to be presented. Zuka remained kneeling on the floor, taking the sand and dirt that had filled the bag and mixing it with water in a loose, wet pile on the chamber's floor. Rashidi stood alone in the center of the room, visibly trembling.

Gabriel's hand tightened on the grip of the rifle in his hand. He would have to act—he had to do something. The only question was when. He could pull his guns now, grab Sheba, try to escape, but even assuming he didn't get them both killed, the best he could hope for was to make it out alive—he'd never know what lay beyond the hole, what the ancient reliquary held. If there was any chance Sheba could coach Rashidi into opening it successfully…

"Inside the hole," Sheba said, "there should be a basin, some sort of recessed area. He should put the offering in that. You'll need to fill it completely," she said to Rashidi. He nodded furiously, desperately. "Make sure you bring enough."

The pile on the ground had grown considerably—Zuka had split open a second sandbag and emptied a second canteen. Anything, to ensure his son's success.

DeGroet flipped a metal pail into the air with the tip of his sword. Hanif caught it. "He can use that," DeGroet said. "Go on, fill it." Hanif fell to the task, scooping handfuls of the mud into the container.

When it was filled, he exchanged a glance with Zuka and handed the pail to Rashidi.

"Go slowly," DeGroet told the young man. "You don't want to end up like the others, do you?" Rashidi violently shook his head. "Then for god's sake, be careful. You understand what you are going to do?" Rashidi nodded. "Then tell me."

"I am going to pour the mud into a basin."

"It may not be an actual basin," Sheba said. "It might just be a, a, a depression, a shallow area. Or a hole—there could just be a hole."

"A hole," Rashidi said.

"Enough," DeGroet said. "In with you." And he struck Rashidi smartly on the backs of his legs with the flat of his blade.

The young man took off his cloak and crawled into the hole, pushing the container of mud before him. It was a tight fit. He wriggled to get his shoulders and head inside, then his torso, and finally his legs. For a moment, his feet remained, sticking out of the hole, but one at a time they vanished inside, too.

A moment later they heard his voice, muffled and echoing in the enclosed space. "I can't see anything," he said.

"Feel for it," Sheba called out. "On the bottom."

Silence.

"Do you feel anything?" she shouted.

"Rashidi?" DeGroet said. "She asked you a question."

"I do," his voice came. "It's like a bowl, with sloping sides."

"Good," Sheba said. "Are you filling it?"

"Yes," came the voice. And a moment later: "It's full." And then: "What should I do now?"

DeGroet looked at Sheba who had nothing to offer but a look of grave uncertainty. "Keep going," he shouted.

"No," Sheba said, "don't, it could be booby trapped—"

They all heard a sound then, a terrible sound, the sound of stone moving against stone deep within the wall, rapidly gathering momentum, like a heavy boulder as it topples off the side of a cliff, gaining speed as it sweeps past; and then the sound of a collision, but only briefly, as though the object in the stone's path had offered only token resistance and been plowed through.

"No!" Zuka shouted, and he ran forward, dived head-first into the hole himself. DeGroet had been right—he could not fit past his shoulders, but he knelt with his head and arms inside, reaching for something, groping, then finally grasping and pulling, extracting. Gabriel saw Zuka's head pop out of the hole first, then his arms emerged, and in each hand one of his son's boot heels. Zuka pulled at his son's body and it came, shins and thighs and lower torso—but where his upper torso should have been there was nothing. He'd been sliced neatly in half at the breastbone.

Zuka fell back, howling.

"Of *course* it's trapped," DeGroet said, disgusted. "Whatever did you think you were here for?"

8

THE SMELL WAS STRONGER NOW, AND NO DOUBT AT
all about its source. Gabriel saw Sheba turn aside, one
hand clapped over her mouth.

"If you insist on being sick, Miss McCoy," DeGroet
said, "please do so quickly. We have work to do." He
swung around, saw Zuka kneeling over Rashidi's
remains, seemed about to say something, then held
himself back. He paced over to the still considerable
heap of mud on the ground and kicked at it, sending a
clod or two against the wall. There was a second metal
pail where he'd picked up the first one, and he snagged
its handle on the end of his sword. Without looking, he
lifted it into the air and sent it flying behind him—in
Gabriel's direction.

"You," he said. "You're not fat, at least. Why don't
you give it a try?"

Gabriel caught the pail against his chest with the
arm in which he held the torch; in the other, he still

held the shovel and the rifle. The folds of the burnoose were wound around the bottom half of his face but Karoly, looking over, recognized him from outside. "Lajos, no," he said in Hungarian, "this man's clumsy as hell, he'll be dead in no time."

"Well, if he is so clumsy," DeGroet said, loudly, in English, "then his death will be no loss." Without looking over at him, he snapped a command at Gabriel. "Fill it!"

Gabriel hesitated a moment, his fist tightening on the rifle's stock. He saw Karoly's hand drop to the sidearm on his hip. With his own hands full like this, there was no way he could beat Karoly to the draw.

He let the rifle down slowly, set it against the wall, then put the pail down beside the mud pile. He used the shovel to fill it, then set that aside, too. The pail was heavy when he lifted it, the metal of the handle cutting into his palm.

He kept his face averted as he walked past DeGroet toward the far wall and its deadly tunnel.

The hole loomed. What had Sheba called it? The portal. For nine men it had been a portal to the underworld, from this life to the next. What chance was there that it would be anything less for him?

Nonsense, he said to himself. You've been in tighter spots. (Though measuring the tunnel's narrow opening against his shoulders, he wasn't so sure.) You've seen traps like this before and defeated them.

Yes, replied a little voice in his head, but all the knowledge and experience in the world won't stop a ten-ton boulder from snipping you in half if you're lying beneath it.

"Miss McCoy, have you got any advice for our newest volunteer?"

Sheba looked up. She'd been leaning against the wall with her eyes closed, her chest heaving. It was one hell of a chest, and Gabriel had to admit that, if this had to be his last sight on earth, there were worse ones to have. With DeGroet behind him, he pulled the burnoose to one side, uncovering his face, and cocked a crooked smile at Sheba. "Do not cry, *effendi*," he said softly in Arabic, and recognition came all at once into her eyes. She started toward him but he shook his head minutely. With an enormous effort she restrained herself, but the look in her eyes changed from momentary relief to terror, a mute pleading.

"No," she said to DeGroet, "no, this man can't go, you can't send him, he'll die—"

"We all must die sometime," DeGroet said. "But if you are so concerned for his well-being, why don't you tell him something that might help him once he's in there?"

"But I don't know anything," she said, and Gabriel could tell that she wished with all her heart that this wasn't so. "A tribute," she said rapidly, running through the text in her head, "an offering to Hathor, the river's wealth, must deposit a heavy burden to make her heart light... that's all it says. Please... please don't send him." Her eyes slid shut again and her voice got very small. "Send me. I'll do it. Send me instead."

"Oh, don't worry, my dear," DeGroet said. "You'll be next."

Gabriel felt the flat of DeGroet's blade strike his calves.

HE HANDED THE TORCH SILENTLY TO SHEBA, BENT TO set the pail down within the hole, and shoved it far enough in that he could squeeze in behind it. The tunnel walls just barely accommodated his shoulders and for a few feet he feared he might actually get stuck, but the tunnel widened slightly after that, the left and right walls angling away from one another at the top, almost like an inverted trapezoid. He found the fit snug but not uncomfortably so. He *had* been in tighter spots—while caving, for instance. And he'd gotten out of those, hadn't he?

With his arms outstretched, he pushed the pail ahead of him, a few inches at a time, and then followed slowly behind it, feeling his way. The darkness was complete, not a trace of light from either end. He dug beneath the fabric of the burnoose to his jacket underneath, straining to reach the closed inner pocket with the Zippo lighter inside. He brought the lighter out and flicked it open. A tiny orange flame bloomed.

The inner walls the flame revealed were smooth, though hand-carved. They were damp, not just beneath him, where the smell of Rashidi's blood explained it, but on the sides and ceiling as well. He could see the pronounced V-shape the walls made—though the hole in the other room had been circular, the tunnel itself was more like a trough or a channel, with the tops of the side walls significantly farther apart than their bottoms. And there were no carvings on either of the walls, no further instructions for those of Sekhmet's priests who made it this far.

He thought about the text Sheba had read, describing the required offering. The opposition of 'heavy' and 'light' wouldn't have been accidental. Not when the instruction involved placing something heavy—he pushed the pail forward another few inches—into a receptacle; not when it was the descent of some sort of heavy mechanism that had separated

Rashidi into top and bottom halves.

He crept another foot forward and then, feeling ahead of him, found the rim of the basin into which Rashidi had poured his bucket of mud. The bucket was nowhere to be seen, and the top half of Rashidi's body, similarly, had vanished.

From outside he heard a voice, DeGroet's. "What have you found?"

"Nothing," he called back. It was the truth.

"Well get a move on," came the shouted reply.

He held the flame of his lighter to the basin—it was empty. How that could be, he didn't know, given that it had been full just minutes earlier. He felt around the basin for any drainage hole through which the mud might have escaped—nothing.

Turning over, he looked up at the ceiling. At a glance it looked no different from the rest of the tunnel, but upon closer inspection he could make out the concealed edges of a distinct block, much like those of the section of the Sphinx's paw Zuka and Hanif had manhandled out of the way at ground level. Clearly this block could move, too—specifically, it could come down, with great force, and anything lying beneath it would get driven violently down along with it.

But what would happen then? Wouldn't the stone block hammering down shatter the basin beneath it when it struck, or at least leave crushed, pulped matter behind when it rose again?

It would—unless, Gabriel realized, the block containing the basin moved as well, swung out of the way at the same time the block descending from above came down. He pictured the block containing the basin and the one above it as teeth on a giant stone gear that rotated when provoked. You poured your mud into the basin, after a moment the weight caused the wheel to turn, the basin block fell out of the way and the new block from the ceiling rotated in to take its place—with a new empty basin of its own on its upper surface.

And anything that happened to be lying between the two blocks at the time got chopped as the upper block rotated down to take the place of the lower.

It was a devilish trap—clever but simple, and a marvel mechanically. The stone gear must weigh tons, many tons; how it had been carved and moved into place and mounted on some sort of axle and hidden within the rock he couldn't imagine. But then no one had figured out how the Egyptians had managed to build the pyramids either. There was no shortage of mechanical marvels on the Giza Plateau.

Of course, the question of how one might build a trap like this was of secondary importance. The first order of business was surviving this one.

So: what to do?

Not pour the mud, clearly; he couldn't even move the pail onto the stone surface surrounding the basin, since the weight would set off the trap. Nor could he put his own weight on it—but how could he make it across to the other side without doing so?

Gabriel thought about it. It had taken perhaps half a minute between when Rashidi had poured the mud and when the mechanism had crushed him. In theory Gabriel might be able to rush across in that time and be out of the way of the descending block before it fell. In theory. And in practice, too, if he'd been upright, with room to maneuver. But not in this tight, narrow tunnel—he couldn't inch his way far enough fast enough, which no doubt had been what the men who built the tunnel had in mind.

But there had to be a way through. Unless the builders were merely playing a cruel game and there was no reliquary to be found, only a tool for slaughtering unwary priests who were foolish enough to follow the instructions you gave them, to deposit the treasure of the Nile in the place you provided for it...

The place provided for it.

If Gabriel had had more room, he might have slapped himself on the forehead. Of course. What if there had been more than one place provided for it? A priest of Sekhmet would know how to follow the instructions properly, while an impostor would make the same mistake Rashidi and Sheba had made, and that Gabriel had nearly made himself.

Where did Hathor's floods deposit the life-giving silt that brought fertility to the Nile Valley? In a basin at the bottom of the river? No—on the river's banks, for Egyptians to find and harvest.

And here he was in a V-shaped channel, with the walls angling away to either side—like a river.

Who said the blocks before him were the only portion of the tunnel walls that could move?

Gabriel reached into the pail, grabbed a handful of mud, and smeared it on the wall beside him, as high up as he could reach. He coated the surface and went back for more. He slapped the mud onto the stone, piling it up, replacing it when bits slid down. Bit by bit, he built up the upper portion of the V, filling in the angle, adding the weight of the mud to the stone surface. He felt it move, very slightly, as the mud accumulated— and as he reached the bottom of the pail, he heard a soft grinding noise deep inside the wall.

This was it. A mechanism was turning.

But *which* mechanism?

He looked up at the deadly stone above him, ominous in the flickering flame of his lighter. If it came down, it would come in an instant, snuffing him out like… well, like the flame went out now as he hastily pocketed the lighter.

The sound grew louder, and apparently it was audible outside, too, because he heard Sheba scream, "Gabriel, no!"

"Gabriel?" DeGroet said, and then he said something else, but Gabriel couldn't hear what it was because the grinding of the stone was too loud in his ears—

And then the angled wall beside him began to turn in earnest beneath its mantle of mud.

As the wall rotated counterclockwise, the top portion headed downwards—but the bottom portion, the portion closer to Gabriel, turned upwards, and it wedged itself under Gabriel as it went, lifting him, till finally a long section of the side wall was horizontal and he was lying on top of it, his burnoose thickly covered with mud.

And it wasn't done yet.

One more turn of the hidden mechanism and the wall was now angled downward again—only in the opposite direction, facing away from the tunnel rather than toward it.

At which point gravity took over, and Gabriel went sliding through the mud, off the edge, and out into space.

9

HE FELL FOR JUST AN INSTANT—THEN LANDED WITH A
thud on a stone floor. Standing, he stripped off the
ruined burnoose, flung it down and flicked open his
lighter again.

The room was large, the flame tiny. But bit by bit it
revealed his surroundings. There was a wall covered
with hieroglyphs beside him and, leaning up against
the wall at an angle, a huge stone carving of a Pharaoh's
face, similar to the face of the Sphinx itself. Just past
that were two upright caskets, both standing open. The
dead body in one was partially mummified, its head
and arms and upper torso preserved in linen bandages,
the rest of its body uncovered and worn down by the
centuries till all that remained were prominent bones
encased in shrunken, leathery flesh. The other casket
was empty but for a handful of broken lengths of bone
at the bottom.

Gabriel picked up one of these, returned to where

he'd landed, and tore the driest strip he could from the burnoose. It took half a minute, after he'd wrapped the fabric tightly around the bone, for the flame from the lighter to catch and the fabric to ignite. What he wouldn't have given for one of those accelerant-treated torches now…

A voice slithered in through the tunnel, a shout in tone but muffled due to the distance it had to travel. *"Hunt! I know it's you. And I know better than to believe you're dead. Say something, damn you!"*

Gabriel didn't say anything. Instead, he took a quick tour of the room. On the surface of one wall there was a recessed rectangular groove, roughly the shape and size of a door—this was the other side of the panel with the writing on it in the entry chamber, Gabriel realized. It was barred crosswise by two long pieces of granite resting in stone brackets protruding from the wall, which suggested that the giant block the groove outlined might be movable, if the bars were removed.

"Hunt!"

The neighboring wall was the one with the hieroglyphics and the caskets. Beside the caskets there were shelves carved into the wall with rows of canopic jars lined up on them, their tops sculpted with images of the sons of Horus: Duamutef, with his jackal's head; Qebehsenuf, with the head of an eagle; and so forth. These would have held the organs of the mummified man in the coffin—or of *some* mummified man, anyway.

"Answer me, Hunt! I can hear you walking, for Christ's sake!"

He kept walking, his flickering torchlight illuminating the walls as he passed them.

The third wall was bare, nothing on it or before it. But the fourth—

The fourth was something else entirely.

"*Hunt,*" DeGroet shouted. "*Hunt, if you don't answer me, I will kill her.*" And he heard Sheba scream.

"You won't kill her," Gabriel shouted back, "or I will destroy what you came here to find."

The canopic jars, the caskets, the half-wrapped mummy—these things were priceless, it was true, and sufficiently impressive additions to any man's collection to warrant the expense and trouble DeGroet had undertaken to find them. But as soon as he had approached the fourth wall Gabriel had known that DeGroet was after a much bigger prize.

The wall was painted, from floor to ceiling, with a map. Or more precisely with part of a map, since what there was ended at a jagged line and was clearly, deliberately incomplete. The outlines of a triangular landmass were traced, and the upper portion of a teardrop shaped island below. But the lower portion of the island was missing.

And seated before the map, directly below this missing portion, was a stone sculpture of a sphinx.

Not the crude sort of monumental stonework that defined the Great Sphinx itself, or even the more careful, delicate sculpture of the canopic jars—that was still stylized rather than naturalistic. But this sculpture… Gabriel approached it, circled around to view it from all sides. It was almost like a piece from Europe's Baroque period, with loving attention lavished on realistically depicting the rippling muscles beneath the skin of the leonine torso, the sunken cheeks and troubled brow and half-open mouth of the human head. It was life-size, perhaps a bit larger—maybe nine feet long and four feet tall. He'd never seen Egyptian sculpture that looked like this. He didn't think anyone had.

And on its flank was carved an inscription. His Ancient Egyptian was rusty—Sheba would have done a better job of translating it. But as best he could make out, it said something like,

> *Here reposes for eternity the Father of Fear,*
> *His mortal portions entombed,*
> *His secrets kept by stone tongue,*
> *His divine treasure returned*
> *To the Cradle of Fear*

DeGroet's voice thundered: "*You wouldn't dare destroy it, Hunt. An artifact this important, you wouldn't—*"

"Let her go," Gabriel shouted, "or I swear to you there'll be nothing here but rubble."

"*All right*," DeGroet said. "*All right*." Then, after a moment: "*Tell him you're free, my dear. Go on.*"

Sheba's voice floated in: "*I'm... free, Gabriel.*"

The tension in her voice made him skeptical.

"There's a hidden doorway to the room you're in, Lajos," Gabriel said. "It's the only way you're going to get in here unless you want to crawl through the tunnel, and I don't think you do." He was still looking at the extraordinary statue. *His secrets kept by stone tongue...* He wondered how literally the inscription was to be taken.

"I am willing to open the doorway," he called, "but only if you promise that no harm will come to either Miss McCoy or myself. Do you agree?" He knew DeGroet's word was worthless and paid no attention to the man's shouted response. Gabriel was just playing for time while, holding the torch close to the head of the sphinx, he stuck the smallest finger of his free hand into its mouth and felt beneath the statue's tongue.

There was something there.

"*I said I agree,*" DeGroet shouted. "*Now open the door, Hunt.*"

"All right," Gabriel said, fishing out the hard, circular, metal object. "Step away from Miss McCoy. I don't want you anywhere near her, and no guns pointed at her either. Do you understand?"

"*Yes.*"

The object was the size of a coin, with an image of a sphinx on one side. A sphinx with wings. A Greek sphinx.

"Sheba," Gabriel called, "have they stepped away?"

Sheba answered: "*A bit. Not very far.*"

"*Enough's enough, Hunt,*" DeGroet shouted. "*Open the door now.*"

"All right." Gabriel returned to the wall separating this room from the entry chamber and lifted the granite bars from the brackets one by one. He leaned then against the wall. Then he put his shoulder to the rectangular block outlined by the recessed groove, braced himself and shoved.

The block rotated a few inches, as if on a central axis, then a few more when he shoved again. One more shove should do it—but Gabriel stepped back instead.

If he pushed it the rest of the way open, he might well find himself walking into an ambush. Whereas if he made them do it...

He darted over to the two open caskets. Ancient Egyptians hadn't been six feet tall—but by bending his knees, Gabriel was able to fit himself into the empty one. He pressed the end of his torch to the ground, stepping on it to extinguish the flame, then dropped it and took his Colt from its holster.

The room was perfectly, completely dark. And for a moment it was silent.

Then a crack of light appeared as he heard the sound of a shoulder ramming against the stone door from the other side. The crack widened into a wedge, and a moment later he saw Zuka charge through the opening holding a torch in one hand and brandishing a deadly looking curved sword in the other. He was wearing an expression that contained all of his grief, transmuted into rage.

Hanif came through the doorway behind him, his red fez tipped slightly forward, tassel soaring, mouth open in a bellow—and in his fist he held a poignard, a short dagger with a silver blade, ready to plunge it down between Gabriel's shoulderblades if only he could find them.

Finally DeGroet entered, forcing Sheba ahead of him at swordpoint.

Gabriel raised his Colt. He aimed carefully at Zuka and squeezed the trigger.

Nothing happened.

The hammer fell—but no gunshot followed. The wrong bullets, damn it! But the sound of the hammer landing had been loud enough to give away his location.

Gabriel dived out of the casket and heard it crash to the ground behind him. He barreled through the semi-darkness directly at Sheba and snatched her out of in front of DeGroet's saber with one arm around her waist. He saw her hands fly up and her mouth go wide in a terrified scream. He leaned close to her ear and whispered, "It's me."

But there was no time for further conversation.

Zuka and Hanif were coming at them from opposite directions, blades held high—and in the tumult he saw Karoly enter the chamber, too. No sword for him: he raised an automatic pistol and leveled it at Gabriel's chest.

Desperately Gabriel raised the Colt and fired again. This time, for whatever reason, the firing pin struck true, and flame spat from the end of the revolver. He saw Karoly's hand jerk back and his pistol go flying. The short man swore loudly, a vicious Magyar curse.

Gabriel lifted Sheba off her feet and swung her toward Hanif. She lashed out with one bare foot at the top of her arc, cracking him across the face and sending his fez flying. Gabriel, meanwhile, kicked backwards with one leg, catching Zuka in the gut. The man collapsed, gasping.

Gabriel set Sheba down on the ground again and whispered urgently: "Run!"

"Where?" she said.

"Out," Gabriel said, and fired another shot in Karoly's direction. He looked around, but couldn't see DeGroet anywhere. Maybe the old man had fled to a safer spot when he realized he was in a situation where a sword couldn't offer much in the way of protection.

Gabriel pointed Sheba toward the doorway and gave her a shove. It was all she needed—she was off and running. Gabriel followed close behind, but was pulled back by an arm around his throat. Karoly? Hanif? It didn't matter which. He swung around and smashed whoever it was into the giant carved stone face behind him, which teetered from the impact. The man's arm didn't release, though. He smashed backwards again and then once more, and finally the man's grip loosened and he tumbled off.

The doorway was just steps away. Gabriel ran through—

—and felt a long narrow blade slide deep into the flesh of his arm.

He jerked free, saw DeGroet outlined by the torchlight from the other room. The sword blade flickered briefly in the darkness like a serpent darting. It caught him across the cheek, opening a gash. He tasted his own blood, running into his mouth.

He remembered Karoly's warning to Andras earlier, at the airport: *Maybe he'll use you for practice. Cut you to ribbons.*

"You've interfered with my plans for the last time, Hunt," DeGroet said, his voice all the more frightening for being quiet and calm. "Now I rid myself of you once and for all." And he gave a little salute with his sword before lunging in for the kill.

Gabriel whipped the bandolier of rifle bullets over his head and caught the blade with it as DeGroet sent it stabbing toward his chest. Sidestepping, he yanked hard, pulling DeGroet's sword arm wide. That gave him room to step in and swing a fist into the side of DeGroet's skull. It wouldn't have been quite as powerful a blow if Gabriel hadn't been holding his gun in that hand; but he was, and DeGroet crumpled to the floor at his feet.

He ran. His left arm ached where DeGroet's blade had penetrated it; his sleeve was slick and heavy with blood. And his cheek felt like it had been split open to the bone. But he couldn't think about any of that now. Behind him he heard voices shouting in Arabic, English, and Hungarian, angry shouts coming closer as he plunged down the stairs in the darkness. He raced across the long tunnel that would return him to the surface, heavy pounding footsteps clamoring behind him and lighter ones pattering desperately up ahead—Sheba's. He caught up with her halfway up the staircase and they plunged through the hole in the Sphinx's paw together.

Dawn was just starting to break over the Nile, the rising sun's rays streaking the sky a hundred shades of pink and purple and amber. It was a staggering sight and Gabriel would have given anything to be able to take pleasure in it. But he couldn't. Their pursuers were only steps behind, and the workers out here, though temporarily startled to see them emerge, wouldn't stay dumbstruck for long.

He grabbed Sheba's arm and steered her down to where the camels and cars stood side by side. The drivers' seats of the cars were empty, but so were the ignition slots. One good thing about a camel, he thought, as he slung Sheba up onto the back of a particularly tall and hardy-looking animal and then vaulted up after her: no key required.

He kicked the camel's sides sharply and they took off into the desert.

"THEY'RE COMING," SHEBA SAID, LOOKING BACK.

"Of course they are," Gabriel muttered. "Why wouldn't they be."

"They're getting in the cars!"

"Naturally," Gabriel said. In the distance he could hear the engines revving. He was holding onto the reins for all he was worth and driving the animal forward at top speed. For the time being their lead was still widening—but that wouldn't last long.

"What are we going to do?" Sheba said, facing

forward again. She was clinging tightly to Gabriel from behind. It was a pleasant sensation, her soft flesh pressing up against his back, but not quite enough to make him forget about the pain in his arm—or about the men coming up behind them.

"Couple of options," he said as they raced over the hard-packed sand. "We can't outrun them, and we won't be able to lose them if we head into Cairo—they'd have the advantage there. But if we can get into an area where this guy can travel but cars can't…"

"Do you know of one near here?"

"No," Gabriel said.

"What's the other option?"

"Get captured," Gabriel said. "Probably get killed."

"Oh," Sheba said.

Gabriel steered them toward a slightly rockier, more mountainous section of the desert in the middle distance. He wasn't at all confident they could reach it before being overtaken.

A gunshot split the air behind them and a bullet sped by near enough that they could feel the breeze from its passage.

"Take my gun," Gabriel said, gesturing with his elbow toward his hip. "Have you ever fired a gun before?"

"Yes," Sheba said, pulling the Colt from its holster. "What? You don't think kids learn to shoot in Ireland?"

"Not at all," Gabriel said. "I just didn't know you had. Glad to hear otherwise." Another gunshot exploded near them. "You might want to start putting that learning to use now."

Sheba had already swiveled in place and braced her arm against the camel's hump, and now she squeezed off a shot that left the windshield of the nearest car behind them shattered. The car wheeled off erratically, its driver losing blood from a wound in his shoulder.

But there were more cars behind that one, more than there were bullets in the gun, and more guns in them, too; and though a racing camel wasn't the easiest target in the world to hit from a moving car, it wasn't the smallest target either, and they wouldn't keep missing forever.

The area of rocky outcroppings was getting closer. It had something of the quality of a canyon, and Gabriel thought it might just be possible to lose the cars in there, if only it would be too dangerous for them to drive into it, for fear of cracking up against the narrow walls. But first he had to make it there. It was going to be close. He kicked inward with his heels again, demanding of the poor beast every last ounce of energy it had.

They were within yards of the first outcropping when he heard the *put-put-put-put* of a helicopter's blades.

His heart fell. *No. Not this close—*

As he watched, a black Sikorsky chopper rose up from behind the rocks, facing them. Beside the pilot, a man stood halfway out of the cockpit, one leg on the landing skid, a machine gun aimed down at them. And painted on the underside of the plane—it couldn't be…

"Gabriel, watch out!" Sheba shouted, pointing.

"Hold onto me," Gabriel said, and urged the animal forward. "Around my neck."

"What are you going to do?" she said, but she followed his direction, looping her arms around him.

"Just hold on," he said. "Don't let go."

The copter was charging downward toward them at steep angle. The gunman hadn't started firing yet, but they saw him take aim. He was almost on top of them.

"Gabriel!" Sheba screamed.

Then the gunman kicked something with one foot,

and it fell, unfurling as it came, dangling below the belly of the copter, and Gabriel let go of the camel's reins to reach up and grab hold as it passed overhead. A rope ladder—and as Gabriel held tight with one good arm and one wounded one to the lowest rung, they were swiftly lifted off the camel's back, Gabriel clinging to the ladder and Sheba clinging onto him, legs wrapping tightly around his waist.

The gunman overhead cut loose with a flurry of bullets that brought the cars behind them to a screaming halt. A few of the drivers reached out through their open windows and fired up at them, but they were firing blind and the bullets missed by a mile.

The copter sped off, rapidly gaining altitude. Looking up, Gabriel saw the man above them toss his smoking gun into the cockpit and begin hauling the rope ladder back aboard.

Gabriel concentrated on holding onto the ladder until the skid was in reach, then carefully shifted his grip over. The man above him helped Sheba into the cabin, then stuck out a hand to help Gabriel.

"Michael send you?" Gabriel asked. The man nodded. Shouting to be heard over the noise of the chopper's blades and engine, he said, "Told me to give you a message. Said keep your cell phone charged next time. We had a hell of a time locating you."

Gabriel hauled himself up and inside. He fell back against the padded seat, breathing heavily.

The gunman pulled the cabin door shut and Gabriel saw in reverse on the glass the same thing he'd spotted painted on the chopper's belly from camelback below: the Hunt Foundation crest.

The pilot called back over his shoulder. "Where we going now?"

"You need a hospital?" the gunman asked, pointing to Gabriel's bloody face and injured arm.

"No," Gabriel said. "I can take care of that myself." He dug into his pocket, passed the ancient coin to Sheba. Her eyes widened as she recognized the symbol on it.

"We're going to Chios," Gabriel said.

10

SHEBA STOOD ON THE BALCONY AND LOOKED OUT
over the cove with its beach of tiny volcanic pebbles
worn smooth by the rolling surf. There was no one on
the beach; no one within half a mile of the beach, in
fact, other than her and Gabriel. The chopper had let
them off in a nearby clearing and they'd walked the
rest of the way. The first thing she'd done when they
reached the house was strip off the satin dress, fill the
tub with warm water, and soak her feet. They'd been
filthy and scraped and bruised and sore and she'd kept
soaking them till at least they weren't filthy anymore.

Gabriel had explored the house, meanwhile, doing
what he could to shore up the security of the place,
which wasn't much—it was a beach house on a Greek
island, after all, not a fortress. Then he'd returned to
the bathroom, where he'd taken off his shirt tenderly,
wincing as the fabric pulled away from where it had
stuck to the wound in his arm. He was for putting on a

bandage and leaving it at that, but Sheba had insisted on dragging him into the tub and washing the wound, and the rest of him, too, while she was at it, and before either of them quite knew what was happening, her aching feet and his bruised and torn flesh were temporarily forgotten.

Now she was standing in the salt breeze wafting off the Aegean, naked as Aphrodite, long hair lying in a damp tangle between her shoulderblades, and Gabriel was seated at a glass-topped table beside her, dressed once again from the waist down, waiting while his shirt dried on the balcony's railing. He was flipping the ancient coin and catching it in his palm.

"It's impossible, Gabriel," Sheba said. "You know that."

"*You* know it. You're the Ph.D. All I know is that this coin was in the statue's mouth."

"Chios was populated that early, but the Greeks didn't start minting coins until the seventh century BC. The Great Sphinx is almost two thousand years older than that."

"Well, maybe it's not," Gabriel said. "Or maybe someone in Chios started making coins earlier than anyone thinks. Or maybe whoever dug that passageway and chamber did it two thousand years after the Sphinx was carved. There's only one thing we know for sure."

She turned to face him. It was distracting to say the least. "What's that?" she said.

"I found this coin," Gabriel said, "in the statue's mouth."

She came over and took it from him. The design depicted a seated sphinx facing to the left beside a narrow wine jug—an amphora—overhung by a bunch of grapes. The sphinx's face was in profile and clearly meant to be female. Her feathered wings coiled up from her shoulders. It was one of the most familiar images of ancient numismatics, the sphinx emblem of Chios.

"What do you think, how did a Greek coin get into a hidden room deep inside the Great Sphinx in Egypt?" Gabriel said.

"There was plenty of contact between their cultures," Sheba said. "As soon as the Greeks started coming over by boat, you see influences from each civilization on the other."

"But a coin in a statue's mouth—is that a ritual you've ever heard of?"

She shook her head. "No."

"Me, neither," Gabriel said. He got up, grabbed his shirt, and headed inside. Sheba followed.

"What about the map on the wall?" Sheba asked. He'd told her about the map during the flight over, while the gunman had been radioing ahead, trying to find an empty house the Foundation could rent on four hours' notice.

"No question about it," Gabriel said, "it was crude, but it was clearly a drawing of the southern coastline of India with Sri Lanka below it."

"The dates are off there as well," Sheba said. "We know there was trade between Egypt and Sri Lanka as early as 1500 BC, but not a thousand years earlier."

"Don't take this the wrong way," Gabriel said, "but I've found when you're dealing with ancient history, plus or minus a thousand years can be well within the margin of error."

"Spoken like a man who flunked history."

"I aced math, though."

"Gabriel," Sheba said, "you can't deny there's

something funny going on here. A statue of a sphinx that's carved in a realistic style that wouldn't be developed till thousands of years later... a map of a place the Egyptians wouldn't make it to for centuries... a coin that wouldn't be minted for centuries..."

"Yeah. Well, we're not going to find an explanation sitting around here." He pulled his shirt on over the thick pad of gauze tapped to his upper arm. Stitches would've been better, but stitches would have to wait. "We need to find someone who can tell us something about this coin. A local expert."

"Where are you going to look for one?"

"Closest town's probably Avgonyma," he said. "Figured I'd head over there, scout around."

"Be careful," Sheba said. "DeGroet might have men here."

Gabriel shook his head. "He never saw the coin. And no one followed us in the chopper."

"DeGroet's even richer than you are, Gabriel," Sheba said. "He could have men on every island in the Mediterranean."

"I'll be careful," Gabriel said. He buckled on his holster and put his jacket on over it. Ninety degrees outside and he was wearing a leather jacket.

"Don't act like you're doing *me* a favor," Sheba said. "Though actually you could do me one if you wanted to. While you're in town."

Gabriel paused in the doorway. "What's that?"

"You could get me a pair of shoes," Sheba said.

LEATHER JACKET OR NOT, THERE WERE WORSE WAYS to spend an hour than on a two mile walk through the sand and scrub of a Greek island, the midday sun shining down on you, no living soul in sight but a pair of goats, the iron bells around their necks clanking as they grazed. Chios lay in the Aegean Sea like a muscled forearm, its elbow jutting toward Turkey, its fist toward the Cyclades. Gabriel's destination was just below the bicep, where a tattoo of an anchor or a mermaid might go if the arm in question belonged to a sailor—or of a sphinx if it belonged to one of the island's traditionalists. The sphinx had been a symbol of Chios dating back to the island's prehistory, when its rocky shores had been inhabited by primitive communities of fishermen and winemakers and farmers. Many amphorae from the period had survived, the clay surfaces of the vessels bearing the same sphinx-and-grapes design as the coin now in his pocket, scrapings of their interiors revealing the ancient residue of wine or olive oil or the peculiar mastic resin native to Chios.

After climbing from sea level up into hills high enough to qualify as small mountains, Gabriel emerged in a clearing surrounded by pine forest, the dusty road leading into a warren of one- and two-story stone buildings. The stones looked to have been quarried from the hills he had just climbed and fit together with the most rudimentary sort of mortar; from their boxy shape and general construction, the buildings looked like they dated back to the medieval period. One or two had thatched awnings and wooden chairs out front, some with wooden tables between them; most of the seats were unoccupied, though in one an old woman slept, baking in the sun with a cat at her feet.

The streets were largely empty, so Gabriel was a bit surprised when, on walking through the arched doorway of one of the buildings, he saw a crowd of perhaps a dozen and a half men breathlessly clustered around a bar. Then he recognized the sound of a transistor radio behind the bar delivering a sports announcer's play-by-play. At one exclamation from the device the men all groaned, except for one who went around the circle collecting money from all the others. The bartender, a bald man with prominent eyes and a heavy five-o'clock shadow even at noon, flicked off the radio and the men dispersed to separate tables around the room, all except for two particularly disconsolate-looking souls who remained at the bar.

Gabriel took a seat beside them and ordered a glass of the local Ariousios Oinos. It was said that the city of Chios had been founded by a son of Dionysus himself, and the Chians were accordingly proud of their wine. It was heavy, heady stuff, a red so dark it was almost black. You tasted echoes, Gabriel thought, swallowing, of Homer's wine-dark seas, on which Odysseus and Agamemnon and so many others came to grief.

"Tourist?" the bartender said, in a thick accent and wearing a cheek-stretching grin. "American?"

"American," Gabriel answered, in Greek, "but not a tourist."

He saw the phony smile on the bartender's face relax into something more like a normal human facial expression. It wasn't a smile anymore so much as a tired grimace. "Would you look at me," he said, "look at what I've come to, playing the monkey when someone comes in. Feh." He spat on the floor from the side of his mouth. "No one comes here anymore. This used to be the high season. Now, maybe once every four days, five days, one tourist, one couple, maybe, they order one drink apiece and don't tip. But I smile, smile, say thank you mister American, thank you for your dollar." He spat again, then slopped some liquor from a jug into a water glass and sampled his own wares. "Cigarette?"

He held a crumpled pack out toward Gabriel.

"Thanks," Gabriel said, pulling one cigarette out and letting it dangle between his fingers after the man lit it with a wooden match. He didn't smoke, but he'd learned over the years that you didn't make friends anywhere in the world by turning down an offered cigarette.

"So what brings you to this rump of a village?" One of the men next to Gabriel looked up angrily at this insult, but said nothing, perhaps because the bartender took the opportunity to refill his glass. "You're a magazine writer, a photographer, what?" The bartender eyed Gabriel critically. "You don't look Greek."

"I'm not. Though I spent a lot of time here growing up. My parents loved it in Greece. They died not too far from here."

The bartender nodded. "Then you are Greek enough. If your dead are buried in our soil."

Ambrose and Cordelia Hunt, two of the bestselling authors of the last fifty years thanks to a pair of improbably successful books of religious history, weren't buried anywhere—they'd disappeared at sea during a millennium-themed speaking tour of the Mediterranean and Gabriel's best efforts had failed to turn up any sign of their bodies. He'd spent eight months searching while, back home, Michael struggled to pick up the pieces of the estate and Lucy—poor Lucy, who'd had a strained relationship with their parents from the day she was born and they decided, oblivious classicists that they were, to name their third child after an archangel in the bible, same as they had their first two, only the choices remaining were Raphael and Lucifer, and you couldn't name a girl

Raphael, could you?—had packed a bag and hopped a plane and severed all contact, taking what had been a family of five down to just Gabriel and Michael. Gabriel, Michael, and a foundation worth one hundred million dollars.

But Gabriel didn't tell the bartender any of this, just nodded as though his parents' graves were right here in Avgonyma, this rump of a village.

He tossed back the rest of his wine, took an obligatory drag on his cigarette, and dropped the coin on the bar. It spun for a second before landing sphinx-side up.

"Know anyone around here who could tell me about this?" Gabriel said. "Specifically, any connection between this sphinx of yours and the one in Egypt."

He saw the bartender's face pale. The man shook his head quickly. "You don't want to ask about this, my friend."

"Why not?" Gabriel said, reaching out to pick up the coin again. Another hand came down heavily on top of his, pinning his to the wood.

Looking to his right, Gabriel saw that the man beside him was standing now, though none too steadily. The other man at the bar got up, too.

"We don't talk about the sphinx with nobody, American." The man pressed down on Gabriel's hand, grinding it into the bar. "You people just don't listen, do you?"

11

"'YOU PEOPLE'?" GABRIEL SAID. "HAS SOMEONE ELSE been asking?"

The man turned to his neighbor, barked out a nasty laugh. "Has someone else...?" Turning back, he swung a fist at Gabriel's head. Gabriel ducked under it and wrenched his hand free. He jammed the coin in his pocket.

"Don't start trouble, Niko," the bartender said, "please. Demetria just cleaned the place—"

"Quiet," Niko roared and barreled forward, his arms wrapping around Gabriel's torso and bearing both of them toward the stone wall. Gabriel snatched a half-full glass off the bar as they passed and smashed it into the back of Niko's head. It got Niko to release his grappling hold but only momentarily while he raked bits of glass and flecks of foam out of his thick mat of hair.

Meanwhile, a young man who shared the bartender's complexion got up from a nearby table.

"Who are you to tell my father to be quiet in his own place?" He came forward.

"Christos, don't," the bartender said, patting the air with one hand placatingly.

"No, papa, this loudmouth can't talk to you this way, not in front of me."

"You just say that," Niko said, "because you like the color of the Americans' money. Show them around the island, take them anywhere they want, tell them anything they want—they feel lonely at night, you get down on your knees for them, too?"

Christos was at the bar in two strides, swinging wildly, but Niko put up his left arm to block the blow, and the man behind him grabbed hold of Christos' other arm.

"Let him go," Gabriel said.

"Or what, American?"

Gabriel's hand dropped to his holster. But before he could get it open, someone leaped on his back from behind.

Gabriel didn't see the free-for-all begin—his face was pressed into the dirt floor. But he could hear it going on above him, the sound of punches landing and glass breaking. He raised one elbow sharply, taking out the man lying on top of him, and rolled over, springing to his feet. He jumped back to get out of the path of one enraged Greek who'd found a cudgel somewhere and was swinging it wildly over his head as he charged the bar. The bartender was nowhere in sight, having either dropped behind the bar for safety or run out into the street for help.

Spotting Christos in the swarm of angry men, Gabriel began making his way toward him, pushing the bodies of combatants to either side. If this Christos was favorably disposed toward Americans and inclined to answer their questions, that made him someone Gabriel needed to talk to before a blow from one his fellow countrymen put him into traction, or worse.

His view was blocked for a moment as someone leapt down from halfway up the staircase to the second floor, the bottom half of of his face smeared with blood. But it wasn't Gabriel he was interested in, and they both darted left, and then right, and then left again, trying to get out of each other's way. Finally Gabriel stopped and stood still, his arms at his sides, and the man ran past, shouting his thanks as he went.

With this gory specter out of his path Gabriel saw Christos again, held between two larger men, each spreading one of his arms wide while Niko lifted a wooden chair and swung it back over one shoulder.

Gabriel got to Niko just as the man completed his backswing. He plucked the chair out of Niko's hands as he was about to bring it down. Niko spun, dumbfounded at finding himself empty-handed. Gabriel gave the chair back to him, full in the face, the wood of the chair's back splintering when it connected with the big man's jaw. Niko slumped to the ground. Gabriel dropped the remnants of the chair and finally drew his Colt.

"Let him go," he told the men holding onto Christos' arms. "Yes, you." He gestured with the gun. The men backed away, hands up in the eternal gesture of surrender. He could have had their wallets if he'd wanted them.

"You," he said, pointing to the one with smaller feet. "Take those off."

"My shoes?" the man said.

"Off," Gabriel repeated, and he accepted the soft gum-soled loafers with his other hand. He jammed them into his jacket pocket. They'd do.

"Thank you—" Christos began, but Gabriel cut him off.

"Later. What's the safest way out of here?"

Christos led him behind the bar, where a wooden panel set into the floor came up when he pulled on the iron ring in its center. A ladder led down to a cellar, and at the bottom they found the bartender, sitting on an empty wine crate, playing solitaire with a filthy, creased deck of cards. "You see what you started, Christos?"

"I didn't start it, papa, Niko did."

The old man shrugged. "Nobody ever starts it. But who's left to clean up when it's finished? Eh?"

"I'll clean up, papa."

"You! That'll be the day. Go on. Get your American out of here before they take him to pieces."

Gabriel reached into his pocket, took out a few of the hundred-dollar bills he had left, laid them down beside the king and queen of spades. "I apologize for the trouble."

"Feh," the bartender said, and spat on the ground, but he kept the money.

THEY CAME UP INTO A REAR COURTYARD BEHIND THE tavern building. Christos had a green-and-white papakia—a souped-up moped—leaning against the wall. The long, narrow padded seat had room for two and Gabriel climbed on behind him, holding onto the young man's waist. He saw a purple knot swelling up on Christos' neck where one of the bar's other patrons had landed a blow. It was ugly and looked painful— but things could've gotten a lot worse, Gabriel told himself. They were lucky to be leaving when they were.

Christos revved the engine and they zoomed off. Two sharp right turns brought them to a steeply rising road through the mountains. Christos seemed to know where he was headed, and Gabriel left him alone to concentrate on driving—until he heard the sound of engines coming up behind them.

"Can this thing go any faster?" he asked. In front of him, Christos shook his head.

Had they been spotted leaving the tavern? There'd been several more of the mopeds leaning against the wall, and certainly some of the brawlers they'd left behind might have been mad enough to follow if they'd seen their prey getting away. Maybe even the man he'd left standing in his socks.

But looking back over his shoulder, Gabriel saw not more papakias come into view but a trio of Ducati Multistrada motorcycles, low to the ground and Corvette red. And their helmeted, black-jacketed drivers were a far cry from the rustics who'd bloodied each other for sport back in the bar.

One of them drew the long barrel of a rifle from a side-mounted holster on his bike's chassis and fired two shots in their direction.

Christos swerved across the opposite lane and back again, tilting the papakia at a precarious angle.

"Don't worry," he shouted back, and then, switching to English, "I drive good—like your Steve McQueen!"

"Great," Gabriel said, pulling his gun. Steve McQueen. He twisted in his seat, aimed carefully at the lead driver behind them and pulled the trigger just as Christos swerved wildly again. The shot went wide.

"Damn it, kid, I've only got three bullets left," Gabriel said.

The bikes were gaining on them, their engines

growling as they accelerated. The driver with the rifle was raising his gun again. Gabriel did the same.

"Keep steady this time," Gabriel said, "or I'll save the last one for you."

"But there's a turn coming up!" Christos said.

"Fine," Gabriel said and squeezed the trigger. The driver went off his bike backwards, the faceplate of his helmet shattered. His rifle spun end over end into the brush on the side of the road.

Christos leaned into the turn, an almost 180-degree switchback zigzagging up the mountainous terrain. Gabriel had to strain to hold on.

The two remaining cycles stayed with them through the turn. Neither of the drivers had rifles, but as Gabriel watched, they both pulled out semiautomatic pistols.

"We've got to lose these guys," Gabriel shouted.

"Hold on," Christos said and, turning off the road, plowed through a field of scrub. The spiny undergrowth tore at Gabriel's ankles and every few feet a rock under their tires threatened to overturn them.

The other bikes were still on their tail.

A bullet flew past just inches away.

The field angled upward before them, a sloping incline, hilly but empty, not a boulder to hide behind, not a tree.

"How's this helping us?" Gabriel shouted.

Without warning, Christos braked. Gabriel slid forward, slamming into Christos' back, and the papakia itself juddered ahead a few feet. The bikes behind them shot past, steering to either side of them to avoid a collision. They began parallel turns that would bring them around again—and then as they passed the crest of the next hill over, they vanished from sight. The sound of metal tearing and twisting and smashing against rock reached them from what sounded like far below. Gabriel jumped off the bike and ran forward, slowing as he got to the place where the other men had disappeared. He stopped at the edge of a crevasse, a sudden rocky sinkhole that bisected the field and plunged at least forty feet straight down. The cycles looked to be very near the bottom. The drivers weren't moving.

Gabriel returned to the bike.

"I grew up just the other side of this field," Christos said as they got underway again. "Papa, he would tell me, don't ever drive in there, no matter what. But I didn't listen. None of us boys did. We all dared each other, who could go the closest. We could find the edge with our eyes closed."

"I guess those guys didn't grow up here," Gabriel said.

"I guess not," Christos said.

THEY WERE BACK ON THE ROAD, CHUGGING UP THE side of the mountain once more.

"How do you think those guys got on our tail?" Gabriel asked.

Sitting in front of him, Christos shrugged. "Someone must have called them, told them there was a man asking questions about a sphinx."

"They tell you to keep an eye out for that?"

"Mm-hm," Christos said. "Said they'd pay, too. Fifty dollars U.S. for any tip, no questions asked."

"That's a pretty good deal," Gabriel said.

"It is."

"Yet, instead of taking them up on it yourself, you just led them over a cliff."

"That's not a cliff," Christos said.

"They're just as dead," Gabriel said. "Why'd you do it? Why not turn me in for the money?"

Christos thought about it for a moment. "You gave my father three hundred dollars when you didn't have to. I'm not going to turn you in for fifty."

"What if they offer four hundred?"

Christos looked back over his shoulder and grinned. "We'll see."

The miles peeled away beneath their tires and the view the road commanded became more spectacular as their elevation rose.

"Where are we going?" Gabriel finally asked.

"Anavatos," Christos said. "To see a man named Tigranes."

"I thought Anavatos was deserted."

"Almost," Christos said. "Still a few people live there."

"And this Tigranes, he knows something about the history of Chios' sphinxes?"

"Oh, yes," Christos said.

"Did you take the others to see him," Gabriel asked, "the other Americans?"

"I tried," Christos said. "And the Hungarian they worked for, too." Gabriel's hands tensed. "But he wouldn't talk to them. Just plain refused."

"I see. And why do you think he'll talk to me? Because I pay better?"

"No—Tigranes doesn't care about money. He wouldn't live in Anavatos if he did."

"Then why?"

"For one thing, you speak our language," Christos said.

"That means something to him?" Gabriel said.

"That means everything to him," Christos said.

12

ANAVATOS CROWNED THE MOUNTAIN THEY'D BEEN ascending, a cluttered, half-ruined collection of cheek-to-jowl stone buildings that made the buildings of Avgonyma look modern by comparison. The only way in was through a steep and winding road that twisted back on itself several times before arriving. The town's name meant "unreachable" or "inaccessible," and never had a place been more appropriately named, Gabriel thought, except maybe Dull, Texas. Built into the mountain, Anavatos was also sometimes called "the invisible city"—if you didn't know it was there, you'd never see it from below, which is why Chians had used it as a hideout or refuge for centuries. This lasted until 1822, when a siege by the Turks had ended in a mass suicide, with the residents of Anavatos plunging to their deaths off the mountain rather than be taken alive. It had been deserted ever since, a ghost town in the most literal sense.

The streets, as they entered, were completely empty—not even an old woman, not even a cat.

Christos drove through them with the confidence of one who knew where he was going and Gabriel let himself be led. He thought briefly about Christos's earlier remark when asked if his allegiance could be bought for $400—*We'll see*—but decided Christos wouldn't have joked about it if he were really leading Gabriel into a trap. He was a local kid, maybe eighteen or nineteen years old, not someone polished in the art of deceit. And even if Gabriel were wrong about this... well, it was too late to do anything about it now.

Gabriel held on till Christos pulled up in front of a two-story building whose stones looked scrofulous with age and wear. There were openings in the walls, but it was an exaggeration to call them windows; there was no glass in them, certainly. And in lieu of a door there was only an uneven archway.

They dismounted and Christos shouted up, cupping both hands around his mouth. "Sir! It's Christos Anninos. There's someone I want you to meet."

No response was shouted back—but after a moment the silence was broken by the sound of a pair of sandals slapping against stone steps.

The man who emerged from the doorway brought the word *antique* to mind, not only because he was elderly—though he was that, his face and hands seamed with countless wrinkles, his hair tumbling gray and untrimmed down to his shoulders, a shaggy white beard resting on his chest—but also because he wore a wool chiton, fastened at the shoulder with a metal clasp and flat sandals held on with straps of knotted leather. He looked like something out of a museum diorama.

In the crook of one arm, he was carrying a U-shaped wooden frame with four strings threaded from a crossbar down to the base of the U—a sort of miniature harp that was just the touch needed to complete the picture of an ancient Greek bard. They might have interrupted him while he was posing for an illustration for a dictionary, Gabriel thought; or perhaps he was like the men who dress up in plastic gladiator outfits and hang around the Coliseum in Rome, bumming cigarettes from tourists and hoping to score a dollar or two posing for photographs. This was Gabriel's first impression, and he cursed himself for having hoped that this local youth might bring him to someone with genuine knowledge of the island's past.

But looking again in each man's eyes, Gabriel saw no sign of a put-on; both seemed in earnest, and Christos in particular had assumed an attitude of respect and deference entirely at odds with his earlier manner when racing up here on the bike. And taking another glance at the old man's attire, Gabriel saw how far from a polished, plastic simulation of antiquity it was; also, how protectively the man cradled his clearly handmade instrument, how worn the bridge was and how calloused were his fingertips. He actually played the thing, apparently. He might well be a lunatic, living out here in an empty town on the top of a mountain—but he did not seem a charlatan.

Tigranes, meanwhile, took a similarly detailed survey of Gabriel, gazing critically at him from head to toe and, unlike Gabriel, looking progressively less satisfied with what he saw as his assessment progressed. He frowned at the leather jacket and the frown deepened when he got to the holster poking out at the bottom.

"Another?" The old man's voice was low and quiet,

almost a whisper. "You bring another to me who cares nothing for my ancient duty, who cares only to satisfy his demands, who will mock and denigrate what he does not understand?"

"No—" Christos began, but Gabriel stepped forward, put a hand on the boy's arm to silence him. Perhaps he was wasting his time—but if, on the other hand, the old man was what he seemed, Gabriel did not want to get turned away at the door as the Americans working for DeGroet had been.

"Honored father," he said, in Greek, "I do not have the privilege of knowing you, but I promise, I mock nothing of the ancient world. I am a student of the ancient ways and hold them in the highest respect."

Tigranes eyed him warily.

"Your instrument," Gabriel said, gesturing toward the harp, "is it a phorminx or a kithara? It's not a barbitos, I don't think... is it?"

Tigranes continued staring at him, his heavy eyelids narrowing to slits. "Of course it is not a barbitos," he said, finally. "I am no woman, playing melodies for the pleasure of the household."

"Then it is a phorminx?" Gabriel pressed.

"Yes," Tigranes said grudgingly. "It is a phorminx."

"And do you... use it?"

"To play merry refrains, you mean?" Tigranes said. "For visitors to dance and drink to? Is this what you have in mind, young man?"

"Of course not," Gabriel said. "That would be an insult to the instrument. You don't dance to the music of the phorminx—you declaim heroic poetry."

Tigranes' eyes widened at this, and he looked to Christos, who nodded.

"Come upstairs," Tigranes said.

* * *

THE MAN'S LIVING QUARTERS WERE AS AUSTERE AS the building's exterior would lead one to expect. There were no signs of electricity or other modern conveniences. Through a rear window in what clearly served as Tigranes' bedroom Gabriel saw a privy out back; in one corner of the room he saw a clay pitcher resting by a straw pallet. This room occupied roughly half of the second floor. Passing through it, Gabriel reached an even emptier sitting room whose only furnishings were drawn on the wall, a crude mural in the Attic style of a young man reclining on a bench before a seated, older man holding a lyre.

Tigranes sat cross-legged on the floor and Gabriel followed suit. Christos discreetly remained in the room outside.

"What is that picture?" Gabriel asked, nodding toward the mural.

"That," Tigranes said, "is my grandfather's grandfather's grandfather. Fifty grandfathers ago."

"He was a bard?" Gabriel said, using the ancient term for it: *rhapsode*, one who sews stories together.

"All the men in my family have been bards," Tigranes said, but he used a term more ancient still: *aoidos*. "From the earliest of days to the present."

"Here on Chios?"

Tigranes nodded, but said no more.

"And your... ancestor," Gabriel said, reaching for a way to draw the old man out, "he... taught pupils?"

"My ancestor did teach a pupil," Tigranes said. "His son. And his son taught his son, and so on. But you misunderstand what you see here. He is not the teacher in this picture." He patted the wall by the image of the boy on the bench. "The young man—*that* is my ancestor."

"I see," Gabriel said. "And who is the old man teaching him?"

"Homer," Tigranes said.

13

"HOMER," GABRIEL SAID.

"Homeros, the prince of the *aoidi*, yes—you did not know he was from Chios?"

Gabriel knew that Chios was one of several places in the region that laid claim to being the birthplace of Homer—it was the Mediterranean's answer to *George Washington slept here.*

"I… I did not," Gabriel said.

"Have you never seen the Daskalopetra? The throne from which Homer taught? It is beside the beach at Vrontados."

He'd seen it, on one previous visit—a jutting stub of stone overlooking the sea. Any man might have sat there, or no man might; none but sea birds rested on it now.

"From father to son for twenty-eight hundred years," Tigranes said, "the words of Homer have passed, a sacred trust. The stories of Achilleus and

Odysseus and Oedipus—"

"Oedipus?" Gabriel said, and Tigranes nodded. He said: "My father taught me as his father taught him, the sixteen thousand verses of the *Iliad*, the twelve thousand of the *Odyssey*, and the seven thousand of the *Oedipodea*." He drew a claw-like hand across the strings of his phorminx and an ancient chord hung in the air. "*Sing, muse, the passion and hubris of Oedipus of Thebes, unhappiest of mortals, whose fate was writ before his birth...*"

As he continued reciting the poem, line after line of hexameter spilling forth, Gabriel felt the hairs on the back of his neck rise. It was the same feeling he got when walking into a sealed tomb for the first time, entering a place no man had set foot for centuries; or holding in his hands an artifact believed lost forever— which, after a fashion, is what this was. You could buy a copy of the *Iliad* or the *Odyssey* in any bookstore, in any language, in any country on the face of the earth. You could find it, god help you, in bits and pixels on the Internet. But the *Oedipodea* was one of the lost works of the ancient world, the only known written copy having been destroyed in the burning of the Library of Alexandria.

"It's... beautiful," Gabriel said when Tigranes reached the end of the introductory *apostrophe* and paused for breath. "And you say it is the work of Homer? I thought I remembered the *Oedipodea* being credited to someone else."

Tigranes made a disgusted sound. "Cinaethon of Sparta," he said, scoffing, "that's what Pausanias said. And Plutarch. But what did they know? Did their fathers learn it at the feet of the poet himself?"

Gabriel understood now why Christos had brought

him here. This was not the improvisation of a madman on a mountaintop—even the portion he had heard so far had the authenticity and coherence of a genuine artifact, a traditional lyric learned by rote as one might memorize and transmit a liturgy, from mind to mind and voice to voice across a sea of generations. It was a record of a forgotten time, one that very likely existed nowhere in the world but in this old man's head. And it was a record with a particular relevance to the question he had posed in the tavern, since whether by Cinaethon or by Homer the *Oedipodea* would have told the story of Oedipus' life—ending, famously, with his killing his father, marrying his mother, and putting his own eyes out when he learned what he had done… but beginning, just as famously, with his triumph over one of Greece's most ancient monsters, the riddle-posing sphinx.

"Do you," Gabriel began, "do you know the whole thing? All seven thousand verses?"

Tigranes' eyes blazed and his chin rose haughtily. "All seven thousand! Of course!" He passed a hand before his eyes. "It is my duty to remember. Until the day I die." His voice fell, taking on a tone of sadness. "I repeat them daily, though only to myself now. For I have no son, no one to teach. They will die with me. But not," he said, rousing some fire again, "a day sooner."

"I would greatly like to hear the rest," Gabriel said.

"Then prepare yourself," the old man said, his voice dropping into a rehearsed cadence, rich in timbre and suffused with pride, "for a story of four nights telling, an adventure unlike any you have heard before, for four nights of bloody deeds and terrible loss, of men brave and desperate, of women cruelly shamed." His hand played among the strings of his phorminx, and the air jangled with a dissonant tune that spoke of distant shores, of men struggling under the heat of a foreign sun. "Prepare for four nights of splendor and depravity, four nights of—"

Christos' voice interrupted then from the other room, where he was standing at the window. "Better make it four minutes," he said. "We've got company."

"EXCUSE ME," GABRIEL SAID. HE RUSHED TO THE window. Through it he saw the alleyway behind Tigranes' home and the rooftops of the one-story buildings clustered around. Past those, he could see a sliver of the entry path leading into Anavatos, and, as they passed, the men coming up along it. Walking two abreast, it looked like a latter-day siege force: a dozen men at least, all armed, and bringing up the rear, standing a foot taller than any of the others, a man Gabriel had hoped never to see again. Andras.

Gabriel ducked out of sight, drew Christos close. "Is there any way out of here other than the way we came in?"

"Out of the building or out of Anavatos?"

"Either."

"No," Christos said.

"There has to be another way out of the building," Gabriel said. "There always is." He looked around. "We can go out the window."

"With an eighty-year-old man?" Christos said. "We can't leave Tigranes here. They'd torture him to make him talk. They'd kill him."

Gabriel ran into the other room, where Tigranes still sat, one hand poised over the strings. The expression on his face said how little he liked being interrupted once he'd begun declaiming, but that he was prepared to forgive all if Gabriel apologized and quietly returned to his seat. Well, he could have his apology, but the rest would have to wait.

"Honored father," Gabriel said, putting one hand under Tigranes' elbow and lifting him to his feet, "I regret that we won't be able to properly begin the *Oedipodea* yet. There are some men on their way, and we can't let them find us here."

"Take your hands off me," Tigranes said, and Gabriel released his arm. The old man smoothed down his chiton.

"We've got a few minutes at most," Christos said.

"You wish to avoid these men?" Tigranes said.

"We have to," Gabriel said.

"Very well. Follow me." And Tigranes headed down the stairs, his sandals slapping against the stone once more.

At the ground floor, he led them past the open front archway (Gabriel glanced outside: no men in sight, not yet), to a small chamber at the far wall. A closet, really—they could barely all fit inside and there was no door to it. As soon as anyone entered the building they'd be seen.

"This is no good," Gabriel said, turning to Tigranes, but Tigranes wasn't there.

Christos and Gabriel looked at each other, baffled— the old man, who had been standing behind them, had vanished somehow while they weren't looking. Then they heard the slap of his sandals overhead.

Gabriel looked up. There was no ceiling to the closet, and Tigranes was ten feet up, climbing the wall using hand- and toeholds carved into the stone like the rungs of a ladder, the phorminx hanging across his back from a leather strap. He was moving quickly; for an octogenarian, the man was remarkably spry.

Gabriel gestured for Christos to go up next, and while the young man did, Gabriel drew his Colt. From the street outside he heard voices. The men were talking, in Greek.

So Andras had rounded up some local talent this time.

Then he heard Andras himself, speaking English, telling them to shut the hell up. And in the quiet that fell he heard one gun after another being armed.

He looked up. Christos was ten feet overhead now and Tigranes was nowhere to be seen. As Gabriel watched, he saw the upper half of Christos' body vanish as well—into what he could only assume, since he couldn't see it from below, was a hole in the wall separating this building from the one beside it.

"Old man!" came a shout from the street. "Come out and talk!"

Gabriel holstered his pistol and began climbing.

"We will count to three and then we will come in. You don't want this, Tigranes. It'll go easier for you if you just come out."

A moment later the counting began, but Gabriel only heard the first number—*Tria!*—before he reached the hole Tigranes and Christos had entered and dove into it himself. Christos was in front of him, crawling swiftly on his hands and knees along a stone tunnel, its inner walls the pink and beige of cut sandstone, light coming in through crevices where the ancient mortar had crumbled away. Past him, Gabriel could just make out Tigranes' chiton-covered rear and the phorminx lying against his back, nearly scraping the ceiling as he crawled.

Judging from the length of the tunnel, it had to pass through quite a few adjacent buildings, turning periodically as the angles of the neighboring houses required. They passed several openings leading down to closets like the one through which they'd entered. Apparently the residents of Anavatos hadn't relied solely on the inaccessibility of their town for purposes of holding out against a siege—tunnels like these would have helped them resist occupation as well.

Though in the end, of course, it hadn't been enough. Gabriel did his best not to think about this.

From some distance back they heard, very quietly, the sound of shouting and pounding footsteps.

"Ask him where we get out," Gabriel whispered to Christos, who passed the question along. He whispered back a moment later: "Next one over."

Then Christos disappeared around a turn in the tunnel, and when Gabriel made the turn himself he saw Christos and Tigranes both on their knees in a wider chamber with a chimney leading up. "Where does this lead us?" Gabriel asked.

"To the end," Tigranes said, and started climbing.

Well, that would more or less have to be the answer, Gabriel supposed: there were only so many buildings standing side by side and no tunnel could go on forever. Perhaps there would be a way for them to climb down the wall of the last building and then get behind Andras and his men, sneak back to the road and return on foot back to a more inhabited part of the island...

Gabriel followed Christos up the short shaft of rock and stepped out onto a flat surface. It wasn't the roof of a building. It was the stony ground at the edge of a cliff.

This was the end, indeed—the end of Anavatos, the edge at which the town's inhabitants had made their final stand, and from which they had leapt to their deaths. Only one hardy tree grew here, its roots clinging to the rock and dangling over the edge.

"What did you bring us here for?" Gabriel said, looking out over the sheer fall and the rocks far below. "There's no way out!"

A shout rose in the distance: "Over there! I see them!"

"There is," Tigranes said, "there *is* a way—"

"Then you'd better tell us pretty quickly what it is," Gabriel said. He pulled his gun. Two bullets—damn it, how did he wind up down to two bullets again? And no telling whether they'd even fire...

"Down the mountain," Tigranes began.

"What," Christos said, the fear evident in his voice, "climbing down the side?"

"To a point," Tigranes said.

"Where?" Christos said.

But there was no time for an answer as men rose into view just yards away, arms and legs pumping as they ran toward the dead end where their prey was cornered.

Gabriel pulled the trigger and a gunshot split the air, taking one of the men down. But the others kept coming.

"Get into the tunnel," he shouted, "we've got to go back—" And he made for the opening of the chimney. But before he could get there, a man emerged from it, a short Greek with hair the color of steel wool and a jagged scar across his forehead. The man was holding a gun and he fired it without pausing even to aim, and it was only that overeagerness that saved Gabriel from catching a bullet in the chest. Gabriel threw himself against the man, knocking his gun away and taking him to the ground. But another came up right behind him. This one did take the time to aim, steadying his gun hand carefully while Gabriel and the scarred man grappled on the ground at his feet.

"No!" Christos shouted, and launched himself at the standing gunman, tackling him around the knees. They fell to the ground in a heap, the barrel of the gunman's pistol just millimeters from where Gabriel lay below the scarred Greek, his throat clutched in the shorter man's hands. Gabriel's saw the gunman's eyes spark with a vicious elation, saw his finger tighten on the trigger—

Desperately, Gabriel rolled over as the gun beside him fired. The explosion was deafening. But it was his enemy's head the bullet entered, not his own. The man's hands fell away from his throat and Gabriel staggered to his feet. He kicked the gun out of the other man's hand while Christos slugged him, hard, in the face.

"Enough!" came a nasal voice and it took Gabriel a moment to realize the word had been spoken in Hungarian, not Greek. He looked up, raising his Colt at the same time. Andras was standing near the edge of the cliff, one meaty arm around Tigranes' throat, the other holding a pistol to the old man's temple.

"Drop your gun, Hunt," Andras said, "or the old man dies."

"Lajos would skin you alive if you killed him," Gabriel said. "He's the only man on earth who knows about the sphinx."

"What Mr. DeGroet does or doesn't do is my problem," Andras said, "not yours. Drop your gun."

Behind him, Gabriel heard the sound of footsteps racing up to within a yard or two, then pattering to a halt. Five men, six men—who knew how many. Too many. One bullet just wasn't enough, even if he'd been willing to risk Tigranes' life. Which he wasn't.

Gabriel reluctantly released the hammer of his Colt and let it slide from his hand to the ground.

He felt men take hold of each of his elbows roughly, felt his wrists drawn together behind his back, felt a length of rope binding them together. A few feet away, he saw another pair of men take hold of Christos.

Andras came forward, dragging Tigranes with him. He bent to pick up Gabriel's gun.

"That's a very nice weapon," he said. "An antique, isn't it? I think I'll keep it."

"You son of a—" Gabriel started, but Andras slapped him brutally across the face with the side of his Colt. He felt the slash on his cheek from DeGroet's sword reopen and start bleeding again.

"Take them away," Andras said, wiping Gabriel's blood off the cylinder.

14

THEY WERE BEING HELD IN ANAVATOS' TALLEST building, a three-story tower near the cliff's edge that during the town's heyday had been the site of an olive oil press, a church, and a school. Today it was an empty shell with a few unbroken benches the only reminder of its earlier functions.

From somewhere Andras' men had found a pair of straight-backed wooden chairs, one with arms and one without, and Gabriel and Christos were tied to these, side by side. Tigranes was seated on the ground across the room, facing them, his hands free, his phorminx in his lap.

On a bench against one wall, Gabriel's Colt lay, tantalizingly out of reach. Andras had placed it there deliberately, Gabriel figured. Just to make a point.

"Tell, old man," Andras said, his Greek crude and heavily accented. He had a cell phone in his hand and, having dialed it a moment earlier, was holding it out in Tigranes' direction. DeGroet was on the other end of the line, waiting silently.

When nothing happened, DeGroet's voice spat from the speaker, thin but clear. "Kill one of them."

"Which one?" Andras said.

"The Greek," DeGroet said. "He wouldn't care about Hunt."

Andras nodded to the men standing behind Christos' chair, and one of them drew a foot-long hunting knife from a scabbard at his waist. He held it to Christos' throat.

"Don't do it," Gabriel said, in Greek, to the man. "He's done nothing wrong. He's one of you."

"He chose his side," the man muttered. His knife didn't budge.

"Boy," came DeGroet's voice, "can you understand me?" His Greek was better than Andras', though still accented.

"Yes," Christos said.

"Tell the old man to begin reciting the poem about the sphinx or my men will cut your head off. Tell him that."

"Tigranes," Christos said. The old man looked over at him. "You heard what they want." His voice trembled. "Don't do it."

"They will kill you," Tigranes said.

"Lajos," Gabriel called out, "you don't need to do this. I know everything you want to know—I already got it out of him. Bring me to wherever you are and I'll—"

"Oh, *now* you wish to cooperate. Imagine that. The great Gabriel Hunt, within an inch of losing his life at last, and now he wants to make a deal. Well, no. I think not. You had your chance—plenty of chances. No more deals. Andras?"

"Yes," Andras said.

"Start a little at a time," DeGroet said in Hungarian. "Cut off the boy's hand. Then the other, then a foot. We'll make the old man talk."

Andras nodded again to the man with the knife and explained partly through gestures what DeGroet wanted. It wasn't a difficult message to convey.

Gabriel, meanwhile, was straining against the ropes holding him to the chair. There was one around his wrists and another tying his ankles to the front legs, and both were taut and unyielding. With enough time and privacy he might be able to introduce some slack, work the knots apart, maybe even inch over to the wall and work the ropes against the rock till the fibers came apart—but time and privacy were two things he didn't have.

One of the men untied Christos' arms and then held them pinned to the wooden arms of the chair. The other, the one with the knife, said to Christos, "You right handed or left? I'll do the other first."

"No," Tigranes said. "No. I cannot sit by while this boy is maimed or killed. Not when all you wish is to hear my poems. I will play." Angrily, he strummed his instrument, and the melody that arose sounded dark, martial.

"There," DeGroet's voice came from the cell phone. "You see?"

"Raise your voice in song, o goddess," Tigranes intoned, *"and tell of Peleus' mighty son, Achilleus, who rained misery untold upon the brows of his fellow Achaeans. Many a hero among them was laid low and brought to Hades, their flesh made carrion for the beaks of vultures and the jaws of wild dogs upon the blood-drenched plains of Troy—"*

DeGroet interrupted, his voice blasting from the

tiny speaker in Andras' hand: "Troy? Troy? I don't want the *Iliad*, you old fool, I want the sphinx—"

"I am very sorry," Tigranes said, his voice soft, his music stilled, "but I am, as you say, old. My memory is not what it was. I cannot enter the old tales anywhere I wish, or that you might wish—I can only remember them from the beginning."

"You're joking," DeGroet said.

"From the beginning," Tigranes repeated. "And that means I have to start on the plains of Troy. And if I am interrupted, I will have to return to the plains of Troy once more, and start over again. From the beginning."

"I will have them kill the boy!" DeGroet shouted.

"You can kill whomever you wish," Tigranes said. "Him, me, yourself. But it will not change the fact that I can only tell the stories in one way: from start to finish, in their proper order."

DeGroet uttered an oath, a fevered Hungarian profanity. The language was rich with them.

"All right," he said finally. "Do it in whatever order you have to, but for god's sake, do it quickly."

"For the gods' sake," Tigranes said, "I will do *properly*."

"Just start already," DeGroet said. "Andras—call me back when he gets to the sphinx." And the connection was broken.

"You heard him," Andras said, pocketing the phone. He looked around the room, the expression on his face making it clear that he'd have to be tied to a chair himself in order to sit through hours of Greek poetry being recited. "Start," he said. "And you—" He pointed to the man with the knife. "Say me when he reaches the sphinx. I go up." He strode out and they all heard his steps on the stairs.

"Sit, gentlemen, sit," Tigranes said, gesturing to their captors, Greek men all, ranging in age from their late twenties to a few in what looked like their late fifties. "We will be here for a while, you may as well be comfortable." Some of the men sat; some remained standing. Tigranes smiled at them. "You know that Homer himself was once a captive, a hostage—it is from this experience that he got his name, *homeros*. He had another name at birth. You did not know this?" He made a clucking sound with his tongue. "You should be ashamed to know so little of your own heritage."

"Stop talking and begin reciting," the man with the knife said. "We don't want to be here all night."

Tigranes shrugged. "As you wish."

His fingers plucked at the strings.

TWO HOURS LATER, TIGRANES HAD REACHED THE bedroom of Helen of Troy and all the men sat at rapt attention. Their eyes were on Tigranes as he sang of her treachery and sadness, of her lover, Paris, and his cowardice, of their dalliance between the sheets while men were dying for them by the score on the battlefield below. His hands alternated between plucking the strings of his lyre and waving in midair to accompany the vivid word pictures he was painting. His voice grew quiet during moments of grieving and loud for the bloody battles, sped up when events took an unexpected turn and lingered painfully when a hero's fatal wounds bled into the Trojan soil.

Glancing to his left, Gabriel saw that Christos was mesmerized as well: he didn't seem anxious for himself any longer, only for the fate of Hector and Ajax and Odysseus. As Gabriel himself might have been—Tigranes was an oddly compelling performer, and there might never be another opportunity to hear the *Iliad* recited in this way, as it was originally meant to be heard. But he had other priorities. He nudged Christos' leg gently with his knee.

It took two more nudges to break the spell. Then Christos looked over. Gabriel jerked his head back very slightly and cast his eyes downward, toward Christos' hands. The man with the knife had retied them behind his back, but he'd done it swiftly—Tigranes' tale had already been underway and he'd been half listening to it already. Perhaps he'd done slightly less thorough a job the second time, had left a bit more slack.

Gabriel's arms were also tied behind his back, and he strained now, stretching as far as the ropes would permit over toward Christos. And after a moment or two Christos got the message and started straining back the other way. Gabriel felt the skin of the younger man's knuckles brush against his own, then they were gone. He redoubled his efforts. He could feel it painfully in his shoulders and elbows, stretched almost to the point of dislocation, and he could see the boy beside him wincing as he tried to meet him more than halfway.

Then Gabriel felt a knot beneath his fingertips.

He seized it, pinched it between forefinger and thumb, grabbed hold and pulled the rope toward him, and Christos' hands with it. Christos took in a sharp breath, bit down on his lower lip. Gabriel saw sweat bead on Christos' forehead, saw the pain in his eyes, but Gabriel held on and mouthed two words: *Untie me*.

Christos blinked tears out of his eyes and nodded, and then his fingers began moving, his nails picking at the rope binding Gabriel's wrists. Gabriel, meanwhile, concentrated on not letting the rope out of his increasingly sweaty grip—if he lost his hold and Christos' hands swung away, Christos might not have the strength to get them back over here again.

Facing them across the room, Tigranes saw what they were doing, or suspected, anyway, and he redoubled his efforts. He stood up, braced the phorminx against his chest with one arm and swept the other in grand theatrical gestures, miming the swing of a sword, a man warding off blows, a wife wiping her husband's battle-weary brow. His beard shook with passion, and the Greeks seated in double rows on the floor and benches before him never looked away.

Half a minute more, a minute—and then finally the rope came free. It slipped from Gabriel's wrists to the floor and he felt blood rush back in where the circulation had been cut off. He flexed his fingers, one hand at a time, then went to work on the rope around Christos' wrists. When that fell to the ground he cautiously reached down to work on the knots at his ankles.

He'd gotten one leg free when heavy footsteps sounded on the stairs outside the door. He and Christos looked at each other. Sitting upright again, they slid their hands behind them, doing their best to look as though they were still tied down.

"Sphinx yet?" Andras asked, barging into the room.

The men all roused, as if from sleep, looking around with a slightly embarrassed expression. Tigranes stopped his song, the last of his notes hanging still in the air. "Not yet," he said. "Now go, before you make me lose my place."

Andras's huge fist rose and he advanced on Tigranes for a step or two, forgetting himself—he was not used to being talked back to by a man twice his age and half his size. But the buzzing of the cell phone in his pocket reminded him of the fate in store for him if he lost his temper. All eyes were on him as he took the phone out and flipped it open, held it to his ear. "No, not yet," he said. "I will. I *will*. Yes, sir." He jabbed the 'END' button with his thumb—and then Gabriel smashed him across the back with the chair.

15

ANDRAS FELL FORWARD ONTO TWO OF THE OTHER men as Gabriel leapt for the bench with his gun on it. He slid across the surface on his belly and snapped the revolver up in one fist, spinning to face Andras as he went off the end of the bench and landed in a crouch.

Christos had taken off the rope around his ankles as well. He ran over to Tigranes and began shepherding him toward Gabriel. He put the old man behind him, protecting him from the blows two of the other Greeks began raining down, getting in a punch of his own whenever one of the midsections before him was unprotected.

"Step back," Gabriel ordered Andras, who'd climbed to his feet once more. The cell phone was still in his hand, its screen broken now, its top half hanging at a crooked angle. He threw it at Gabriel and reached for the gun at his hip.

"Uh-uh," Gabriel said, catching the ruined phone

in his free hand and pulling the Colt's hammer back. "Hands up by your shoulders."

Andras sneered, disgusted—but he put his hands up.

Gabriel moved toward the room's one window, inching along the wall so no man could get behind him. He fanned the Colt left and right in tight arcs, sending each man who'd dared to venture a step forward shrinking back. He saw Christos inching toward him from the other direction, Tigranes shielded behind his broad shoulders. "Let him through," Gabriel said, and the men pressing around Christos fell back a step or two, their hands up, as Gabriel's gun swept over to cover them.

"You're a fool," Andras said as Gabriel and Christos closed in from either side on the window, a narrow arched opening in the tower wall that looked out over a rear courtyard. "Where are you going to go?" They were on the ground floor, so even Tigranes could go out the window here—but ten yards away was the cliff where they'd been captured, and past it, nothing but open sky.

"What, are you going to jump," Andras said, "like those old Greeks did? Kill yourself to get away?"

"Maybe," Gabriel said. "Like someone once told me, what I do or don't do is my problem, not yours."

"Kill yourself if you want, Hunt—I don't care. But if you take the old man, that makes it my problem. My boss is not the sort of man you want to disappoint. He can be very nasty when someone disappoints him."

"I'm sure that's true," Gabriel said. Beside him, out of the corner of one eye, he saw Christos climbing out the window, then reaching back in to help Tigranes through.

Andras darted an involuntary glance down toward

where his gun hung at his side. Gabriel knew what he was thinking: could he get to it in time?

"Don't do it, Andras," Gabriel said.

"You're going to have to leave the old man here, Hunt," Andras said. "I don't like the idea of being cut into little pieces by Lajos DeGroet." And he went for his gun.

He managed to get it out of its holster before Gabriel pulled the trigger. Andras spun toward the wall and collapsed, Gabriel's last bullet in his chest. "Well," Gabriel said softly, "you don't have to worry about that anymore."

THE GREEKS STOOD AROUND FOR A MOMENT IN stunned silence, the man who'd been paying them and giving them their orders lying lifeless at their feet. Gabriel took the opportunity to vault over the sill of the window and into the courtyard. He hit the ground running. Christos and Tigranes were already twenty feet away, speeding for the cliff's edge as fast as Tigranes could go. Which was pretty fast, Gabriel was happy to see.

Would the Greeks follow? They had no real reason to—he'd have thought they'd have had more loyalty to a couple of their countrymen than to Andras and DeGroet.

But a moment later the question was answered. A chorus of angry voices arose behind them and then gunfire followed as the Greeks poured out the window and gave chase.

He hastened to the edge of the cliff, where Tigranes and Christos were on their hands and knees, facing away from the vertiginous drop. Tigranes had his phorminx slung across his back once more and his tough, gnarled hands wrapped tightly around a brown root, similarly tough and gnarled, that trailed across the ground and over the edge. "Follow me closely," he said. "We are only going a short distance down."

"I certainly hope we are," Gabriel said, looking at the long fall to the mountain's base.

"Hold tight," Tigranes said and, letting himself down the root hand over hand, dropped out of sight. Christos looked up at Gabriel nervously and then followed suit, holding onto a neighboring root. That left Gabriel by himself on the clifftop—but not for long, since the first of the men who'd pursued them from the tower was upon him in seconds.

It was the man with the knife, and he swung its blade before him, back and forth in wide sweeps, like a thresher looking for wheat to cut down to size.

"Where are they?" he shouted.

"Gone," Gabriel said, stepping back to stay out of the blade's reach. "Over the side." With each step backwards he took, the other man took one forward, matching him stride for stride. And there wasn't much striding room left.

"You lie," the man said. Then, looking down at the ground, he saw one of the roots shift slightly, as though under a heavy burden. "Or... maybe you don't," he said. "An old man, hanging like a child from a tree limb." His voice rose to a shout. "You should be ashamed of yourself, Tigranes!" He raised his knife overhand and brought his arm down forcefully, releasing the blade so that it plunged downward and landed, quivering, in the center of the root. It was the thinnest of the roots, and it split as the blade went in. The severed portion snaked toward the edge of the cliff. Gabriel leaped after it, skidding along the ground and grabbing hold of the root just as it plunged over the edge. But when he grabbed it, he found it weighed practically nothing—and looking down he saw there was no one holding onto the other end.

He heard a sound beside him—*hsst!*—and turned his head to see Christos just inches away, clinging desperately to the next root over. Tigranes was hanging onto one a few feet further down the rock face, his sandaled feet twined in its length, one hand feeling for something among the rocks beside him.

"Now you, American," came a voice from behind him, and Gabriel felt hands at his ankles, lifting his feet high in the air and tilting him forward. "You can join them."

Gabriel dropped the cut root and scrabbled with his hands at the rock before him, but he couldn't get a grip as the Greek behind him tipped him over. His chest slid roughly down the stone surface till he was hanging headfirst, arms dangling toward the ground far below.

Looking to the side where Christos and Tigranes were, he saw the strangest thing then: Tigranes, who had continued feeling among the edges and protrusions of the cliff's face, apparently found what he'd been hunting for and, reaching with one arm and one leg, he pulled himself over to it—and vanished. The root he'd been hanging on swung back toward Christos, empty.

Above him, Gabriel heard another Greek voice back on the clifftop shouting breathlessly, "Don't do it! Don't let him go! The Hungarian wanted them alive!"

"Not this one," said the man holding onto Gabriel's boots—but he kept holding on, for now. "He wanted the old man. This one he was happy to see dead."

"Still," the other Greek said, uncertainty creeping into his voice.

Beside him, Gabriel saw Christos nervously reach out for the root that Tigranes had vacated. Carefully, oh so carefully, he shifted his weight over to it and slid down its length to where Tigranes had been feeling around the rocks.

Meanwhile, the argument continued overhead.

"You want him? You hold him," the man with his hands on Gabriel's ankles said.

"*I* don't want him," the other man said.

"You don't want him? I don't want him. Andras didn't want him. No one wants him. You hear that?" the man shouted down at Gabriel. "No one wants you. Goodbye, American." And he gave Gabriel's ankles a heave toward the sea, letting go when they were out over the edge.

As he fell, Gabriel reached out desperately for the root Christos had been hanging from. He grabbed hold of it at the very bottom, turning end over end till he was hanging upright. His momentum carried him bruisingly into the rock, but he held on tight, his fingers clenching for all they were worth.

But the momentum had been transmitted along the length of the root and had not gone unnoticed overhead.

"Son of a bitch," came the Greek's voice, and Gabriel heard him walking over to where he'd left the knife. A moment later, Gabriel felt the root he was hanging from shift downward as the man started hacking at it.

Below him, he saw Christos feeling among the rocks where Tigranes had disappeared. A gnarled, clawlike hand popped out from behind one of the protrusions on the cliff's surface, took hold of Christos' forearm, and pulled him toward itself.

This root was thicker and wouldn't part quite as easily as the last one—Gabriel heard the sounds of hacking overhead replaced with sawing, the knife's serrated blade biting into the thick tendril. With each stroke, he felt the root's purchase on the cliff's surface become weaker.

Christos was stretching out a leg now, as Tigranes had.

Gabriel braced his feet against the cliff wall. He'd only have one shot at this—

Christos vanished behind the same outjutting stretch of rock Tigranes had, and the root he'd been hanging from swung back, liberated from his weight. At that instant the root from which Gabriel was hanging was liberated, too, from the trunk of the tree it had supported for a century or more. Gabriel kicked off with both feet and, reaching out, seized hold of the swinging root as it came toward him.

His palms were slick with sweat and raw with abrasions. He slid down the root, trying to cling, straining to hold on, finally getting a good grip only inches from the end. He was breathing heavily, rapidly, his heart hammering in his chest. Beneath his boots, he saw the hundreds of feet of empty air he'd be falling through if he slipped any further. Far, far below, he saw the root he'd been hanging from a moment earlier still plunging toward the rocks.

"Goddamn it," came the Greek's voice from overhead—and Gabriel knew his move to the new root had not gone unnoticed. "You're a stubborn bastard, aren't you?" And the man began sawing at this final root, the thickest of the three.

Gabriel looked to the side, where Christos and Tigranes had gone, and used his feet to pull himself over toward the spot. There was a prominent outcropping of rock there, blocking his view. Concealed behind it, what would he find? A space large enough for two, apparently; hopefully enough for three. A crevice or fissure in the cliff wall, perhaps, maybe even a small cave—trust an old mountain rat like Tigranes to know the location of every cranny and tunnel in the place. Of course how they'd get down from there was one hell of a question, but right now that was far from Gabriel's biggest worry.

He could feel the root beginning to come apart. It slipped an inch, two inches—it had to be hanging by its last tough fibers now, and Gabriel knew his weight would swiftly part those even if the knife blade didn't.

Next to him, he saw a hand appear from around the rock—a young man's hand. He let go of the root with one of his own and swung his arm over, grabbing hold of Christos' hand, palm to palm.

Then the root snapped.

He fell with a sharp jerk but held onto Christos' hand, squeezing tight, clawing with his other hand against the rock and trying to get purchase on the surface with the soles of his boots. He caught hold of the outcropping itself and, using it for leverage, heaved himself around it.

On the other side, there was a ledge. Christos was kneeling on it, one arm braced against the outcropping, the other extended out into space. This was the one Gabriel was holding onto with a bone-crushing grip. Tigranes stood behind Christos, his wiry arms encircling the younger man's chest, leaning back with all his might. Behind him, a dark, crooked opening led into the mountain itself.

Gabriel found the ledge with one foot, then the

other, and Christos helped him up onto it, dragging him the last few inches. Then all three of them fell back into the cool darkness, the blessed solidity of stone beneath their bodies.

From up above, sounding far away, they heard the voice of the man with the knife: "*Can you see them? Can you see where they fell?*"

"*No,*" came another voice.

"*Then,*" said the man with the knife, "*where in the holy hell are they?*"

16

IN THE LIGHT SPILLING IN FROM THE OPENING, Tigranes held up the broken frame of his phorminx. Its strings hung loose, the wood around them splintered.

He laid it down on the ground sadly, folding the strap over it like the corner of a shroud.

"I'm sorry," Gabriel whispered and Tigranes nodded. None of them wanted to speak too loudly or too much, not while the men above were still hunting for them.

Tigranes gestured for them to follow and, with one hand on the wall to steady himself, led them deeper into the cave. It went on for quite a while, enough so that the light from outside dwindled to a white patch in the darkness—but there was a flickering orange light growing larger from the other direction.

They reached the end of the narrow cleft and made a ninety-degree turn. The sight that greeted them stopped Gabriel and Christos in their tracks.

It was more cavern than cave, a chamber at least fifty feet around and thirty high, seemingly naturally formed, with a pool of water at the center of it; and rising from this pool was a short pedestal of stone carved into the broad, ridged shape of an Ionic column. The capitals of this abbreviated column curled to either side like the horns of a ram. There was a marble seat on top of the capital, a squarish throne, and a larger-than-life-size statue of a muscular man reposed upon it, bare-chested, a stone lyre gripped in one arm. His face was long, his nose and brows prominent. Carved locks of hair tumbled about his ears and down his neck, while a chiseled beard roiled beneath his jaw.

Flame spouted from a pair of shallow stone bowls carved into the wall beside the room's entrance—natural gas, Gabriel judged from the smell, an eternal flame ignited untold lifetimes ago that had cast its flickering light on this hidden temple ever since.

"What *is* this place?" Gabriel said.

"It is our Homereion," Tigranes answered, stepping into the pool, which was only ankle-deep. He walked to the base of the statue, touched his fingers to his lips and pressed them to the carved throne. "A tribute to Chios' glorious son. There was one like it at Alexandria, greater even than this, built by Ptolemy—the fourth Ptolemy. There was one in Smyrna, one in Ephesus... but this was the very first, built just fifty years after the master's death. My father brought me here when I was a child of three or four. He carried me in his arms and laid me down right here." He reached up to pat the statue's lap, where the stone folds of a toga cast undulant shadows across the figure's carved knees.

"Why didn't the residents of Anavatos come down here?" Gabriel said. "In 1822, when the Turks came—

rather than leaping to their deaths?"

"Some did—a few," Tigranes said. "Those who knew of its existence. We kept it secret. Only the Homeridae were permitted to know. The children of Homer."

"Allowing hundreds of people to die, just to keep a secret—"

"I may be old," Tigranes said, walking back out of the pool, "but I am not quite *that* old. Please don't blame me for something that happened a century before I was born."

Gabriel nodded. "Of course," he said.

"Anyway, what do you think would have happened if its existence had been widely known? The Turks would have found out, just as they found out about Anavatos in the first place—by bribing some foolish woman who gave the secret away in return for a few drachmae. They would have come here and slaughtered everyone, and destroyed the Homereion, too. This way at least the handful of people who did know about it were able to survive. And the Homereion as well."

He found his way to a dry spot at the margin of the room, sat down, and took off his sandals, wiped them on the hem of his chiton. Christos sat beside him. Gabriel remained standing.

"The men who were chasing us," he said, "the ones working for Andras and DeGroet—they're going to come back. They may not have the equipment they'd need here—ropes, rappelling gear—but they can get it at Avgonyma, and then they'll be back. We might have a couple of hours, but not more."

"Why would they come back?" Christos said. "Why not leave us in peace?"

"You know the answer to that," Gabriel said. "Because DeGroet will punish them brutally if they let us escape, and pay handsomely if they deliver us to him." And, Gabriel thought, just imagine what he'd pay to see this place.

"Is there any way out of here," Gabriel asked, "any back entrance, any way out other than the way we came in?"

Tigranes shook his head. "There is only one other chamber—and the only way in or out is through here."

It was as bad as he'd feared. Still—

"Might as well see it," Gabriel said, offering Tigranes a hand to help him to his feet. Tigranes pointedly ignored it and got up on his own. Gabriel found himself hoping he'd be in the shape this old fellow was in when he turned eighty. Then he chastised himself for foolish optimism. What made him think he'd live to forty, never mind eighty?

Tigranes led them around the edge of the room till they were behind the statue. He stopped when he came to an opening in the wall, a low archway he had to duck to pass through. Gabriel bent and followed close behind.

The room beyond the archway was small and dark, lit only by reflected light from outside.

There was no pool in this room, no column, no oblate bowls with dancing flames.

But there was a stone figure.

And behind it, painted on the wall, there was a map.

GABRIEL APPROACHED THE STATUE SLOWLY, WALKING in a careful circle around it, looking at it closely from all angles, or as closely as the limited light would permit. The carving, the artistry—it was the same, unmistakably so. And while the Greeks of Homer's day had surely been more sophisticated sculptors than the Egyptians of Khafre's, the style here was still incongruous. This was more the vital realism of a Michelangelo, a Bernini. And the figure—

It was the figure of a lioness, lying prone upon the ground, her paws outstretched; except that two-thirds of the way up, her torso became that of a woman, sleek fur replaced by hairless skin, small high breasts bare; and from her human shoulders sprouted a pair of stone wings, which lay neatly folded along her spine. Her head was thrown back, her eyes closed, her mouth slightly open, as though she were calling out for someone. On her brow the sculptor had given her a diadem, a band to hold back her intricately carved ridges of hair. The statue of Homer outside had been idealized—he looked practically like a god, like Poseidon on his throne looking down upon the waters at his feet. This figure, this sphinx, was more modest— smaller, for one thing, and somehow, though it seemed perverse to think in these terms, less fantastical. Her eyelids, Gabriel noted, had wrinkles at their edges— he ran a finger over them and felt the tiny grooves in the stone. Her breasts—the nipples drooped slightly, as with age. The row upon row of feathers on each wing—each had been carved with meticulous care and craftsmanship.

On her flank, an inscription had been chiseled in angular Greek letters:

Accursed daughter of Echidna, rest eternal be yours
Your people shall forget you not, though
generations pass
Your precious one shall hold your image close
where you hold his

And your holy treasure speeds on Hermes'
wings to Taprobane,
Returning to the Cradle of Fear

Gabriel reached into the statue's open mouth.

"What are you doing?" Tigranes said. And Christos said, "You shouldn't—"

Gabriel pulled his hand away and came toward them. He held between his fingers a silver coin. On one side was an image of an eagle; on the other, a male face, in profile. He extended it toward Tigranes, who shook his head, and then to Christos, who peered closely at its surface. "The writing on it… is this coin Greek?"

"Egyptian," Gabriel said.

HE TURNED HIS ATTENTION TO THE WALL. IT HAD BEEN painted with a single enormous teardrop shape; above this, in the uppermost corner of the wall, was the hint of a coastline to the north. It was the reverse of the map he'd found in Egypt: this one showed the island in full and the landmass of India only in part. It also had details painted in—not many, but enough to indicate a path from a spot on the coast to a location inland, very near the center of the island. If this was supposed to be Sri Lanka—Taprobane, as it was known in the days of Alexander—the destination marked would be just northeast of Dambulla. He'd been there once, in pursuit of a priceless wooden Bodhisattva figure stolen from the famous Golden Temple. He hadn't paid much attention to anything else while he was there—but he did see the occasional sphinx mixed in among the other figures on wall murals and carvings.

As he recalled, the legends of Sri Lanka spoke of it

as a 'man-lion'—*narasimha*—and it played the role of guardian, much as it had here in Greece. Across the sea in southern India, they gave it a Sanskrit name, *purush-amriga*—the human-beast. Under one name or another sphinxes popped up throughout the lands of Asia. But just what the connections were between the island of Sri Lanka, the Egyptian sphinx, and the sphinx depicted here—presumably the one from the *Oedipodea*—was a mystery to Gabriel. And if there was one thing he couldn't abide, it was a mystery. Especially one people were willing to kill each other over.

"I think the time has come for us to find out a bit more about this sphinx," he said to Tigranes. "If you know anything—"

"I do," Tigranes said, nodding slowly. "The tale of Oedipus is but half the matter of the *Oedipodea*. The poet also told the story of the sphinx: her birth, her fierce defense of Thebes, her departure thence for Chios' shores—"

"We don't have four nights, I'm afraid," Gabriel said.

"That's quite all right," Tigranes said. "I'll begin where you wish."

"I thought you said you couldn't do that," Gabriel said, "that you could only recite the entire poem from the start."

"Do you believe everything someone tells you?" Tigranes said with a sly hint of a smile. "Here, let us go out into the main chamber again. I will feel my instrument's absence less in the shadow of my master."

They returned to the room with the statue of Homer in it, sat down at the edge of the pool. Tigranes began to speak, to sing, his voice echoing gently from wall to wall. Gabriel looked up at the statue. With the firelight playing over its carved features, you could almost imagine that it, and not Tigranes, was reciting the ancient words.

And the story of the sphinx unfolded. Gabriel didn't interrupt, just listened, and as he did, pieces of the puzzle finally began to fall into place.

17

"ARE YOU SAYING SHE REALLY EXISTED, ALL THOSE centuries ago?" Christos said when Tigranes fell silent. He'd been listening even more intently than Gabriel, if that was possible. "She really lived?"

"What, the sphinx? She was as real," Tigranes said, "as Oedipus—as real as the Minotaur and the Lernean Hydra—as real as Zeus and Apollo and all the rest of them. How real that is, each man must decide for himself. I, for one, am prepared to believe she was as real as you or I. This world has many strange things in it, and one must never fall into the trap of saying, 'I have never seen it, so it follows that no man has; and as no man has ever seen it, thus it cannot be.' "

This was a lesson Gabriel had learned many times himself over the years, when his voyages to some of the world's more obscure corners had brought him face to face with things other people might say were impossible. Why, earlier this very year he'd fought side by side in the Guatemalan jungle with a man no less than 150 years old, kept youthful by the waters of, well, if it wasn't literally the Fountain of Youth it might as well have been. Cierra Alamanzar had been with him; they had both witnessed it. But could they tell anyone what they'd seen without being called liars or worse? They could not. That didn't mean it wasn't true.

Still, a sphinx—an actual, living beast, half lion and half human? If ever something deserved to be called impossible...

"So you're saying," Christos began again, "that—"

"I am saying nothing," Tigranes corrected him. "It is Homer who said it. I merely recount what he reported."

"And he reported," Gabriel said, "that the island of Taprobane, source of cinnamon and spice, of coconuts and tea, also bred sphinxes for export to Egypt and Greece?"

"Not just sphinxes," Tigranes said. "All manner of monstrous crossbreed. The men of Taprobane were the greatest breeders of the ancient world. You could not get a sphinx anywhere else—not for all the gold and rubies in the richest treasury on Earth. So great men came to Taprobane in secret, and not only the rulers of Egypt and Greece, either—every kingdom from the Indies to Ultima Thule came."

"To the cradle of fear," Gabriel said.

"Yes. The cradle of fear. The place every king and sultan and emperor the world over sent to for his guardian beasts, his fearsome defenders of temples and labyrinths, of secrets great or small."

"And how did this island come to develop this... specialty?" Gabriel said.

"How did the men of Arabia come to tame stallions? Who knows? Homer does not say. He merely tells us that they played this role for longer than man's memory can tell."

Gabriel pondered the story. No doubt it had its roots in some germ of truth, but how much or how little those roots resembled the distant branches that had flowered elaborately in the millennia since, there was no way to know. No doubt the early Sri Lankans had bred *something*, perhaps a variety of fearsome beasts, perhaps ones their visitors from far-flung lands found strange and unfamiliar, and that fact had blossomed in the telling into a reputation for breeding monsters. Or maybe, who knows, the men of Sri Lanka might have been extraordinary sculptors, ones who traveled the world overseeing the creation of monumental statues like that of the Great Sphinx at Giza, and over time their reputation for fashioning beasts of stone and clay got transmuted into a reputation for breeding their living, breathing counterparts. It was easy to imagine how that might happen.

Still... the story, true or false, unquestionably had the power to compel the imagination, to enthrall—and perhaps not just credulous youths such as Steve McQueen here. Even a worldly sort like Lajos DeGroet might find his attention seized by all this talk of holy treasure.

"Do you have any idea what the treasure is that the inscription speaks of? And who it was that was supposed to return it to Taprobane?"

"The story goes," Tigranes said, "that the men from Taprobane made the long voyage here themselves to collect it, and left behind them the map and the inscription you see as a reminder that they'd been. Directions, if you will, that they might be found again should the need for their services once more arise.

But as for what the treasure was, no one knows. Some have speculated that it was wealth that our sphinx had received in tribute, some that it might have been a religious artifact created in her honor. Some…"

"Yes?"

"Some think it refers to some part of the sphinx herself, collected at the time of her death—her heart, perhaps, or her eyes. They were thought to be the seat of her power, you see."

"Power? What power?"

"All sphinxes were said to have the power to destroy their enemies with a glance," Tigranes said. "By rendering them physically paralyzed with fear."

Gabriel thought of the Great Sphinx of Egypt, called Abul-Hôl, the Father of Fear. And his Greek counterpart, called "Strangler" after her method of putting victims to death—perhaps the ancient Greeks had meant not literal, physical strangulation but the inducement of a terror so extreme its victim couldn't breathe?

The children of the cradle of fear, bringing fear to the four corners of the world.

Gabriel felt a chill go down his spine. Was Lajos DeGroet simply after new trophies for his collection or was he searching for something considerably more sinister—more dangerous? Certainly the amount of firepower he'd flown over to Egypt had suggested something deadlier than your average relic-hunting expedition. But what could this man possibly have hoped to find in the belly of the Sphinx? Some artifact that might give him this legendary power of the sphinx, the power to terrify with a glance? And if so… to what end? To what use would a man in possession of ungodly wealth, a private army, a staggering ego and unmatched ambition put such a power? Gabriel didn't know the answer—he just knew he was glad DeGroet hadn't yet found what he was looking for.

But of course now—

Damn it, now he *would* find it. The one advantage Gabriel had had was that back in Egypt DeGroet hadn't found the coin in the statue's mouth. He'd only found the partial map the chamber had contained, and no clue as to where the remainder might be located. But now he knew that Gabriel was on Chios… and soon his men, in searching for the three of them, would stumble upon this temple. And then the rest of the map would be his.

They hear a sound then.

It came from outside, where the tunnel began. It was the sound of a heavy rope uncoiling and slapping against the stone wall. And then a second one.

They all looked at each other.

"Come on," Gabriel said.

"What are you going to do?" Christos whispered.

"I don't know," Gabriel said. "I'll think of something."

They retraced their steps through the tunnel, watching the white patch in the distance grow larger as they neared it. They could see the two ropes, hanging in front of the opening, and as they watched, a figure carefully let itself down on one of them in a mountaineering harness. The figure was brightly backlit, so Gabriel couldn't make out the person's features; he only hoped this meant he had the benefit on his side of being hidden in relative darkness. He flattened himself against the tunnel wall and drew his Colt, empty though it was. Sometimes you played a weak hand just because all your chips were in the pot and it was the hand you had.

He cocked the pistol loudly. "Set one foot in here and

you're a dead man," Gabriel said, his voice bristling with as much self-confidence as he could project.

"That's a hell of a way to greet an old friend," a familiar voice replied, somewhat unsteadily.

And then Sheba unlatched herself from the rope and stepped into the tunnel.

GABRIEL RUSHED FORWARD. HE SWEPT HER UP IN HIS arms and lifted her off her feet, buried his face in her hair. He could feel that she was trembling. "How... how did you get here?"

"A girl could grow old waiting for you to bring her a pair of shoes."

He unzipped the pocket of his jacket, found the pair of loafers crumpled beside Andras' broken cell phone. He took them out. "I got you these."

"That's all right," Sheba said. She took a deep breath, let it out. Her voice steadied. "I took care of myself."

She had. She was wearing khaki pants and a ribbed white tank top under a lightweight jacket, and on her feet she had what looked like steel-toed climbing boots. Gabriel tossed the loafers aside.

"Sheba," Gabriel said, switching back to Greek for the purpose of making introductions, "this is Christos." The young man extended a hand, and she shook it. He seemed to be having some difficulty raising his eyes higher than the snug fabric of her tank top. "And this is Tigranes."

"Tigranes?" she said. "That's an interesting name. You know they say that was Homer's name, originally, before—"

"Before his captivity, yes. I know." Tigranes smiled. "I am surprised, however, that a young woman such as yourself, a foreigner, would know this."

"Sheba's a surprising young woman indeed," Gabriel said, "and she knows practically everything." He pulled her to one side. "I think," he whispered in English, "you just made a friend for life."

"Who are they?" she whispered back.

"They're on our side. That's all that matters." Gabriel walked closer to the ledge, inspected the ropes. Reaching out, he tugged on each in turn. They were both solidly anchored. But thinking back to Sheba's terror on the battlements in Hungary, he knew that climbing down the face of a cliff—even a short distance, even on a well-anchored rope—couldn't have been easy for her.

"Where did you get the equipment?" he asked.

"Same place I picked up your trail. You'd said you were going to Avgonyma, so I followed you there—"

"Barefoot?"

"I found a pair of sandals in the house," Sheba said. "Pretty flimsy, but good enough to get me to Avgonyma."

"Where you found…?"

"Everything you see. The boots were the hardest to come by, but I found a merchant who had hiking and climbing gear. The most interesting thing happened while I was there haggling with him, though—these two trucks drove up and a dozen men poured out with a story of having been through a gun battle and trapped 'the American' on the side of the mountain."

"The American," Gabriel said. "You didn't think it might be some other American?"

"Trapped on the side of a mountain after a gun battle? Not for a moment."

"And all this equipment—how did you get your hands on it? I would have expected the Greeks to grab whatever the guy had."

"Oh, they did," Sheba said. "They grabbed it and loaded it into one of the trucks."

"And?"

"And I stole the truck," Sheba said.

"You stole the truck," Gabriel said.

"That's right."

"But didn't you say they had another truck?" Gabriel said.

"They did," Sheba said. "What they have now is a gas tank full of sand."

Gabriel kissed her, hard, on the lips. "You're something else," he said when they finally came up for air. "I owe you one."

"You owe me two," Sheba whispered. "But who's counting?"

"Let's get out of here," Gabriel said. "Why don't you go up first? Christos and I can follow and then we can pull Tigranes up—"

"You don't need to *pull* Tigranes anywhere," Tigranes said. "I can climb a rope, young man."

"All right," Gabriel said. "Why don't you go first, then."

Tigranes clamped his weathered palms around the rope and was up it in a flash. Christos followed, more slowly, and then it was time for Sheba to go. She took care reattaching her safety harness.

"I appreciate what it meant for you to come here," Gabriel told her, steadying the rope so she could climb on. "I know you're no fan of heights."

"Heights are okay," Sheba said, her voice trembling again. "It's just falling I can't stand." And she began the short climb, pulling herself up hand over hand.

Gabriel took one more look around, at the broken phorminx lying on the ground and the dark tunnel beyond. A more ruthless sort, he thought, might try to arrange some sort of rockfall, some way of closing up the opening forever so DeGroet's men couldn't find it. But DeGroet had been right, back in Giza. Even if there had been a way, he couldn't bring himself to do it—not if it meant destroying something this precious and irreplaceable.

There'd be another way to stop DeGroet. There always was another way.

He grabbed hold of the rope with his hands and feet and climbed it to the top.

18

THE TRUCK ONLY HAD A QUARTER OF A TANK OF GAS
and lousy brakes, but Gabriel figured the former
would be enough to get them to the docks at Chios
Town if the latter didn't cause them to drive off the
side of the mountain first.

Sheba was sitting in the passenger seat behind him,
the two lengths of rope coiled in her lap. Tigranes
and Christos were in the back of the truck, enjoying a
bumpy ride. Gabriel kept the gas as close to the floor
as he could while still making all the hairpin turns
and switchbacks necessary to get to the bottom of the
mountain. There was no telling how long they had
before DeGroet's men regrouped, found another truck
and more supplies, and headed back up this narrow
road. He really didn't want to meet them head on.

As he drove, Gabriel filled Sheba in on what she'd
missed. Her eyebrows rose quizzically when he came
to the part about the living sphinxes.

"Really," she said. "He told you there was a real sphinx."

"Two of them. A boy sphinx in Egypt and a girl sphinx in Greece."

"And they met."

"Well, when Oedipus chased her out of Thebes, she had to go somewhere, didn't she?" Gabriel slowed to take a particularly nasty turn, then sped up in the straightaway that followed.

"I thought the story was that she threw herself to her death off the side of a cliff after he answered her riddle," Sheba said.

"She threw herself, but not to her death. Wings, remember?"

"Ah. Of course."

"After a stop in Chios for, oh, a hundred years or so, she headed over to Egypt where she met her counterpart in Giza."

"A hundred years? Just how long are these sphinxes supposed to live?"

"Oh, a few thousand years, give or take," Gabriel said.

"According to the old man in the back of our truck," Sheba said.

"According to Homer," Gabriel said. He was silent for a moment. "If you ask the old man in the back of our truck."

"All right, let's say, just for the sake of argument, that I buy it. The lady sphinx spends a hundred years in Chios, then heads over to Giza, where the old Father of Fear wines and dines her, shows off the nifty statue of him they've got over there, and then what?"

"Back to Chios. She stays there for the rest of her life, from about 900 BC till about 250 or so, inspiring art and architecture and lending her face to the city's coins. And somewhere in there she meets a young local boy and tells him her story… and he eventually tells it to the rest of the world when he grows up to become Homer."

"I see," Sheba said.

"Well, that makes one of us," Gabriel said. "I don't know what's crazier, the idea of a three thousand year old monster telling her story to a young Homer or the idea of a seventy year old monster chasing around after her lost treasure today."

"Well, crazy or not, we know at least the second part's true," Sheba said.

"Yeah," Gabriel said. "And if we knew it was just some archaeological treasure he was after, maybe we could let him have it. But it's not. Or *maybe* it's not—nobody knows. But we can't take the chance."

"Of what, exactly?" Sheba said. "Letting DeGroet get his hands on something that would give him the power to terrify with a glance? It's not like the man isn't plenty scary as it is."

"It's not a question of being scary," Gabriel said. "If you believe Tigranes, it's the power literally to paralyze with fear. And not just one person—a hundred people, a thousand at once, however many the sphinx looked upon. And with modern technology at DeGroet's disposal, the ability to broadcast to millions…"

Sheba laughed, then stopped when she noticed Gabriel wasn't laughing along. "Come on," she said. "You can't be taking this seriously."

"I don't know," Gabriel said. "I grant you, it could all be nonsense—DeGroet could be chasing after a myth. But if it's not and he's not… we can't let him find what he's after."

"And how are we supposed to stop him?"

"By finding it ourselves first," Gabriel said. "And while we're at it, by finding him."

"Oh, yeah? Did that map on the wall show you where he is?"

"No," Gabriel said. "But I've got something that will."

He reached into his pocket and held up Andras' cell phone.

THE SUN WAS HANGING LOW BEHIND THE MOUNTAINS when they pulled up to the ferry landing. The ferry was there, bobbing in the water and bumping against the row of old Goodyears lashed to the pilings as a cushion. Across the way, through the late afternoon haze, the coast of Turkey loomed. He could see the battlements of Çeşme Castle faintly in the distance.

"Book passage for four," Gabriel said, passing Sheba a handful of money, all he had left except for a single hundred-dollar bill. "I'll join you in a minute."

"They're coming with us?"

"We can't leave them here. We'll find a safe place for them on the other side."

"And where are you going?"

"To find a telephone," Gabriel said, and he headed off toward a low bunker with cement walls that looked as though it served some official function. It was a law the world over: officials had telephones.

He had to ask several people dressed in crisp uniforms before being directed to a payphone hanging from a wall. Stickers on its side advertised taxi services and island tours. Gabriel dialed the operator and asked to place a collect call to New York.

The phone rang four times before Michael answered it. "Hello?"

"Will you accept a collect call," the operator asked in heavily accented English, "from a mister Gabriel—"

"Yes, yes, absolutely, operator—put him through. Gabriel? Gabriel? Are you there? Are you okay?"

"Calm down, Michael. I'm fine."

"Is Sheba…?"

"She's fine, too. We're both a little banged up—"

"I knew it," Michael said miserably.

"—but nothing that won't heal. Now, listen, Michael, I need something from you."

"Anything."

"I need the name of someone in this area who could hack into a busted cell phone and tell me what the last number it got called by was—and then trace that number."

"Where are you?"

"Chios. But in a few minutes I'm going to be headed to Turkey."

"Çeşme?"

"That's right," Gabriel said. He heard Michael typing on a computer keyboard.

"Mm," Michael muttered to himself. "No, he's… no…"

Gabriel turned to look out the window. Dusk was descending suddenly, as it always did in this part of the world; one minute it was still light out, the next you'd be looking at a starry sky.

"Do you think you could make it up to Istanbul?" Michael asked suddenly.

"If we had to," Gabriel said. "Why? Who's in Istanbul?"

"There's someone the Foundation has used before—

he goes by the name 'Cipher,' moves around a lot, but last we heard he was in Istanbul. Never met the man myself, just e-mail back and forth, but he really knows his stuff. Computers, phones—what you're talking about would be right up his alley."

"How'd you find him?"

"He came to us," Michael said. "Couple of years back, offered to help with a project we were working on at the time. Don't know how he found out about it… but then he wouldn't be very good at what he does if he hadn't been able to, right?"

"I suppose," Gabriel said, not much liking the sound of it. He preferred dealing with people who went by their names, not clever handles like "Cipher." For that matter, he preferred dealing with almost anything to dealing with computers and cell phones. But sometimes you had to. "Can you send him a message, let him know I'm on my way?"

"Already done," Michael said. "How can I contact you to let you know what he—" Michael stopped in mid-sentence. "Well, well, will you look at that."

"What?"

"I just got a message back from him," Michael said. "Literally, right now. From Cipher."

"Well, that should make you feel important," Gabriel said.

"You, too—listen to this: 'The famous Gabriel Hunt, coming here? How could I say no?' That's what he wrote. 'Tell him to meet me at the Basilica Cistern at midnight.' The famous Gabriel Hunt. How do you like that?"

"Not much," Gabriel said.

"Can you make it there by midnight?"

Gabriel looked at his watch. "Only if I hang up now," he said. "Tell him I'll be there. And Michael—"

"Yes?"

"Thank you." He hung up.

He returned to the pier, threaded his way through a small crowd to where the ferry was tied up. Tigranes and Christos were already on board. Sheba was waiting at the foot of the ramp, two tickets in her hand. Her face lit up when she saw Gabriel coming toward her—but then her expression changed to one of alarm.

Gabriel looked back over his shoulder. Coming up the long road to the docks was a jeep and at its wheel was a man he recognized even at this distance—it was the knife artist from Anavatos, the one who'd thrown him off the cliff.

"Come on," he said, "get on board." He hustled Sheba up the ramp and, reaching over to the bitt the ferry's hawser was coiled around, he yanked the great rope free.

"We are not ready to depart yet!" a crewman said, rushing up.

"Hundred dollars says you are," Gabriel said and handed over his last bill. He patted the man on the shoulder. "Go."

The man scurried up front and a moment later the engine sputtered to life.

By the time the jeep squealed to a stop by the dock, the ferry was twenty yards out to sea and plowing toward Turkey. He saw the driver leap out of the truck and run up to the water's edge. He tore the cap he was wearing from his head and dashed it to the wooden planks at his feet. "We will find you!" he shouted at the departing ship. "*Wherever you run, we will find you!*"

"Or vice versa," Gabriel whispered.

19

THE BASILICA CISTERN HAD STOOD IN MORE OR LESS
its present form, Gabriel knew, since the sixth century,
when the Byzantine Emperor Justinian the Great had
had it constructed. It was hard to imagine that it had
once served a municipal function, supplying water
to the Topkapi Palace. A grand underground space
filled with ranks of colossal columns, hundreds of
them, each thirty feet high, stretched as far as the eye
could see beneath an arched and vaulted ceiling. The
Turks called it *Yerebatan Sarayi*, the sunken palace. Each
column was lit from below with flame-red lights, giving
the space an ominous appearance. You expected a man
in a cape and domino mask to step into view at any
moment from behind one of the columns, carrying a
wax-sealed missive—or a dagger to slip between your
ribs. Which no doubt was why this man Cipher had
chosen it for their meeting. His name itself suggested
his taste for the dramatic.

In one corner of the space, a quartet was playing for an appreciative audience of tourists seated in metal folding chairs, the sounds of lute and zither, flute and fiddle filling the air with mournful Ottoman melodies. Gabriel steered clear of the area. Cipher wouldn't be caught out in the open like that, he felt sure; men who spent their lives behind the screens of laptop computers infiltrating global telecommunications networks generally don't congregate with tour groups at midnight concerts.

Although you never knew. Gabriel didn't generally congregate with tour groups himself, yet he'd spent most of the past five hours on a bus with a church group out of West Virginia who'd taken a day trip to Çeşme to see the castle and the museum and the seaside and now had the long trip back to Istanbul to look at each other's digital photographs and share loud anecdotes about the marvels they had seen. Sheba had been the one to spot the coach parked outside the castle, its side painted with the VARAN TURIZM logo, its door open, the driver standing outside having a smoke. She'd also been the one to talk him into letting the four of them occupy the uncomfortable pair of benches in the rear by the lavatory in return for what little cash they had left and an extorted kiss on the cheek. Christos and Tigranes had piled on board gratefully and slept through most of the ride, the younger man leaning up against the window and snoring softly, the older sitting stock-still and silent in his seat.

"Your father?" one of the women from West Virginia had asked, and Gabriel had said, "My rabbi," and she'd left him alone after that.

It was just as well that they'd made the trip, Gabriel thought as he circled around the interior of the cistern, pausing to look at every man who was there by himself and giving each a chance to look at him. In order to get a flight out to Sri Lanka they'd have had to make their way to one of the larger cities eventually, either to Istanbul or Ankara, and the drive would have been just as arduous either way. Still, around the end of the third hour, when the hymns had started, he had found himself wishing that they'd turned up some other form of transportation.

As he completed one full circuit of the space, he spotted a man standing between the two Medusa-head pillars in the rear corner, his face lit by the glow from a palmtop computer, his stylus clicking away across its illuminated surface. Gabriel walked over, stood beside him, waited for him to look up. He wore thick glasses and had his hair cut short, with a cowlick standing up in back. The stubble dotting his lantern jaw said he hadn't shaved in a day or two. Finally he put the stylus away and thumbed off the light. "Do I... know you?" he said.

"Cipher?"

He looked blank. "Excuse me?"

"Oh, this will be perfect, darling," a woman's voice interrupted. Turning, they both saw a petite brunette approaching. She was carrying a camera in one hand and had a notebook and pen in the other. "I can have them hide in here from the guards when they're being chased—" Then she noticed Gabriel. "Hello," she said. And to the man: "Want to introduce me?"

"I'd love to," the man said, "but we hadn't quite gotten to the point of introducing ourselves."

"I'm sorry," Gabriel said, "I thought you were someone else—"

"I'm Naomi," the woman said, extending a hand.

"We're here doing research. I write historical fantasy novels and my husband here writes adventure stories." Gabriel took her hand, shook it briefly, released it. "And you're...?"

"Gabriel," he said reluctantly.

"I knew it," the man said. "I *do* know you. Gabriel Hunt, right? Darling, you remember, that book with the Phoenician temple art. You wrote that, right?"

"No," Gabriel said.

"But I recognize you, from the photo on the back."

"I just wrote the introduction," Gabriel said. "The publisher slapped my picture on it. Now, I'm sorry but I really have to go—"

"So soon?" came another voice, and a second woman walked out from behind the nearer of the columns with the fearsome head of Medusa carved at the base. She was slender—no, more than that, she was skinny, almost gaunt; even in the red-tinged light Gabriel could see that her skin was pale, her cheeks hollow. She wore her dark hair chopped in a spiky pixie cut with ragged bangs and had a row of four or five silver rings in each earlobe. A tattoo of a serpent with a flicking tongue trailed down her throat, its tail disappearing beneath her chin. She was wearing jeans and a black t-shirt, both of which looked battered enough that they probably wouldn't survive another laundering, which made it just as well that they didn't seem likely to get one any time soon. Her heavy boots added at least three inches to her height, but even so she only came to Gabriel's chin. Over one shoulder was slung the strap of a bulging canvas satchel whose contents looked like they might weigh almost as much as she did.

But none of these things about her were what made Gabriel take a step back in disbelief.

He did that because he recognized her.

"The famous Gabriel Hunt," she said. "Stay a while, why don't you? Greet your fans."

"*Lucy?*" Gabriel said, and a wicked smile crossed her face.

"Cifer," she said.

"EXCUSE US, PLEASE," GABRIEL SAID AND PULLED HIS sister by the arm toward an empty section of the cistern.

"That wasn't very polite," she said.

"What are you *doing* here?"

"I live here," she said. "For now. You're the one who's dropping in out of nowhere and heading right back out an hour later."

"Does Michael know…?"

"What, that the mysterious guy who's been helping him out with one thing or another for the past two years is his kid sister? Not a chance. And you're not going to tell him, either. Not if you ever want to get your e-mail delivered again."

"I don't have e-mail."

She rolled her eyes. "Figures. Fine. If you don't want a tax audit each year for the next decade. Computers are powerful things, Gabriel."

"I'm sure," he said. "Well, don't worry. I wouldn't dream of telling Michael. It would break his heart."

She looked off to one side. "He wouldn't care."

"Are you kidding? He hasn't seen his sister in nine years, hasn't heard from her, not a letter, not a call—as far as he knows. If he found out you've been playing him for a fool—"

"That's not fair," she said. "I've been helping him."

"You've been lying to him."

"Helpfully," Lucy said.

Gabriel shook his head. He gave her a long look, taking her in from head to toe. "What's happened to you? You haven't been eating well."

"I eat fine," she said. "Just, you know, vegan. It's a bitch getting your protein. But on the other hand the food's cheap."

"Cheap?" Gabriel said. He lowered his voice. "My god, Lucy, you shouldn't be worried about money. You could have all the money you want—more than you could want—"

"Not that money. I don't want it. It's theirs, not ours."

Gabriel put a hand on her shoulder but she shook it off. "They're dead," he said gently.

"They're *missing*," she said.

"It's been nine years," Gabriel said.

"It's been nine years since you saw me, too. Am I dead?"

"Pretty close," Gabriel said. "Look at you." He pulled her heavy bag off her shoulder, slung it over his. She let him. "Come on. I'm buying you a proper meal." Then he remembered he had no cash left. He went through a mental list of places he knew in the area that would be open at midnight and where the proprietor might throw the bill away. "Devrim. He'll feed you."

She followed him up the stairs to street level. "No meat," she warned. He didn't say anything. "Did you hear me? I'm serious. Not on my plate, not on yours, or I'm walking."

"All right, princess," Gabriel said.

"Call me that again and—"

"I know," Gabriel said, "you're walking."

"No," Lucy said. "Call me that again and you're *not* walking, because I'll break both your legs."

They stared each other down. Then a crooked grin crept onto Gabriel's face and, reaching out, he pulled her into a hug. After a moment, he could feel her thin arms digging hard into his back.

"My god, Lucy, it's so good to see you again."

She burrowed her forehead into his chest. When she spoke he could barely make out the words. "Why couldn't you find them?"

He stroked back her hair. "I tried, Lucy. I tried."

DEVRIM'S PLACE WAS OFF TEVKIFHANE STREET, UP A flight of stairs. You couldn't see it from outside. You just had to know it was there.

The big man greeted Gabriel warmly, slapping a meaty paw on either side of Gabriel's hand and shaking vigorously. Then he turned to Lucy. "And who is this creature you bring to me, this starved thing? We fatten her up, no?"

"Gabriel—" she said, but he shushed her. She crossed her arms over her chest and tapped one foot.

"This is my sister," Gabriel told Devrim.

"Ah. My apologies, miss. Any relative of Gabriel's..." His voice trailed off. "Sit, I bring wine."

They took a table in the corner farthest from the door and turned a pair of high-backed wooden chairs to screen them from view. Not that there was anyone else here at the moment, and not that Devrim himself would pry, but—

When Lucy began unpacking the satchel, Gabriel felt a bit like a surgical trainee on his first day in the OR, watching the doctors lay out instruments of which he didn't even know the names, much less the functions. He sipped from the fat-bellied goblet of wine Devrim had brought and watched Lucy hook cables from this device to that, looked on as a little screen flickered to life and text began racing across it. "Spill that wine on anything you see and you're a dead man," Lucy said, her fingers darting nimbly over a keyboard.

"Not a problem," Gabriel said, and drained the glass.

It was good wine. Devrim always managed to get his hands on the best.

"So Michael says you need a phone number traced," Lucy said. "You've got what, a cell phone that called the number?"

"I've got a broken cell phone," Gabriel said, "that was called by the number." He took Andras' phone from his pocket, set it down, and slid it across the scarred wooden surface of the table. Lucy looked at it. The screen had a jagged crack down its center and the phone's hinged top half hung lopsidedly from the bottom. Lucy pressed the power button a couple of times and nothing happened.

"You don't make things easy, do you?"

"Rarely," Gabriel said.

Lucy pried open a panel at the back of the phone, popped out the battery, and dug around inside the body of the phone. She slapped it twice, hard, against the heel of her hand, as though trying to jar something loose, then went digging again.

"Go talk to your friend," she said, not looking at him as she poked at the phone's innards. "I'm going to be a while."

"Okay," Gabriel said. "Take your time."

He found Devrim at the top of the stairs, smoking a

long, thin, brown cigarette, the heavy smell of Turkish tobacco hanging in the corridor.

"Your sister, huh?" Devrim said. Gabriel nodded. "Looks nothing like you."

"She takes after our mother," he said.

"And you look like your father?"

"I look like the milkman," Gabriel said, and Devrim gave him a confused look. Then he laughed, a single loud bark. "The milkman! Hah! You are a devil, Gabriel."

Gabriel rotated his shoulder and flexed his arm, which was getting stiff where the blade had gone in. His palms were still raw from hanging onto the roots in Anavatos and his cheek ached every time he opened his mouth. "I must be," he muttered. "I feel like hell."

"Hey," Lucy's voice floated in from the other room, "I've got it. Wanna see?"

Gabriel levered himself to his feet again and returned to the table. "I thought you said it would take a while."

"It did," Lucy said. "Just not a long while. Sit." He sat, stared at the screen she was pointing to proudly. It showed a Mercator map of the world with two blinking white symbols, one an X, the other an O. The X was sitting, pulsing, on the northern coastline of Turkey. The O was just off the eastern coast of Chios—and moving, slowly, one tick at a time, toward the X.

"That's us?" Gabriel asked, pointing at the X.

"Right," Lucy said. "And that's the person you're looking for. Though it looks more like he's looking for you." They both watched as the O came another tiny notch closer to the X.

20

DEGROET WAS COMING.

It was hardly a surprise—he needed to get to Sri Lanka as well, and Istanbul was the nearest major international hub. But Gabriel couldn't help the feeling that there was more to it, that DeGroet had been briefed by the man they'd left behind on the pier, that he was coming via Turkey in part because he knew this was where they'd fled. Hell, maybe they'd somehow been followed into Turkey by one of DeGroet's agents or their trail had been picked up once they arrived by someone he already had in place. There could be men closing in as they sat here—on Gabriel and Lucy in Devrim's, or on Sheba in the hostel where he'd left her to arrange a room for Christos and Tigranes.

"We've got to go," Gabriel said.

"What?" Lucy said. "This instant?"

"I'm sorry. It's just not safe. Devrim," he called, "you'll take care of my sister another night, right?"

"Any night," Devrim called back. "Every night. Till she weighs as much as my own daughter."

"Thank you." Gabriel shot a lingering look at the screen with its handy little map as Lucy began disconnecting her machinery and stuffing it back in her bag. This was exactly the sort of technology he hated—and yet... it wouldn't hurt to know where DeGroet was at any given time. "I don't suppose there's any way I could take this with me," he said, lifting the unit.

"No," Lucy said and plucked it out of his hands. "The way you carry on? It'd be smashed in five minutes."

"Yeah," he said. "You're probably right. Well—"

"This on the other hand," Lucy said, holding up a black plastic box the size of a pack of playing cards, "you can bang around till the cows come home and you won't break it. Doesn't have the fancy map on it, but what it's got's just as good." She flicked a switch on the bottom of the box and a single row of red digits lit up along one of its shorter sides:

178SW

Then after a second the display changed:

177SW

"Miles?" Gabriel said.

"You prefer kilometers?"

"No," Gabriel said, "I prefer miles."

He slipped the box into his pocket beside his Zippo. "How long will the battery—"

"A week. If you keep it on the whole time, maybe a little less." She finished packing, looked around for anything she'd missed. "You want me to show you how to change it?"

Gabriel shook his head. "This'll all be over in a lot less than a week. One way or another."

An anxious look crossed her face. She reached up a hand and stroked the side of his jaw, avoiding the raw slash that was just beginning to heal. "Just how much trouble are you in?"

"Oh, nothing too serious," Gabriel said, and he worked up a smile he hoped didn't look too phony. "You know better than to worry about me."

She nodded, and the trust in her eyes took him back fifteen years, to when he was twenty-three and she was eleven and he'd keep her up past her bedtime with stories about the places he'd been and the dangers he'd faced. But there was a measure of concern in her expression, too. "I know you can take care of yourself. But—"

"But what?"

"I follow what you do, Gabriel. Newspaper articles, the things you publish, people posting online that they saw you one place or another—"

"Computers are powerful things," Gabriel said.

"Yeah. Well. Any time your name pops up on my screen, there's part of me that's excited, but there's part of me that's sure each time it's your obituary I'm going to read." Her voice fell. "The famous Gabriel Hunt, clawed to death by wild dogs in Zambia. The famous Gabriel Hunt falls from the wing of an airplane. Something."

"I always wear my seatbelt on airplanes," Gabriel said. "And dogs love me."

"Well that's a relief," she said. "But I'm just talking the law of averages. You can be the best in the world at what you do and there'll still come a day when you get unlucky."

"Is that why you agreed to see me when Michael sent his note?" Gabriel said. "After all this time? Because you thought it might be your last chance?"

"Of course not," she said. She wouldn't meet his eyes. "I was just thinking, how many times are you and I going to be in the same place. The way you move around. The way I do."

Gabriel lifted her chin with his knuckle. "Don't worry about me, kid," he said. "I always come out on top."

"Well, good. You can prove it," she said, tapping a forefinger against the pocket where the little box lay, "by not getting yourself killed before that battery runs out."

THEY SEPARATED ON TEVKIFHANE STREET. GABRIEL watched her back recede as she walked quickly in the direction of the Blue Mosque, that Laurel-and-Hardy contraption of slender minarets and squat domes. It was brightly lit and stood out against the pitch black of the sky like a picture cut out from a magazine and pasted on a scrapbook page.

When he could no longer see her, Gabriel turned in the other direction and headed toward the hostel where Sheba was waiting. On the way he passed the Four Seasons hotel, located in what had once been a prison building. The man at the front entrance, who looked as though he might have held the same job back in the building's earlier incarnation, touched two fingers to the brim of his cap and nodded as Gabriel went by.

A moment later, Gabriel heard footsteps behind him. Two men, he thought—possibly three. Trying to keep their steps quiet.

So the nod hadn't been for him.

He risked a glance back, saw two men directly behind him, maybe ten yards away, and a third across the street. He didn't recognize the first two—but the third was Mr. Molnar, the round-faced Magyar whose brother had had the bad sense to charge at him in Budapest when his Colt had still had a bullet in it. Their eyes met, and even at this distance Gabriel could see that the intensity of his feelings had not abated.

"Hunt!" he bellowed, followed by another of those curses that seem so ubiquitous in the Hungarian tongue. Then he and the other two started running toward Gabriel, who took off as well, racing toward the nearby intersection with Kutlugün Street. It was a dark street of short, red-roofed buildings, mostly little hotels and cafes, all of them shuttered tight at half past one in the morning. Gabriel kept going, sprinting for the nearest corner. Sheba was on the next street over, Akbiyik Caddesi, the Street of the White Moustache; it was a slightly less reputable avenue, where the hostels were dingier and the proprietors asked fewer questions, like why a young American woman might be renting a room for two Greek men using another man's credit card number.

He could hear his pursuers' shoes pounding against the paving stones close behind him. That they hadn't pulled pistols and started shooting at him yet Gabriel attributed entirely to the late hour: they wouldn't want to wake the entire neighborhood with the sound of gunfire. But if they managed to get their hands on him, Gabriel knew, Molnar wouldn't need bullets to exact revenge for his brother's death.

Gabriel skidded to a stop beside a shuttered store. There was a narrow alleyway between it and the next building over and he darted into it, leaping up at the far end to catch hold of the curlicue grillwork at the base of a second-story balcony. He pulled himself up, his arms complaining at the strain. From the balcony he was able to climb onto a bit of ornamental stonework that decorated the building's wall, testing it first with one foot to make sure it was secure. Then from there he was able to grab hold of the edge of the roof and haul himself up.

Down below, he could hear the three men pouring into the alley. The footsteps stopped and the cursing resumed. They wouldn't be stymied for long: it was a dead end and the only direction Gabriel could have gone was up. But every second counted, and Gabriel used the next few to sprint to the edge of the building and leap across a narrow airshaft onto the neighboring roof.

He landed badly, twisting his ankle.

Damn it—the law of averages hadn't had to choose this moment to kick in, had it? He hobbled away from the edge of the roof, putting weight on his left foot only gingerly, twinges of pain shooting up his shin each time he did so.

He was close to Sheba's hostel (the Sultan—but then every other building in this city was called "the Sultan"). On one hand, he didn't want to bring Molnar and the other two to her doorstep—that could put her and Tigranes and Christos all in danger. On the other hand, they might be in danger already, if DeGroet had sent a separate team after them, and if so they might need him there to help. There was no way to know what the right decision was. Except that standing still wasn't it. He limped on, telling himself that the pain in his ankle was already lessening a bit, even though it wasn't.

At the edge of the building he reached a gap too large for him to jump even if his leg had been fine, so, looking around, he yanked open the only door he could see on the roof and clambered down the stairs he found inside. Behind him, as the metal door slowly swung shut, he heard the running footsteps of his pursuers, coming closer. By the time he reached the bottom of the stairs, he could hear them at the top. Then the explosion of a gunshot rang out and a bullet chewed bits of metal, plaster, and paint from the doorframe beside his head. Apparently they didn't mind waking the people here.

Gabriel ran out into the street. The Sultan Hostel was just two buildings away and he made for it at what passed in his current condition for top speed, his gait a loping, uneven thing. Sweat beaded on his forehead. His ankle wasn't broken, he was fairly sure of that, but it felt like a knife blade was jabbing into it at every step, and the pounding he was giving it surely wasn't helping speed the healing process.

A ten-hour flight to Sri Lanka, he kept telling himself, *plenty of time to rest it, get a bag of ice from the stewardess for the swelling…*

But first he had to make it to the airport and onto a plane alive.

He ducked inside the front door of the hostel just as Molnar burst out into the street. Gabriel saw him looking left and right and hid behind one of the columns in the entryway. A heavy potted plant provided a bit of extra cover—but only a bit.

Behind him, the lights in the hostel's lobby went

on. A sleepy-eyed attendant shuffled up beside him, a saucer with a flickering candle on it in one hand. "Can I help you?" he said, blowing out the candle.

"Some friends of mine are staying here," Gabriel said, through clenched teeth. "I've come to see them."

"Rather late to be dropping by," the attendant said. "I will have to see if they—"

A hammering came at the door then, and peeking around the column Gabriel saw through the glass of the door that it was Molnar, flanked on either side by his henchmen. "Don't open the door," Gabriel whispered.

"What do you mean?" the attendant said, turning the knob. "Of course I'll open the—"

A moment later, the saucer slipped from his fingers and smashed against the tile floor. The man backed up, his hands in the air, his jowls trembling. Molnar followed, the barrel of his revolver planted squarely in the middle of the man's face. Together, Molnar and the attendant walked past the corner where Gabriel was hiding and the other two men followed, drawing their guns as they went. If any of them had looked to the side they'd have seen Gabriel—but they didn't. He shot a glance at the still open door. He could dash out, maybe make it to the next street before they noticed...

But he couldn't leave this guy with a gun in his face and a homicidal Hungarian itching to pull the trigger. Not to mention Sheba just a few flights up with only an eighty-year-old man and an eighteen-year-old kid for protection.

Grimacing silently, Gabriel lifted the potted plant in both hands.

The attendant looked over at him, his eyes widening at the sight as Gabriel swung the heavy stone pot up in the air. It provided enough warning for Molnar to turn and swing his gun around, but not enough for him to pull the trigger. Gabriel launched the pot at him and it caught him in the face, knocking him to the ground with its momentum. The attendant jumped out of the way as the pot landed, cracking the tiles beneath it.

The two other gunmen spun around now, too, but Gabriel was upon them, throwing a powerful right cross at the first man's jaw and getting the second in the throat with his elbow on the backswing. Neither man was incapacitated by the blow and both brought their guns into play, one firing wildly and missing, his shots tearing up the wood of the reception desk and shattering a lamp as Gabriel ran ahead of them, the other swinging his gun like a metal extension to his fist and catching Gabriel on the side of the head with it. Gabriel reeled, fell back. He dropped into a crouch and pistoned outward with one fist, sinking it deep into the man's gut. He could hear the forceful expulsion of breath, feel the spray of spittle from the man's lips. Gabriel followed up with a second punch, and a third, and then the man fell before a fourth could land.

Gabriel made to stand up, but was driven forward as the second man jumped on his back. The extra weight hit his ankle just right, and he collapsed to one knee.

Before him, the other gunman lay prone, his arm outstretched on the floor. Gabriel grabbed the gun from his hand, reversed it in his own, and aimed it back over his shoulder. When he felt the barrel press against something soft that wasn't part of his own body, he pulled the trigger with his thumb. The weight vanished from his shoulders and a low moaning began behind him.

Standing up, Gabriel limped over to the wounded man. He was leaking blood from a nasty wound in his upper chest. He still held his gun, loosely, in a trembling hand, and Gabriel bent to take it away from him. He broke it open: no bullets left. Every one of them spent on the desk and lamp. He tossed the useless gun into a corner of the room, held onto the other one.

"Who... who *are* these men?" the attendant said, his voice rising siren-like as he surveyed the damage. "What did they want?"

"I don't know," Gabriel said. "They started following me a few blocks away." He limped over to the bullet-scarred desk, leaned his weight against it. On the stairs winding up to the second floor he saw a man creep cautiously into view, a corpulent ex-military type in a gray bathrobe. He had a white moustache, fittingly enough. "Go back to bed," Gabriel told him. "It's all over."

The man cast a critical eye over the scene before him. "I hope so," he said, his British accent icy. "I didn't pay to be woken by gunfire and fisticuffs. If I'd wanted that I could have stayed in Brixton. Excuse me, miss." As he climbed the stairs, hugging the wall, another figure passed him on the way down. It was Sheba, wearing an identical gray robe—they must have had them hanging in all the rooms. Who would have thought it, amenities in a place like this.

"Gabriel?" Sheba said. "You okay?"

"I'm still standing," he said. "More or less."

"DeGroet?"

"On his way," Gabriel said. He took Lucy's box out of his pocket, glanced at it. "Just a hundred fourteen miles off."

"How do you know that...?" Sheba asked and

then raised a hand, palm out. "Never mind. I'll go get dressed. We're in 304." She vanished up the stairs.

Gabriel walked from one of the bodies to the next. The man he'd shot had stopped moaning; he seemed to have slipped into unconsciousness. He'd live, though. The same couldn't be said for Molnar, who'd joined his brother at last. Gabriel stopped beside the third man, who was conscious but curled up on the floor, both hands pressed to his abdomen. Gabriel aimed the gun down at him. "What did DeGroet want you to do?"

"Bring you…" The man coughed, spat a bloody wad onto the tiles. "Bring you to him."

"Just me?"

"The woman, too."

"Not the old man?"

"What old man?"

Gabriel nodded. Maybe now that Chios had given up its secrets, DeGroet had decided he didn't need Tigranes anymore. On the other hand, maybe he just hadn't told this guy about him.

"Well, tell DeGroet," Gabriel said, "that we're leaving the country tonight. That we're going back to Cairo. If he's so eager to see us, he can find us there." When the man didn't respond, he thumbed back the gun's hammer. "Got that?"

The man nodded violently. "To Cairo." He didn't sound as though he believed it, and Gabriel knew better than to think DeGroet would—but he had to try. Maybe DeGroet would at least divert some of his men to Cairo, evening up the sides a little.

"Now get up," Gabriel said.

"I can't…"

"Yes you can," Gabriel said and nudged him forcefully with his foot. The man struggled to his knees, then to his feet. His face was ashen, clammy.

When he reached the door, the man turned back. "He'll kill you," he said, quietly. "You know that."

"I know he'll try," Gabriel said. "Now, go."

UP IN ROOM 304, THE GRAY ROBE WAS ON THE FLOOR and Sheba was back in her khakis and tank top. Tigranes was asleep in one of the room's two twin beds. Christos was standing at the window, looking out at the street below.

"You think it's safe for us to stay here?" Christos said.

"I wouldn't," Gabriel said. "DeGroet's got other things on his mind now, like the treasure and the two of us, but just to be safe—" He handed Christos a slip of paper with a phone number written on it. At least it wasn't torn from a sandwich wrapper this time. "That's my brother's number. Explain what you need and he'll take care of it. Stay any place you like." He paused for a moment. "Just not the Four Seasons."

"Of course not," Christos said, "that would be much too expensive—"

"That's not why," Gabriel said. "Oh, and tell Michael, when you talk to him, that the man you're rooming with has the *Oedipodea* committed to memory. My guess is you'll get some professional recording apparatus in the mail the next day, and a job putting it to use if you want it."

Christos looked over at the old man where he lay. "I don't know how he'd feel about being recorded," he said.

"Then I hope you've got a good memory," Gabriel said, "because it's got to be preserved somehow."

Christos nodded uncertainly.

"Listen," Gabriel said. "What's in that man's head is a priceless, priceless treasure. And he knows it. When you first brought me to Anavatos, he told me about having no son to pass the poem to. He doesn't want it to die with him. If you explain to him that you'll be keeping it alive, that you'll teach it to *your* son someday... trust me, he'll do it." He turned to Sheba. "You could stay, too, you know. The Foundation could certainly use a linguist working on the project. The first translator of the *Oedipodea*—it could make your career."

"That it could," Sheba said, a hint of her long-buried Irish accent coming out in her fatigue. "And perhaps it will. But I'll never feel safe unless I know this is over. And I can't let you face it by yourself."

"Don't be silly," Gabriel said, "I can—"

"You can, you can... do you ever listen to yourself?" She came over to him, put a hand on each of his shoulders. "You're hurt, you're tired. You're not going to be alone, too. Besides," she said, "I already got us on a plane leaving in—" she glanced over at the clock on the bedside table "—forty-seven minutes."

"You got us on..." Gabriel said. "Who has a flight leaving Istanbul at three AM?"

"FedEx," Sheba said.

"You got us on a *FedEx* plane?"

"The Hunt name really opens doors," Sheba said. "You should try it sometime."

He gathered her up in his arms, kissed the top of her head. So much for stewardesses and icepacks— but with a non-stop cargo flight they might be able to beat DeGroet to the island, even if he flew one of his own planes.

"Sheba McCoy," Gabriel said, "have I ever told you how impressive you are?"

"Why don't you hold that thought," she said. "Just till we're safely in the air."

21

"YOU REALLY ARE," GABRIEL SAID, "IMPRESSIVE, I mean," and this time Sheba just nodded. They were sprawled in the cargo hold of a huge FedEx plane, surrounded by cardboard boxes, bulging sacks, and the occasional wooden crate, all secured in a web of plastic netting. Sheba leaned back against a stack of padded envelopes, her shoes and socks beside her, a blanket wrapped around her against the unheated cabin's chill. Gabriel had his boots off as well and was winding an Ace bandage around his left ankle. The co-pilot had found it in the first-aid kit mounted above the emergency exit hatchway.

The first hour of the flight had been consumed by the crew filing back, one by one, to ask Gabriel about some of his more notorious exploits, like the expulsion from Libya in 2004 and the time he'd fled Peru on horseback with half the army chasing after him. That incident had made the *Times* and each of them in turn wanted to know about it. But after a while the questions petered out and eventually the crew returned to the flight deck and left them alone. There was a pair of empty jumpseats they could have used but as long as there was no turbulence it was actually more comfortable sitting on the floor, and so far the flight had been smooth. They might as well have been sailing a ship over a calm ocean.

"Most people," Gabriel said, "facing half the things you have in the past forty-eight hours, would've fallen apart. Believe me, I've seen it happen."

"Oh, I've seen it, too," Sheba said. "You met my sisters. Growing up, not a one of them was worth a damn in a scrape."

"How'd you escape turning out like that?" Gabriel asked.

"It was my dad's decision," Sheba said. She opened the blanket and spread it to cover both of them. "He wanted a son so badly, and he kept trying, and what'd he end up with but a house full of women? It was him, my mother and my three sisters. Finally I came along and he decided he'd had enough. So from the time I was six or seven, he'd take me out with him when he went shooting and driving and fishing and living off the land." Sheba shrugged. "I enjoyed it. My sisters thought I was mental, and maybe they were right, but…"

"But you enjoyed it."

"And now I know how to reload a rifle or hook up a climbing harness or change a flat tire—"

"Oh, that, too?"

"I'm a whiz with flat tires." She snapped her fingers. "On and off like that."

"Is there anything you can't do?"

"Wait tables," she said. "I'm a real bad waitress. Did it for a summer, and my god, I was awful. Made no tips."

"All right," Gabriel said. "Anything else?"

She bent over him, brought her lips close to his. "Taking no for an answer. Not getting what I want. I'm terrible at that."

Gabriel smiled. "I'm not too good at it myself," he said.

THEY LANDED IN KURUNEGALA, ON A PRIVATE AIRSTRIP near the train depot. The town was centrally located at the intersection of the A6 and A10 motorways, within reach of all parts of the country. Dambulla was just thirty miles away to the northeast, and the spot marked on the map, Gabriel estimated, would be another ten miles or so past that.

On the way out of the plane, he rummaged through the emergency supplies cabinet by the door. Flares, life jackets, a long-handled flashlight—plenty of things that might be useful in a pinch. No ammunition for a Colt Peacemaker, though. That would have been too much to hope for.

Gabriel asked the pilot if he could grab a few things, and the pilot nodded. "Whatever you need. We'll restock at the hangar."

Gabriel took a couple of items, handed some to Sheba. Then he handed a cardboard box to the pilot. There'd been a rack of shipping supplies against one wall of the plane and he'd prepared the package while they were in flight. The account number he'd filled in was the Hunt Foundation's and the address the package was going to was the Discoverers League building in New York. No point lugging two guns around when one of them was empty. And Andras had been right. The Colt *was* an antique, one that (the story went) had once belonged to either Wyatt Earp or Bat Masterson. Who knew if it was true—but if he wasn't going to be able to use the thing, he might as well keep it safe.

The pilot smiled as he accepted the package. "It'll be there tomorrow," he said. "Guaranteed."

THEY STEPPED OUT INTO NINETY-DEGREE HEAT AND humidity so powerful that a layer of moisture formed on their skin in seconds. It was late afternoon, so they were at least spared the glare of the sun directly overhead, but walking through the damp, warm air felt uncomfortable enough. In the distance, beneath the thrumming of airplane and truck engines, they heard a raucous chorus of chirps and caws mixed with the periodic screech of a monkey.

Kurunegala was shaped roughly like a flat-bottomed bowl, the plain the town was built on being surrounded by tall rock outcroppings the locals had named after the animals they resembled. The town's name itself meant "Tusker Rock," since the tallest of the outcroppings, a grim thousand-foot cliff, was said to resemble a *kurune*, a tusked elephant. Gabriel squinted, but he couldn't see it. There was also a Tortoise Rock, a Goat Rock, a Beetle Rock, an Eel Rock, and a Monkey Rock, all of which looked to Gabriel like rocks. There was even (the railroad stationmaster told Gabriel in a fit of garrulousness) a Yakdessa Rock, at which point Sheba needed to translate for him since the stationmaster was at a loss to explain what sort of animal a Yakdessa might be.

"It's not an animal," Sheba said. "It's a man. Like a shaman—he would help afflicted people who were possessed by *Yak*."

"Possessed by yak," Gabriel said.

"It's the name of the Devil in Sinhala," Sheba said.

"That certainly makes more sense," Gabriel muttered.

He wasn't used to not being able to speak the local language well enough to get by. Over the years he'd picked up at least a few words and phrases in most languages and was passably fluent in more than a dozen. But he'd never had the need or the opportunity to pick up Sinhala or Tamil, the languages of Sri Lanka. The one time he'd been here he'd managed to get by with a mixture of English, Urdu, and hand gestures. And pistol gestures, when he'd finally tracked down the statue. Those were understood everywhere.

He snuck a glance at the tracking device Lucy had given him, then returned it to his pocket. DeGroet was just 141 miles northwest. And closing.

"Can we use your phone," Gabriel asked the stationmaster, a younger man no more than five feet tall who squinted up at him myopically any time he didn't understand what he was hearing, almost as though it were his eyes that were at fault. He was squinting now. "Your telephone. We need to make a telephone call, to Dambulla."

"Dambulla?"

"Yes, Dambulla."

"Train does not go."

"No, I know that," Gabriel said. "We want to use—"

"Highway," the stationmaster said. "You must drive." And he made steering wheel motions with his hands.

"You want to try?" Gabriel asked Sheba.

"If they'd had telephones back when they had yakdessas," she said, "I'd know the word for it."

Gabriel mimed picking up a phone receiver and dialing a number, then realized that gesture might not mean anything anymore, not to someone raised on cell phones. He mimed unfolding a cell phone and talking into it. The stationmaster's eyes unclenched happily. He reached under his counter and pulled out a phone with a scratched and faded plastic case. He opened it, pressed a button, and handed it over.

Gabriel punched in a number he remembered well from his last time here and was relieved to hear a woman's voice answer on the third ring. "'Allo," she said, a hint of a French accent surviving the transit through the cheap loudspeaker.

"Dayani, this is Gabriel Hunt," Gabriel said.

"Gabriel! My goodness. How *are* you? Are you thinking of coming back to our island for a visit sometime?"

"Actually, I'm in Kurunegala," he said, "right now. How would you feel about dropping everything you're doing and driving out here to pick me up?"

She didn't miss a beat. "I'm not sure my coworkers will like it so much, but I would feel just fine about it. Want to wait for me by the clock tower? I can be there in forty minutes."

"I wish we could," he said, thinking about his ankle. Taped up, it did hurt less, but it still hurt, and waiting would feel better than walking. "But we can't. We're going to start walking along the A6, just look for us on the side of the road."

"Are you in some sort of trouble, Gabriel?"

"Some sort," he said.

"*Naturellement*," she said. "I'm leaving now." And the connection broke.

Gabriel handed the phone back to the stationmaster.

"You...go to Dambulla?" the young man said. Gabriel nodded. "You go quick. Quick? Understand? Before rains come."

"Rains," Gabriel said.

The man squinted, searching for a word. "Later, big rains," he said. Then his face relaxed. He knew the word he wanted.

"Monsoon," he said.

22

"THIS WOMAN WHO'S PICKING US UP," SHEBA SAID, and Gabriel said, "Dayani."

"Who is she?"

They were walking along the side of the highway separating Kurunegala from Dambulla, a long, straight stretch of asphalt that cut like a knife blade through the heavy jungle cover that began in earnest just outside the town. Less than a mile from the train station, you couldn't see anything in any direction but leaves and vines and trunks and undergrowth. That, and the occasional animal passing in your peripheral vision, the occasional car zooming past on the road.

"She's a translator," Gabriel said. "Spent ten years working for UNESCO out of Paris—that's where I met her. She transferred back here a year or so ago to work on a set of documents discovered at the Golden Temple."

"And you came for a visit to... assist her with the translation."

"She called me to see if I'd help out when one of the Temple's statues was stolen."

"I see."

"I got the statue back."

Sheba nodded.

"What?" Gabriel said.

"Nothing," Sheba said. "I was just thinking how strangely specific a man's tastes can be. Some men have a thing for feet. You seem to have a thing for linguists."

Gabriel smiled. "What can I say? I like smart women."

She patted him on the shoulder. "And apparently we like you."

The jungle thinned and was replaced by farmland, tidily cultivated fields stretching for miles on either side of the road. With the sky visible again Gabriel saw clouds massing heavily overhead, moving swiftly as the wind picked up. The sun was dropping and the undersides of the clouds were stained with shadow, dark russet streaks that made them look lower than they were.

When the first drops fell, it was almost a relief, cutting the heat and releasing some of the humidity. But drops were soon replaced by sheets of water pounding into the ground, a torrent that would have resembled a flash flood if Gabriel hadn't known it was likely to continue unabated for the next five hours. He was soaked through in an instant; Sheba, too, though her jacket at least had a hood that she was able to put up. Of all the supplies they'd taken off the plane, some of which he was carrying strapped to his belt, some worn over his shoulders like a backpack under his leather jacket, some in a satchel slung over Sheba's shoulder, none was an umbrella. And there had been one, too. He kicked himself for not taking it.

Instead, he took out a safety blinker from Sheba's bag, activated it, and clipped it to one of the bag's straps. It was a square plastic box that flashed a bright red light every three seconds. Even with visibility cut by the downpour, Gabriel figured it should be enough to keep strange cars from hitting them—and Dayani from missing them.

It also attracted notice from other drivers. One car pulled up alongside them and cracked the window, the driver asking in a shout whether they needed help, first in Sinhala and then in halting English.

The temptation to accept his offer was great—but they couldn't get any wetter at this point, and since they'd been walking almost half an hour now, Dayani should be driving by any minute.

"Thanks, no," Gabriel shouted back. "Someone's picking us up." He had to shout it again to make himself heard. The driver shrugged, rolled his window up and drove off.

"You're sure your friend's coming?" Sheba asked, leaning close to his ear.

Gabriel nodded.

"I hope so," she said, pulling her jacket tightly around her, for what little good that did.

A moment later Gabriel pointed at a shape looming out of the gray wall of water before them. "Here she is." He pulled a road flare from his belt and activated it, waving it overhead till Dayani's white Indica pulled to a halt. They piled into the back seat and slammed the door shut behind them. Water ran off them, soaking the mats on the floor. They were both breathing heavily, as if they'd just come from running a footrace.

The woman in the driver's seat turned to face them, a towel in one hand. "Here, you can use this." She looked from Gabriel to Sheba and back again. "I only brought one."

"That's okay," Gabriel said. And to Sheba: "You use it."

"And this is…?" Dayani said.

"A friend of mine," Gabriel said. "Sheba McCoy. She's a linguist."

Dayani's eyebrows rose. "Oh, is she?"

Sheba snatched the towel out of her hand and began drying her face and hair, which had gotten drenched in spite of the hood.

"Thank you for picking us up," Gabriel said. He took one of Dayani's hands, squeezed it and, leaning forward, kissed her on the cheek.

"*Pas de problème*," Dayani said. "Want to tell me what's got you in such a hurry that you'd walk through a monsoon to get there?"

"I found a map," Gabriel said, sitting back as Dayani made a U-turn and got underway again. "Partly in Egypt and partly in Greece. It pointed here."

"Here to Sri Lanka? Here to Kurunegala? To Dambulla?"

"To a spot maybe ten miles northeast of Dambulla," Gabriel said. "Give or take. Do you have any idea what might be there?"

"Of course," Dayani said. In the rearview mirror, Gabriel saw her dark brown eyes narrow. "Ten miles northeast, that's where Sigiriya is."

The name rang only the faintest of bells. "Sigiriya?"

"It's an ancient rock fortress in the middle of the jungle," Dayani said. "The locals sometimes call it Lion Rock."

* * *

"A MAN NAMED JOHN STILL DISCOVERED IT IN 1907," Dayani said, speaking slowly, her attention focused on the road. "Not the rock itself, of course—that's never been a secret. A 370-meter volcanic rock towering over the surrounding treeline, you're not going to lose track of that. What Still discovered were the ruins on top of the rock, and the remains of some artwork on the way up—paintings, mostly."

"Do any of these paintings depict monsters? Animals with human heads?"

"No. You mean like a sphinx?"

"Exactly like a sphinx," Gabriel said.

"Well, most of them have been lost—the paintings were done directly on the side of the rock more than fifteen hundred years ago, and there are only twenty-two remaining out of what we think were something like five hundred originally. The ones that are left are mostly images of women—bare-breasted concubines, that sort of thing. But who knows what the ones that were lost depicted."

"Are there any sculptures, by any chance?"

"One," Dayani said. "Halfway up, there's a shelf with two monumental stone paws—lion's paws, each one taller than a man. And there's a flight of stone steps between them, leading further up the rock. But that's all that's left—the rest of the figure is missing. Clearly there used to be a head there, probably made of fired clay or brick; to get to the top you'd have had to climb up into the lion's mouth. But it's all long gone. There's no record of what it looked like."

Or whether it was a lion's mouth at all, Gabriel thought. As frightening as it might have been to ask visitors to allow themselves to be swallowed by a giant stone lion, how much more so would it have been to ask them to climb into the mouth of a man with a lion's body?

Just the thing to set the proper tone for foreign emissaries coming to the Cradle of Fear.

"Has the site been thoroughly explored?" Gabriel said.

"Depends what you mean by thoroughly," Dayani said. "It's rather enormous. The upper surface has been mapped and the grounds around it, but the rock itself is riddled with caves—monks were using it as a shelter for nine hundred years before King Kasyapa ever built the palace on the top, and after his death they used it for nine hundred more."

"Only monks?" Gabriel said.

"Why? What else did you have in mind?"

"Breeders," Gabriel said. "Animal breeders."

"Well, monks in Sri Lanka often did raise animals," Dayani said.

"Not the kind I'm thinking of," Gabriel said.

"And what kind's that?"

Gabriel shook his head. "I'm sorry, Dayani. The less you know, the better. There are men coming here who have already killed at least nine people in pursuit of a relic of some sort that's connected to Sigiriya. I don't want them to have a reason to come after you."

"Gabriel," Dayani said patiently, "if they find out I drove you, they'll have all the reason they need. You may think you're protecting me, but you're not. At worst you're endangering me and at best you're annoying me." She swerved onto the shoulder to give a wide berth to a truck that had loomed up out of nowhere. Honking, she swerved back on once it was past. "So for the sake of all that is holy, *mon âme*, would you please just tell me what the hell is going on?"

Sheba put down the towel. "Oh, I like this one, Gabriel," she said.

SO HE TOLD HER—THE WHOLE STORY, STARTING WITH the call from Jim Kellen in Dublin and the midnight flight to Hungary, then the abduction in New York and the plane ride to Egypt, the secret chamber deep inside the Sphinx and the cavern beneath Anavatos. He told her about the two sculptures he'd found and the two coins, and the two maps, too, with their inscriptions pointing to ancient Taprobane. Dayani listened to it all without any change in her expression, concentrating on her driving, until finally she pulled to a stop in a lot behind the Golden Temple, put on the parking brake, and turned the keys in the ignition. The car's engine grumbled once and was silent.

"Gabriel," she said, turning to face him over the back of the seat, "that's the craziest story I've ever heard. It's madness—sheer madness. Grown men chasing about, getting killed, over a fairytale about monsters and treasures… how could anyone believe anything so, so *détraqué*?"

"You asked," Gabriel said. "You wanted to hear it. Now you've heard it. Maybe it's crazy and maybe it's not. But it's true—I can promise you that. The men who are looking for this treasure are real, and the bullets in their guns are real, and they're all of—" he checked the unit in his pocket "—ninety-one miles away. Which probably means they've just landed in Colombo. We'd better get going again."

"You can't even wait for the rain to let up?" Dayani said.

"They won't," Gabriel said.

She looked over at Sheba. "Have you tried to talk some sense into him?"

"Hey," Sheba said, "you spend some time with a gun to your head or a sword at your throat, sister, and then you can talk."

Gabriel saw Dayani's eyes blaze and he put a hand up between the women. "We don't have time for this. Dayani—can you let us borrow the car? Actually," he said, "I guess I should start by asking whether you can even get there by car."

"You can get pretty close," Dayani conceded after a moment. "You'll have to walk the last half mile or so."

"Then you'll let us borrow it?" Gabriel said. "Please, Dayani. It's important."

Dayani stared into Gabriel's eyes half regretfully, as though she could read there some terrible future consequences of her decision. "You think I can say no to you?" she said. "Just be careful, for heaven's sake. Bad enough to get yourself killed over something real, something that matters. To die for a rich man's fantasy..."

"Many have died for less," Gabriel said.

"*Oui*. And many have died for nothing. But I don't care about many. I care about you." To Sheba she said, "Close your eyes, dear. You won't want to see this."

Sheba didn't close her eyes as Dayani planted a palm on each of Gabriel's cheeks and pressed her lips to his, but when the kiss lasted past the ten-second mark, she turned to look out the window. At twenty seconds she said, without turning back, "Maybe you can enlighten me, Gabriel, on just what we do and don't have time for."

"Sorry," Gabriel said, pulling away.

"Be safe," Dayani whispered. "You too," she said to Sheba, and gripped her hand briefly. Then she was out of the car and heading through the pouring rain toward the back door of the administrative building by the Temple's side. She looked back once, then went inside.

"All of us," Gabriel said, and he climbed into the front seat.

23

THE READOUT OF THE TRACKING UNIT, WHICH GABRIEL
had propped upright between them, was slowly
counting down. When they'd gotten back onto the
highway it had said *83SW*; now it was down to *77*.

The pitch-black sky overhead was lit suddenly by
the jagged forks of a lighting strike, followed seconds
later by a monstrous crack of thunder and the sound
of a tree smashing through branches and leaves to the
jungle floor. It sounded just yards away, and Gabriel
half expected to see a portion of the tree's massive
trunk drop into view in their path. The car's headlights
illuminated only a few feet ahead of them; it felt like
anything might be out there, just out of sight, a collision
waiting to happen.

He felt the slope of the road increase as they went, the
little car's brakes straining harder to grip the surface, its
engine straining to make some of the steeper climbs. It
was a Tata Motors import from India, the best Dayani

could afford, no doubt, on the amount UNESCO paid her, and it probably did fine for ferrying her to and from work. It was waterproof; the windshield wipers worked. But it had surely never been tested under the sort of stress cars regularly were forced to endure under Gabriel's hand, and he very much doubted this one could take the punishment. Just as well, then, that they'd be leaving it at a safe distance from their destination.

They came to the turn-off from the highway and shot through a muddy patch at the start of a road whose paving was cracked and uneven. Municipal services were not the country's strong suit and road repair took a back seat in the fight for what resources there were. But the rains kept coming, seven months out of the year, battering each manmade incursion into the jungle as if eager to erase its presence. They drove over potholes that would make even a New Yorker look twice. You could've bathed a baby in some of them.

But even cracked pavement was preferable to an unpaved dirt road, and Gabriel braked to a halt when he realized that was what he was driving on. Already, the mud beneath their tires was dragging at them, making progress difficult—he didn't want to get the car stuck entirely. Revving the engine, he switched into reverse and backed up out of the muck till he was on asphalt again and under the overhang of a healthy-sized tree limb. Pocketing the keys, he got out. Sheba followed, the towel held over her head.

"We walk from here," Gabriel said, and led the way.

THEIR FIRST SIGHT OF SIGIRIYA CAME WITH A SUDDEN strobe of lightning overhead. The rock didn't look like a lion. It looked a little like Devil's Tower—that same impression almost of a geyser of stone spouting from the ground, like a gargantuan oil strike frozen in mid eruption. In front of the rock, a space had been cleared in the jungle, a thousand feet of little square gardens and paths and ponds, all of them now awash with rainwater. He strode quickly along the main path, mud sucking at his boots, the bandage around his ankle waterlogged and cold. Sheba walked beside him, hugging the bag from the plane to her side. Gabriel reached into it and drew out the flashlight—rubber-sheathed and waterproof and with a beam roughly as effective as the car's headlights had been. It was better than nothing.

The rock grew in stuttering snapshot steps as they approached it, larger each time it was made visible by a crooked branch of lightning zigzagging through the sky. In certain spots the highest levels of the rock overhung the lowest, and Gabriel made for one of these. Though the wind continued to blow the rain against them, here at least was some small shelter from the storm. He could see how Sigiriya would have recommended itself to monks in the fourth century—BC or AD, it didn't matter which—desperate for relief from the island's thunderous deluges. That there were caves, too—warm, dry, possibly home to a local animal or two who could be cooked over a fire for dinner—was all the more reason.

But he and Sheba didn't have the luxury of crawling into a cave and waiting out the storm. Shielding it with one hand, he drew Lucy's device from his pocket once more. Sixty miles exactly. That wasn't much time at all.

Squeezing through a narrow opening between two tall walls of rock, Gabriel found a set of shallow stone steps leading up along the side. He put out one hand to steady himself against the rock face and shouted back for Sheba to do the same. For a moment she held onto the waterlogged towel, then she crammed it in the bag. "Hell with it," she said. She didn't bother putting up the hood. Her hair was plastered to her scalp within seconds.

They climbed slowly, carefully. The path wound around the huge boulder, narrowing as it went till there was no more than a person's width of stone beneath their feet, and nothing to their left but a sheer drop. The rock they walked on was slick and slippery, and pitted with shallow depressions that had accumulated puddles but looked solid in the flashlight's glare. A misstep, a loss of balance, a moment's error, and they'd be falling through the darkness. But not for long. Gabriel thought of the man who'd plunged to his death in front of his eyes back in New York. Even a fall of a hundred feet would take just two or three seconds, not long enough even to mouth a prayer. Not that Gabriel was a praying man, and he didn't think he'd turn into one at the end, but—

He hugged the rock and climbed in minute steps. He didn't want to find out.

Behind him, Sheba was saying something but the powerful winds were snatching her words away before they could reach him. He hung back so she could catch up. When she did, he could hear the fear in her voice. "Can you see… how much farther…?"

"Not much," he said, though the honest answer would have been, *No, I can't see.*

"Really?"

"Yeah," he said, and reached out a hand to stroke her shoulder gently. "Just pretend you're taking a walk down Grafton Street on a Sunday afternoon. Sidewalk there's not a whole lot wider than this."

"Maybe," Sheba said, "but stepping off the curb's not such a big deal."

"I thought you said your father took you climbing and such," Gabriel said, "and that you enjoyed it."

"I enjoyed it when he took me hunting and fishing and camping out," Sheba said. "I always hated the climbing."

"Well, there's not much of it left," Gabriel said. "Just a little bit."

"You're fucking lying to me, Hunt," she said.

"Yes," Gabriel said.

"Well, thank you," she said. "Keep doing it." And she put out a hand again to find the wall beside her.

But it didn't land on stone.

A noise arose as her hand hit the side of something soft and fibrous, an angry buzzing sound like a hundred cell phones set to vibrate going off at once. Gabriel swung the beam of the flashlight around and it slid across a cluster of dark misshapen sacs hanging from the underside of a small ledge of rock. Sheba's palm had landed directly on one of them, crushing the side, and through the hole was streaming a cloud of—

"Move!" Gabriel shouted. "Now!"

Wasps. The so-called 'wild bees' of Sri Lanka were legendary for their viciousness—some years back there'd been a newspaper article about a wasp attack that had left two hundred tourists in the hospital with swollen limbs and constricted breathing passages. And if you had the misfortune to be allergic to their venom—

He grabbed Sheba's arm and pulled her around in front of him, putting himself in the raging insects' path, an act of chivalry that was rewarded instantly when he felt a stinger plunge into the flesh of his neck. He swatted wildly over his shoulder till he felt the back of his hand collide with the wasp's body, then slapped his hand against the rock, crushing it.

But there were too many to kill one by one. There were too many even to *see* one by one—what he saw, silhouetted against the general darkness, was a cloud with undulating edges made up of hundreds of enraged wasps unleashed into the thunderstorm. The rain was probably confusing them, but not enough— several dozen came flying toward Gabriel, who threw up one leather-jacketed arm in front of his face and slapped a flurry of the bugs aside.

"The towel," he shouted, "hold it up and climb as fast as you can."

He felt Sheba move beside him, saw the white of the towel out of the corner of one eye, heard her taking small but rapid steps along the precarious path.

A wasp darted in under his guard and jabbed into his chin. He could feel the swelling begin immediately.

He turned and ran, the wasps screaming angrily behind him, and not far behind at that. He felt his injured foot slip and caught himself with one hand, digging his fingers desperately into a crevice in the rock. Wasps flung themselves by the dozen against his back and legs, unable to penetrate the thick leather of the jacket or the fabric of his pants. But he felt one in his hair as well and another at his neck, which was already swollen and painful from the earlier sting. He brushed the one in his hair away and kept going, urging Sheba along when he caught up to her.

They rounded a corner and found themselves facing a passage between the rock face on one side and an artificial wall erected on the other. It was a huge barrier, like a restraining wall or a dam, five feet thick at the base and tapering toward the top some ten feet overhead. In the flashlight's beam it looked like it was made of fired clay with some sort of glaze or veneer, and on the rock behind the wall, sheltered by it and by an overhang above, Gabriel glimpsed the paintings Dayani had mentioned, the maidens of Sigiriya with their jeweled headdresses and lotus blossoms between their fingers and no shirts on. He ran past them, Sheba in the lead and going even faster, neither of them at risk of falling off the mountain, temporarily, because of the wall to their left. The wasps continued to race after them—some hadn't made the turn, but most had. Sheba came to a set of stairs carved into the rock and took them two at a time, and Gabriel followed, close on her heels. Then off to one side Gabriel saw the narrow entrance of a cave. Sheba ran past it, but Gabriel reached out, snagged her arm and pulled her back toward him. Squeezing inside the cave opening, he flattened himself against the wall on one side and motioned for Sheba to do the same on the other. He grabbed one corner of the towel from her hand and held it up against the wall at the edge of the opening. Sheba followed his lead, the towel hanging between them, covering the opening to about three feet down from the top. Gabriel shut off the flashlight and they waited in the dark.

They heard the sounds of wasps winging past, felt small collisions as some hurled their bodies against the towel. It took a minute or two for the sounds to die down and the collisions to stop. Still, Gabriel whispered "Wait," and gave it another two minutes. When he'd heard no sounds for that long, he switched on the light again and let his end of the towel fall. The flashlight's beam revealed, hanging from the fabric, the bodies of ten or eleven fat wasps, their stingers trapped in the towel's fabric. Sheba threw the towel to the ground. Then she stepped on each one, grinding it to a bloody smear on the cloth.

"Did you get stung?" Gabriel asked.

She nodded. "Hurts like hell. You?"

He reached back to massage the inflamed lump on his neck. "I'll live."

"I'm sorry—I should have been more careful—"

"Stop it," Gabriel said. He stepped outside. The storm was still raging, but the water almost felt good on his neck and chin. He glanced at the tracker. Fifty-two miles. It ticked over to fifty-one as he watched. Driving quickly, DeGroet might get here in less than an hour. "Come on," he said and held his hand out. Sheba took it, and they continued along the winding path up the side of the rock.

"Not much longer now," Gabriel said after a bit. He'd just reached the top of a set of stairs and Sheba was a few steps behind.

"I'm not falling for that again," Sheba said.

"Good for you," Gabriel said. "Except this time it's the truth."

And as Sheba climbed the last few steps a shattering bolt of lightning lit the sky, revealing the shelf of rock they stood upon—and at the far end, where the rest of the mountain still towered above them, two vast and trunkless feet of stone, the three carved claws on each gleaming, shining in the rain.

24

THEY WERE BETTER PRESERVED THAN THE PAWS OF the Great Sphinx in Egypt—but as Dayani had warned, the well-preserved paws were all that remained. The steep stone stairs between the paws led only to a rock ledge that in turn led to more stairs winding further up the mountain—the monumental head the stairs must once have passed through was completely gone.

Gabriel walked over to what would have been the figure's left paw and crouched beside it. Rainwater ran down its sides and pooled at his feet. He shone the flashlight on the wet surface and felt along it with one hand, inching his fingertips from the base of the claw all the way back to the rock wall the paw emerged from. Then he did the same thing again, a few inches lower.

"What are you doing?" Sheba said.

He didn't answer, just kept feeling along the surface for any irregularity in texture, any indication of a seam. He stopped about halfway down. "The men of

Taprobane," he said, pulling from his belt the other tool he'd hung there on the way off the plane, a spring-loaded emergency window punch, "were creatures of habit." He set the tip of the punch to the section of the stone where his finger had halted and triggered its action. The point shot out, chiseling into the stone. "Two temples, separated by hundreds of miles and hundreds of years, but they had matching maps and matching statues inside, matching inscriptions." He pried the punch out, reset it, moved it a few inches away, and triggered it again. "I figure if they built a secret entrance into the Sphinx's left paw in Giza, they'd probably—" he moved the punch once more, triggered it again "—do the same thing here."

After a few more shots, the outline of a seam began to emerge. "Here, hold this," he said, and Sheba took the flashlight from him, aiming it down to illuminate the surface. "A little higher." The beam moved. "That's it." He drew the point of the punch along the seam, clearing it of the compacted stone dust that had filled it in for so long. The rain was helping, by washing particles away as he dug them out.

Yes, there was definitely a separate block here, no question about it. The question was how he could get it out. In Giza it had taken two strong men to lever the stone slowly out of its hole—and that had been a smaller block that had already been removed and replaced several times. This one had probably never been moved since first being sealed up who knew how many centuries ago. Even if Sheba helped, they'd be at a disadvantage. And they didn't have an unlimited amount of time. Hunching over to protect it from getting wet, he looked once more at the device Lucy had given him. *40SW*, it said. Forty miles—it meant DeGroet was in Kurunegala already. Even in the rain it wouldn't take him long to cover the remaining distance…

Gabriel froze.

He'd heard a sound, faintly, from the direction of the stairs, one that chilled him in a way that an hour spent out in the rain and wind had not. Or had he just imagined it? He looked down at Lucy's device again. It couldn't be—

Slap, slap, click.

He looked up—and, noticing him do so, Sheba did, too. She was still aiming the flashlight down at the stone of the lion's paw, but enough light leaked past to outline the figures at the top of the steps. The man in front was small and slender and stood stiff-backed with a walking stick in one hand.

Lajos DeGroet.

DEGROET SWITCHED ON A SMALL FLASHLIGHT IN HIS other hand. There was a bigger man standing behind him, holding an umbrella over DeGroet's head. To one side of DeGroet and one step back, holding his own umbrella, was Karoly, a cigarette smoldering in a corner of his mouth, a pistol in his hand.

The man behind DeGroet, Gabriel saw, had a gun on them as well.

"You look surprised," DeGroet said.

He walked slowly down the steps, clipping the flashlight to his belt as he went.

"Do you think I am an idiot, Hunt? Did you think I wouldn't notice that Andras' cell phone was gone? Or that maybe it wouldn't occur to me that you could use it to track mine?" DeGroet stopped a foot away, flanked by his men. "Have you never played chess, Hunt? I know you're not the intellectual your brother is, but I would have thought you might have picked up some of the basic principles over the years. One of which is lulling your opponent into a false sense of security."

He extended his free hand, palm up.

"Your gun, if you please."

Gabriel unsnapped his holster and handed over the gun he'd taken from DeGroet's man in Istanbul, butt first.

"Where's your Colt, Hunt? I hope you haven't lost it. That was a fine piece. A fine piece." He turned the gun over in his hand a few times, then tossed it off the side of the mountain.

"How did you beat us here?" Gabriel said.

"How do I beat everyone at everything? I just do. It is my gift." He turned to Sheba. "I am sorry we didn't meet under better circumstances, my dear. You are a very lovely girl and I can be most generous to my friends." He gestured at the man holding the umbrella over him. "Istvan, help Mr. Hunt get that stone out, will you? Here, I'll take that." He took the umbrella in his free hand. "Go on."

Istvan slipped his gun into a shoulder holster under his jacket and knelt on the ground beside the paw. Both DeGroet's light and Sheba's shone on the block. Istvan felt around the edges of the seam Gabriel had uncovered, tried to slip his thick fingers inside. It was impossible—the groove was too narrow. He looked back at his boss somewhat helplessly. "How am I supposed to get it out?"

"Well, Hunt? How were you going to do it?"

"Frankly," Gabriel said, "I hadn't figured that out yet myself."

"Well, figure it out now, or your lovely friend goes where your gun just did."

Karoly took the bag off Sheba's shoulder, transferred it to his own, and pressed the nose of his revolver into her back. Gabriel could see that his hand was bandaged. "Did that hurt," Gabriel said, "when I shot the gun out of your hand?"

"Quit stalling," Karoly said, his voice a low rasp.

"Oh, good," Gabriel said. "It did." He turned back to the block, thought about the options for getting it out. With a drill and some anchored screws it might be possible to gain purchase on the stone and draw it out; with an explosive, of course, you could blast it out. But with neither…

"Lie down," he told Istvan. "On your back."

"What?" the big man asked.

"On your back, next to me," Gabriel said, and demonstrated, lying down with the soles of his boots up against the stone block.

"What are you doing, Hunt?" DeGroet wanted to know.

"We're not going to be able to pull it out—we don't have the tools. That means we'll have to push it in."

DeGroet thought about it for a moment, then nodded. "Do it," he told Istvan.

The big man lay down, braced his feet against the stone. Gabriel briefly considered the possibility of rolling over on top of him, trying to get to the gun in his holster, but he discarded the idea. Even if he succeeded in taking Istvan by surprise and could overpower him and get to his gun—none of which was a sure thing—doing so would take time, and with Karoly's pistol millimeters from Sheba's spine, it was time they didn't have.

Gabriel said, "Count of three, push. Okay?" Istvan spat to clear rainwater from his mouth, then nodded. "One," Gabriel said. "Two…"

He saw Sheba move. She spun and broke free of Karoly's grip and started running for the stairs. DeGroet reacted swiftly: he swung his walking stick out, slipping it between her legs in mid-stride and, with a snap of his wrist, sweeping her ankle from under her. Sheba fell to the ground with a crash.

Gabriel jumped to his feet, but Karoly stepped forward with his gun aimed squarely between Gabriel's eyes. "Just give me a reason," he growled.

DeGroet stood over Sheba where she lay sprawled, her breath knocked out of her, her hair a wet heap against the stone. He put the tip of his walking stick against her throat. "Don't do that again. Next time it'll be my sword you'll feel. Get up."

Sheba climbed unsteadily to her feet. Karoly grabbed her arm roughly and pulled her to him.

"Where were we," DeGroet said. "Ah, yes. You were counting to three?"

Gabriel looked from DeGroet to Karoly and then to Sheba. Her eyes shone apologetically. "Don't," he told her. "It's all right." He resumed his position on the ground, steadied his feet against the stone.

"One," he said. "Two…" He looked over at Istvan, who nodded. "Three—"

He pushed with all the strength in his legs, and beside him he saw Istvan doing the same. Judging by the size of the man's legs, he had no shortage of strength in them. The block moved—but only infinitesimally. "Again," Gabriel said, and counted. It moved a bit more this time, sliding inward by a few inches. "One more. Kick this time."

They both brought their knees to their chest and, when Gabriel called "Three," kicked out, their soles landing sharply against the stone. The block slid in by half a foot or more—and then, after teetering for a second, fell inwards. There was silence for several seconds, then a large, reverberating thud that sounded like it had come from a long way below them.

Gabriel rolled over and approached the opening. Istvan was right behind him, gun in hand once more. Gabriel took his Zippo from his pocket, lit it. Inside, a corridor led along the length of the paw and deep into the rock behind it—but first there was a gaping pit, beginning an inch from the opening, and it was into this pit that the stone block had fallen. If they'd managed to pull the block out rather than push it, whoever had been the first to step into the opening would have fallen similarly.

"I need more light," Gabriel said. He picked up the flashlight Sheba had been carrying from where it had fallen when she'd taken her spill. Shining it at the corridor's ceiling, Gabriel saw a series of crossbeams stretching from wall to wall as well as columns supporting the ceiling. It looked almost like a tunnel in a mine, propped up to ensure stability.

The first of the crossbeams was directly above the pit.

Gabriel walked up to Karoly. "I need something from that bag. You can get it for me or you can let me get it myself—your choice."

"What is it?"

"A coil of rope."

"Get him the rope," Karoly said to Sheba. "Nothing else. I see anything else come out of that bag, you're a dead woman."

"Understood," Sheba said. She unzipped the bag and pulled out a hank of nylon rope.

Gabriel carried it back to the opening. It took three tries to get the end of the rope over the crossbeam and then much fishing with the middle portion of the rope to snag the far end and pull it far enough back across the pit for him to grab it. When he did, he tied a quick six-loop hangman's knot and drew the rope tight around the beam, like a noose. He tested it with a few strong tugs. The beam held.

"Okay," Gabriel said. "Who goes first?"

They all looked at each other. Gabriel pictured DeGroet running scenarios in his head along the lines of the old missionaries-and-cannibals puzzle: If he sent Gabriel first, Gabriel could keep the rope on the far side and escape along the corridor, if he were willing to sacrifice Sheba, and DeGroet couldn't be certain he wouldn't; on the other hand, if DeGroet sent one of his men across first, he'd no longer have the advantage in terms of numbers back on this side of the pit...

"Ladies first," DeGroet said, and he pulled Sheba toward the opening. She took hold of the rope, wrapped it several times around one fist, then grabbed it with her other hand as well. She gave Gabriel a concerned look, then lifted her feet and swung across. She staggered a bit when she landed and for a moment Gabriel thought she might slip backwards—but she steadied herself and remained upright. When she'd regained her balance, she threw the end of the rope back. Karoly caught it and, after pocketing his gun, followed her across.

Next came Gabriel. He tossed the flashlight across to Sheba, who shone the beam downward so it wouldn't get in his eyes. Gabriel gripped the rope firmly and pushed off. He noticed as he swung that the crossbeam didn't seem quite as stable as it had when he'd first tested it. But he made it safely across. When he landed, Karoly made a point of showing him that he had his gun out again and his finger tight against the trigger. "I see it," Gabriel said. "You don't have to wave it around."

"Just as long as you don't get any bright ideas," Karoly said.

"If I were the type to get bright ideas," Gabriel said, "I wouldn't be here, would I?" He swung the rope back across the pit.

DeGroet caught it, handed his walking stick to Istvan, moved his grip around a bit till he got comfortable with it, and then swung across, the light hanging from his hip brushing a reflected arc against the stone wall. When he had landed, he had Istvan throw the walking stick to him. He snatched it one-handed out of the air.

Then he sent the rope back. Istvan took hold of it and walked up to the edge. He tugged on the rope a couple of times, wrapped it around one hand as Sheba had, held on with the other hand, and launched himself across.

When he'd made it halfway, the crossbeam snapped.

He vanished in a split second, plummeting into the pit. He screamed all the way down.

It took him as long to hit bottom as it had taken the stone block to fall. The sound of his impact, when it came, was quieter. That made it no less painful to hear.

"Unfortunate," DeGroet said, after a moment. He aimed his stick down the corridor. "Now get moving."

25

KAROLY HAD TAKEN THE FLASHLIGHT BACK FROM
Sheba and was shining it between them, lighting the
path a few feet ahead. They were walking two abreast,
Gabriel and Sheba in front, DeGroet and Karoly in the
rear, the clicks of the old man's stick against the stone
floor punctuating their progress as they went.

The main corridor ended at an archway that led
into a circular chamber, though there were other,
smaller archways branching off to the left and right
as well. Prodded by Karoly's gun in his back, Gabriel
walked forward.

The room was large enough that it took them some
time to explore it all. There was no map on any of the
walls, Gabriel noted, and no sculptures, of sphinxes
or otherwise. What they did find was cages, their bars
extending all the way from the rough-hewn floor to a
ceiling some fourteen or fifteen feet overhead. In each
there were metal shackles attached to the walls by

heavy chains, the circular bands lying open and empty on the ground. Some cages had just one pair, some had two. One had three. And the walls were covered with the intricate swoops and whorls of the Sinhala alphabet, the faded ink showing dimly in the yellow beams of the flashlights.

"Please do us the kindness of translating this... this scribbling," DeGroet said to Sheba.

"I'm no expert—" Sheba began.

"Come now," DeGroet said. "We both know that an expert is precisely what you are. I seem to recall seeing a paper of yours on Sri Lankan vowel variants in the *Journal of Phonetics*, and though I didn't understand two words of it, I trust the peer reviewers wouldn't have accepted it if its author had been illiterate in the languages it purported to analyze. Now—what does that say?" And he swung his stick to point at a passage inscribed beside the largest of the cages.

Sheba read it over twice. "It's a... a feeding guide. It specifies a diet of one whole cow and two goat flanks daily, to be provided freshly slaughtered but not prepared in any other way."

"Provided to *what*?" DeGroet said.

"It doesn't say."

"All right. How about this one?" DeGroet pointed out a bit of text a few cages down.

"Same thing. Only this one got goats and sheep, one of each in the morning and then again at night."

"That's all?" DeGroet said.

"It says they're to be brought to the cage alive," Sheba said.

"Not a word about what it was that would eat all these goats and sheep?"

Sheba shook her head.

"You wouldn't lie to me, would you?"

"I'm not lying," Sheba said. "That's what it says."

DeGroet looked around at the rows of empty cages. His face betrayed a strange mix of elation and disappointment. "It's proof," he muttered, half to himself. "It's proof enough."

"Of what?" Gabriel said. "That thousands of years ago, they bred sphinxes here? I don't think so."

"It's proof they bred something, Hunt. Something big. Look at the size of those shackles. Something carnivorous, too—we know that, thanks to Miss Mccoy. What do *you* suppose it was they were breeding?"

"I don't suppose anything," Gabriel said. "If I had to guess, I'd say maybe lions. Or maybe they brought some tigers over from South India. Or jackals—they have those in India as well."

"You ever see a jackal eat a cow?"

"Actually, yes," Gabriel said. "I have."

"By itself? One jackal, a whole cow?"

"No," Gabriel said, "there were a few of them, but—"

"You wouldn't build a cage like this to house a jackal," DeGroet said, and silently Gabriel had to admit he agreed. "And you couldn't sell a jackal for much at all. No prince would come across the sea to buy one. No, the inhabitants of these cages were far rarer than that."

"Maybe," Gabriel said. "But they were not monsters. Terrible creatures, perhaps. Fierce ones trained to attack or to guard. But not crossbreeds between animals and men."

"You are so very sure of yourself," DeGroet said. "It must be comforting at a time like this." He gestured toward Karoly. "Let's go on."

Karoly prodded Gabriel into the next room. This one

seemed to have once been an antechamber of some sort, smaller than the previous room and with stone benches where the other room had cages. Between each bench and its neighbor a metal rack stood, covered thickly with dust and cobwebs and crammed with various tools and implements. In the brief glance he got as the flashlights' beams swept past, Gabriel spotted a sort of halberd or poleax in one, with both a blade and a point at the end—the sort of thing you might use to keep a large animal at bay. He also saw what looked like a branding iron, and something else that resembled a long-armed pair of pincers, and—was that a rack of swords and armor pieces? But DeGroet and Karoly pressed them onward and the narrow shafts of light moved on as well.

In the center of the room there was a circular platform made from what looked like a single thickly varnished slab of wood, with vertical chains attached to the perimeter at regular intervals. Karoly angled his flashlight up to see what the other ends of the chains were attached to, but they receded into darkness too far above for the light to reach.

A long metal lever abutted the platform and DeGroet approached it, struck it ringingly with the side of his walking stick. "Interesting," he said. "Interesting." He turned in a tight circle, the light on his belt traveling along the walls. "What do you think, Hunt? If you were going to hide an ancient treasure somewhere here, where would you put it?"

"Can I ask what it is you're looking for?" Gabriel said. DeGroet didn't answer him. "You don't know, do you?" He felt a jab from Karoly's gun but he went on anyway. "I don't think you have the faintest idea."

"Oh, I have as much of an idea as you have," DeGroet said, "and that was enough to bring you

halfway around the world, wasn't it? It's a treasure—
we know that. Is it a mechanical device of some sort? A
religious artifact? Some physical relic of a living sphinx?
No one knows. But there is no question that a treasure
of some sort was taken out of Egypt and brought back
here—and apparently one from Greece, too. Something
precious. And powerful—very, very powerful."

"You believe that?" Gabriel said. "This business
about the power to terrify with a glance?"

"I have what you might call an open mind,"
DeGroet said.

"But what would you even want with it?" Gabriel
said. "Did you suddenly wake up one morning and
decide you wanted to rule the world?"

"Rule the world? Me?" DeGroet laughed, a sincere,
full-throated laugh that echoed against the ancient
stone walls. "I'd sooner hang myself. No, Mr. Hunt,
I don't want this power for myself. I'm quite content
living a life of leisure. Ruling the world would be a
terrible chore."

"Then why…?"

"*I* don't wish to rule the world," DeGroet said, "but
that doesn't mean no one does. And while some of the
men who do are penurious madmen living in squalid
apartments in third-world slums, with no possibility
of paying someone who could help them realize their
ambition, others are quite wealthy and would give
a large fraction of that wealth for a treasure of the
ancient world that might confer upon them the power
to terrify an army into immobility."

"You want to sell it," Gabriel said. "You don't even
know what it is or what it can do, but you've decided
you're going to sell the thing to some dictator to use
against his enemies—"

"Did I say 'dictator'? That is your word, not mine. I just said he had to be wealthy, not what his politics needed to be. And if there are two of these treasures to be found, as I believe there should be, I will gladly sell the other to his opponent—let them be locked forever in a stalemate of induced terror, I don't care. Just as long as their payments clear."

"And if this mythical power of the sphinx is just that—mythical?"

DeGroet smiled. "Then I'll have a pair of relics that will still fetch an excellent price at auction, won't I?"

"You'd kill nine men for that?"

"I'd kill ninety, Mr. Hunt," DeGroet said.

Behind him, Gabriel felt the point of Karoly's gun jab him again. But it was no longer poking squarely into the small of his back; it was nearer to his side now—and to his elbow. It was too good an opportunity to pass up. He moved swiftly, pinning the barrel between his arm and his side. Then he wrenched his torso to the left, holding tight to his grip on the gun. Karoly howled as the metal twisted in his injured hand. The beam of the flashlight in his other hand swung wildly. The gun fired, then fired again, as Karoly desperately squeezed the trigger, but the bullets sped into darkness, hitting only the far wall. Gabriel felt the heat of the gun's barrel through his jacket, smelled scorched leather beneath the stronger odor of gunpowder. He squeezed harder with his elbow and bent forward sharply. He heard the bones of Karoly's wrist snap. The gun clattered to the floor.

"Run!" Gabriel shouted over Karoly's screams and he saw Sheba dart out of sight, her footsteps speeding back toward the room with the cages. Behind him he heard the sound of DeGroet's walking stick unlocking and the deadly saber sliding out of its metal sheath.

Gabriel raised his other arm and smashed his elbow backwards, connecting with Karoly's face. The man fell, the flashlight tumbling from his hand and spinning across the floor, coming to a stop against the wooden platform. Gabriel bent forward and reached down for the gun—but his foot connected with it before his groping hand did, sending it skittering into some dark corner of the room.

He heard the swish of DeGroet's blade then, flashing through the air where his head would have been if he hadn't been bent double. He launched himself into a shoulder roll, coming up against one of the stone benches. He reached over to find the metal rack beside it. Was this the one with the halberd? No—his hand closed on one arm of the giant pincers. He saw DeGroet's light coming near, bobbing as the man ran forward. Gabriel yanked the pincers out of the rack and swung them at the light, but DeGroet stepped nimbly out of the way and they swept through empty air. A second later DeGroet's blade struck from the side, slicing through one leg of Gabriel's pants and the flesh of his thigh underneath. He felt the wound open, felt blood run warm and sticky down his skin. It was his injured leg, too. He limped out of range as fast as he could, pulling over the rack behind him with a huge clatter of metal against stone. Anything to slow DeGroet down.

He staggered to the end of the next bench over and felt for the rack that should be there. Which one was this? He felt a surge of relief as his hand closed not on the shaft of a branding iron or some other bit of paraphernalia but the hilt of a sword. He drew it quickly. Ancient steel and probably fragile, not the thing you wanted most when facing a former gold medalist in fencing—but it would have to do. For good measure, he grabbed a second sword in his other hand, swinging one overhead and the other at chest level.

DeGroet loomed suddenly out of the darkness, his blade striking mercilessly toward Gabriel's face. Gabriel parried it at the last second, the saber's narrower blade clashing noisily against the steel of the curved sword in his left hand. He feinted with the one in his right, aiming high at DeGroet's shoulder, and then when DeGroet angled his torso to dodge it, Gabriel changed course, tilted the blade down, and used it to sweep the flashlight off his hip. It flew through the air and smashed against the floor, leaving them in darkness.

He heard DeGroet's blade coming and reached up blindly to meet it. The blades struck with a clang of metal against metal, and DeGroet's slid off. Two parries in a row—Gabriel congratulated himself. Some of the finest fencers in two Olympics hadn't managed that against DeGroet. But the second time had just been blind luck, Gabriel knew—and he couldn't count on getting lucky again. He took several rapid steps backwards, heard DeGroet coming after him.

Neither of them could see, which negated DeGroet's advantage in terms of pure swordsmanship. But fighting in the dark like this for any real length of time was no good. It left survival up to chance—and Gabriel had never been one to bet his life on the toss of a coin.

Orienting himself against the one light remaining in the room, he ran toward the flashlight lying against the wooden platform. If he could get hold of it, maybe use it to locate the gun... But as he got close, he saw

DeGroet racing for the same spot. DeGroet saw him as well, and poured on extra speed Gabriel wouldn't have thought the man was capable of. They stepped onto the wooden platform at the same instant.

Lit indirectly from below, the combat between the two men took on an almost dreamlike quality, their blades slashing in and out of visibility, cutting brief blazing arcs and vanishing again as they passed beyond the cone of light. DeGroet swept his sword down from above, an angled stroke of the cutting edge that could remove a man's head; but Gabriel crossed his blades and caught DeGroet's in the crook of the X they formed. DeGroet yanked the saber free and sent it darting at Gabriel's chest. Gabriel sidestepped, parried with the flat of one blade and lunged with the other. The point streaked against DeGroet's cheek and blood welled up.

"A touch," DeGroet said grimly, raising a finger to his cheek. "It will be your last." And he lashed out with his sword, spiraling it around the blade in Gabriel's left fist once, twice, and suddenly the sword flew from Gabriel's hand, yanked out of his grip by expert pressure against the blade in just the right spot.

Now it was down to one blade against one—a contest Gabriel knew he couldn't win.

He kicked out with one foot, planting his boot in DeGroet's midsection. DeGroet flew backwards, fetching up against one of the chains, grabbing onto it with his free hand to keep himself from falling off the platform. Before he could come back, Gabriel leaned out past the platform's edge and took hold of the lever by its side. With a mighty heave, he pulled it toward him.

It didn't want to move, but Gabriel left it no choice, dragging it along the channel in the floor in which it was lodged. It came, scraping with a horrendous squeal. DeGroet, meanwhile, had regained his footing and had his sword poised for another stroke—but a sound from overhead stopped them both. It was a loud grinding of stone against stone, not unlike the sound they'd heard in the chamber within the Great Sphinx, just before poor Rashidi had been chopped in half. They felt a tremor beneath their feet—and then suddenly the platform they were on lifted into the air, the chains rattling as they got forcefully yanked upwards.

Gabriel grabbed hold of one chain, DeGroet another; they both clung desperately as the platform sped through the air, the solitary light of the flashlight dwindling far below them. They were being drawn up a stone shaft at tremendous speed, as though a mammoth counterweight had been dropped from some vast height and was now plunging into whatever stygian depths Istvan had fallen to.

They couldn't see—not just each other, but anything. Gabriel brought his sword up in front of his face and he couldn't see the blade. The walls of the vertical tunnel through which they were rocketing might have been feet away or inches—there was no way to know, other than to reach a hand out, and Gabriel wasn't about to try that experiment. Looking up, he saw no sign of what waited for them overhead—

But then a crack opened, a narrow line above them, lit by a concussive string of lightning strikes. It widened from a hairline to a handsbreadth and from there to a doorway's width, two slabs of stone above them separating and tilting to either side to make room for the platform to emerge.

What had this been used for, Gabriel wondered,

this primitive but effective elevator—raising beasts to the upper surface in dramatic fashion, to impress prospective purchasers?

The opening continued to spread wider and rainwater gushed down on them, the monsoon having reached its full strength while they were sheltered within the belly of the mountain.

The platform slowed, some sort of baffle kicking in. It shuddered to a halt when it was level with the upper surface. Gabriel stepped off between the chains, his legs unsteady.

The sight that greeted him in the next flash of lightning was extraordinary—all of Sri Lanka spread out below them, a thousand feet below or more, the treetops a vast furred carpet, the snaking lengths of highway and river like veins on an anatomy chart. The winds were powerful, gusting this way and that, buffeting him from behind, pushing him toward the rock's edge. He saw DeGroet run toward him and raised his sword to meet the charge.

But it was hopeless. He parried high and DeGroet swung low, the point of his blade shredding the front of Gabriel's leather jacket and the shirt and skin beneath. Gabriel tried to control his blade, to swing carefully rather than wildly and not give DeGroet any openings, but it was like a novice at chess playing against a master, his desperate attempts at strategy countered and foiled effortlessly.

He saw a cruel smile emerge on DeGroet's lips as he pressed Gabriel back, back, till they were both near the edge. Glancing down, Gabriel saw they were at one of the mountain's overhang points—no slope at all that he might roll down safely, not even a sheer face he might dream of climbing if the rains hadn't made that impossible. Just a fall—an endless, open drop into eternity.

There was still a way out, of course. There always was. But as DeGroet teased him with his blade, drawing blood here and here and there, he began to fear he might not manage it.

"Lajos," he shouted, his words stripped almost to silence by the rushing winds. "Lajos!"

"Yes, Hunt?"

"I know where the treasure is," he shouted. "I've figured it out!" The older man's blade darted in again, nicked a bit of flesh from the side of Gabriel's neck.

"You know what, Hunt? I don't believe you. And even if it's true… I don't care. I'll figure it out for myself. Or I'll pay someone to do so. *I don't need you.*" And with that he sent his saber's blade spiraling out again, as he had in the chamber far below, and swept Gabriel's sword out of his hand. They both watched as it spun end over end into the darkness.

Gabriel whipped off his jacket and threw it at DeGroet, who batted it aside with his sword. It landed at his feet. "That the best you can do? I am disappointed in you, Hunt."

Gabriel looked behind him—only inches remained.

"There's no wire for you to grab hold of here, is there?" DeGroet taunted.

Gabriel dropped to his knees.

"Oh, for heaven's sake, don't beg," DeGroet shouted. "Meet your death like a man."

"Just give me a moment, please," Gabriel said. "One moment, to say a prayer."

"One moment," DeGroet said. "No more."

"And please," Gabriel said, "when you do it… swing hard. Make it clean."

"Oh, I'll swing hard," DeGroet said and raised his sword high overhead.

THERE IS A REASON THEY SAY THAT IN A LIGHTNING storm it is unwise to be the tallest thing in sight. How much less wise, Gabriel thought, to stand atop a thousand foot boulder in a raging thunderstorm and raise a metal bar above your head?

He knew it wasn't possible—he knew that lightning travels much too swiftly for its motion to be seen—but looking up at DeGroet standing over him he could have sworn he saw the charge gather in the clouds, saw the forked serpent's tongue of electricity streak down, aimed unerringly for the point of DeGroet's saber, saw it kiss the metal with its deadly, incinerating charge.

But it couldn't be. Not just because of the speeds involved—but because he wasn't there to see it.

The same people who said you shouldn't be the highest point in a lightning storm had a thing or two to say about kneeling in a puddle of water beside a man being struck by lightning, too, and none of them were good. So before he could get incinerated along with DeGroet, Gabriel kicked off, hard, from the surface of the rock and flung himself outward into space.

Beneath his leather jacket he'd been wearing one last emergency supply he'd taken off the plane, a slender knapsack, and he reached now for the metal ring attached to one of the straps. Finding it, he tugged firmly.

And behind him a compact stream of folded fabric unfurled, blossoming with a satisfying *whoomp* into an airtight canopy that lowered him gently through the storm.

26

HE LANDED WHERE THEY'D BEGUN THEIR CLIMB, AT the foot of the mountain. As the folds of fabric pooled around him, he stripped the parachute off and squeezed between the walls of rock, beginning the laborious ascent once more. He was tired, he was wounded, he was weak—he would have liked nothing better than to make his way back to Dayani's car and drive it to Dambulla, get help that way. But he couldn't just leave Sheba alone in a dark cavern at the heart of a mountain fortress. And worse, she wasn't alone. Karoly might have a broken wrist, but he might also have a flashlight—and a gun.

No, there was nothing for it but to climb, and he did, as quickly as he could without losing his footing or his grip, hugging the wall as he went. He passed the wasps' nests, careful not to disturb them again; he passed the lacquered wall and the painted ladies; he passed the tiny cave with the bloody towel lying at its entrance. Rainwater washed his wounds clean as he went, and when twice he felt a moment of dizziness he leaned against the rock and waited for it to pass.

Eventually he made it to the lion's paws. He staggered to the opening, waited for a lightning strike to illuminate the interior, showing him both the corridor and the gaping hole he'd have to cross to get to it. There was nothing for it—he had no rope, and the crossbeam was gone anyway. He judged the angle as best he could, got a running start, and leaped.

He landed short, his chest hitting the floor, his legs dangling into the pit. He scrabbled with his hands as he felt himself begin to slide backwards. The floor was craggy, but the crags were low and worn, and his fingers, wet from the rain, couldn't get a solid grip.

No—

No. This wasn't how he'd go, lost in darkness, buried beneath ten thousand pounds of stone. It couldn't be. He bit down hard with his fingertips against the rock, squeezed till they caught hold of *something*, till he was hanging literally by his fingertips—but hanging all the same, not falling, not anymore. He took a deep breath, let his racing heartbeat slow for half a second, and then began the process of inching his fingers forward. After an eternity he managed to get one elbow up over the edge... then the other... then his wet and battered trunk, and finally his legs.

He rolled over onto his back, breathing heavily, his chest heaving, his eyes closed. Too close. He'd had too many close calls over the past few days, and this one may have been the worst. Or maybe it was just the accumulation that had worn him down. On a good day he would have made that jump easily.

Of course, on a good day he wouldn't have been attempting it with a bandaged ankle and a lacerated thigh.

He got to his feet and felt his way along the corridor till he came to the branch at the entrance to the cage room. There was no light at all—and his Zippo was up on the top of the mountain, in his jacket pocket.

He opened his mouth to call out, then hesitated. If Karoly was nearby and heard him…

But what was the alternative? Blundering around in the dark?

He shouted: "Sheba!"

At first there was no answer. Then he heard footsteps running toward him, and saw a light approaching from the left-hand passageway. He backed up against the wall and raised a fist in case it was Karoly his call had attracted.

But a moment later he heard Sheba's voice. "Gabriel, thank god," she said, sounding every bit as exhausted as he felt—and something more than exhausted, too. Frightened? That would be natural enough. But it was somehow not just fear he heard in her voice—it was something worse.

"What is it?" he said, stepping into her path. She fell into his arms. He could feel her shaking. "Is it Karoly, is he—"

"Karoly's dead," she said, her words muffled against his chest.

"Then what…?"

"It was a mistranslation, Gabriel," Sheba said, her voice more unsteady than he'd ever heard it. "You said it was the power to terrify—but it wasn't, Gabriel, it wasn't that at all. It was the power to *petrify*."

"What are you talking about? The treasure?"

Gabriel said, and he felt her chin move as she nodded. "You found it?"

"Karoly did," she said.

"But… terrify, petrify," Gabriel said, "what's the difference?"

Sheba raised her head. There was a brittle edge of panic to her voice. "Petrify, Gabriel—from the Greek, 'petra,' meaning rock or stone. Gabriel, the sphinx's power wasn't the power to frighten men—*it was the power to turn them to stone.*"

And she swung the flashlight's beam around.

There was a statue in the passageway, just a few feet away. It was exquisitely detailed, as naturalistic as the ones Gabriel had found in the chambers in Egypt and Greece. But this one didn't depict a sphinx.

It was Karoly.

HE WAS FROZEN IN AN ATTITUDE OF TERROR, ONE hand flung up before his face, the other—the one with the broken wrist—dangling crookedly by his side. But his body, his clothing…

Was stone.

Gabriel ran his fingers over the surface. His heart began triphammering again, worse even than when he'd been dangling at the edge of the pit. "What happened? Did he touch something? Did he… did he step on something? Inhale something?"

Sheba shook her head vigorously. "I was running away. I heard him coming after me, and then a sound…"

"What sound?"

She didn't answer. But, then, she didn't have to. Because they both heard the sound then. It was a low, rumbling growl, accompanied by the slow padding of clawed footsteps against stone.

"Get back," Gabriel said, taking the flashlight from her.

The footsteps came closer, then stopped, just out of sight.

"*And you,*" came a voice from the darkness. "*Have you come to disturb my peace as well?*"

It spoke in Greek. Not the modern Greek the men of Avgonyma had used—the voice had the same ring of antiquity about it that Tigranes had had when declaiming his verses of heroism and disaster.

"No," Gabriel responded in the same tongue, "we do not wish to disturb anything."

A shape appeared then at the edge of the pool of light the flashlight cast. The figure was low and muscular—an animal's body. And when it moved it was with the languorous rippling grace of a jungle cat, a jaguar or a lion. But its torso rose higher than any cat's, and the silhouette of its head was…

Gabriel gripped the flashlight tighter.

The silhouette of its head was a man's.

"You speak the language of Olympos like a foreigner," the sphinx said, stepping forward into the light. "Like an *invader*."

It reared up, its paws extended fully. It was almost Gabriel's height this way—and clearly many times his weight. The hair cascading over its shoulders was as gray as the fur upon its chest, and its face was lined, drawn. But its eyes were fierce and clear, their irises a piercing sapphire blue. And stretching along the creature's back Gabriel saw a folded pair of wings.

He blinked to clear his vision, thought back to the brief moments of vertigo he'd felt climbing the mountain, the stings he'd suffered from the wasps, the hours since he'd eaten. Could he be hallucinating? But if he was, Sheba seemed to be as well, judging by the strength with which her fingers were digging into his arm from behind.

Gabriel made himself step forward. "It's true," he said, "that we are not from Greece. But we are no invaders."

"You come here," the sphinx said, its voice rising as it spoke, "you discharge your weapons, you shatter a peace of centuries, and yet you say you are not invaders! How dare you?"

"We came to stop this man," Gabriel said, gesturing behind him, toward Karoly's remains, "and another you'll find dead on the mountaintop. They were the invaders—they were searching for your treasure, to use it for terrible ends."

"My treasure? I have no treasure." The sphinx shook its head roughly, and its hair flew about.

"Maybe you don't think of it as treasure," Gabriel said. "But whatever you used to… to do this." And he gestured backwards again.

"All men have stone within them," the sphinx said brusquely. "All living creatures do. When I wish, I bring it out. I don't *use* anything to do so."

"You do it just by… by looking at them?" Gabriel said.

"What does *looking* have to do with it? I could make a statue of you just as well with my eyes closed," the sphinx said. "Both of you. Any of you! I could salt the earth with statues! I could end all of your kind at once, however many millions you now pestilentially represent. Or is it billions now, I wonder? You multiply so…"

"That can't be," Gabriel said. "It can't. You can't turn billions of people to stone." But hearing himself say this he wondered—a day ago he'd have said it was impossible to turn even one person to stone. Was a billion less plausible?

"Don't test me, human," the sphinx said. "You will rue it. Perhaps I will leave you alive, the last of your kind as I am of mine, to lament to the end of your paltry days that you doubted me."

"I don't," Gabriel said quickly. "I don't doubt—"

"You lie!" the sphinx roared. It began pacing, walking in a tight circle around them. It had a musky, unwashed smell, a smell of exertion and lassitude. For all its explosive anger, Gabriel got a sense of fatigue from the creature, of extreme age and isolation.

"You lie," it repeated. "And you must pay for it." It leaned in close to Gabriel, its breath hot on his cheeks. "But I shall be fair. My kind always has been—we have always dealt by the rules we're bound by, though we suffer grievously for it.

"I will pose for you a question, a simple question. It calls for a simple answer, and if you give it I will let you live—all of you. But if you do not answer, if you cannot answer, if you choose not to answer, if you fail to answer, then, human, I will let *only* you live—you alone of all humanity, and a world of stone to keep you company in your grief."

"Gabriel, you can't—" Sheba said.

"Ah, the female speaks as well," the sphinx said. "It is unfortunate she counsels you so poorly." It turned a baleful glare upon her. "Not only *can* he, he *must*. It is my will."

"What's the question?" Gabriel said, thinking of all the legends he'd read, all the stories about the Theban sphinx. There was the famous riddle: *What walks on four legs in the morning, two in the afternoon, and three in the evening, and is the weaker the more legs it has?* The answer being man: the crawling infant, the erect adult, and the infirm elder. And there was its sometime corollary: *What two sisters are they, the first giving birth to the second, and then the second once more to the first?* To which the answer was night and day. Either of those he could answer, and he thought he could manage others of their ilk.

"The question is this," the sphinx said. "What is my name?"

"Your name?" Gabriel said.

"*My name!*" the sphinx screamed, its voice echoing from the walls. "You will know my name. I will *teach* you my name. But—" it put a paw against Gabriel's chest "—only when you fail to *guess* my name."

Rumpelstiltskin, Gabriel wanted to say. Your name is Rumpelstiltskin, and you can spin straw into gold...

Your name. Your name. How in God's name, you'll pardon the expression, am I supposed to pull the right answer out of the thousands, the hundreds of thousands, the almost infinite possibilities? This is no riddle! He wanted to shout it: this is a fix-up, a fraud, a pretext for slaughter!

But no—it wouldn't be. If the beast had wanted merely to kill them it could have. If it really had the power it claimed, it could have slaughtered all humanity at any time. It needed no pretext. If instead of killing it had asked this question, there had to be a way to answer it—a clue, a hint... something. Gabriel thought back to his first glimpse of the Sphinx in Egypt, the great and terrible Abul-Hôl, looming in the night. He thought back to the inscriptions, to their talk of a divine or holy treasure, and to the statues into whose flanks they were carved—which statues, with their impossible degree of sculptural perfection, must, he now knew, have been actual, living sphinxes once. And he thought of the story Tigranes had recounted, of the Theban sphinx's journeys and her tribulations.

And then suddenly he realized he knew the answer.

"Your name is Fear," Gabriel said.

THE SPHINX STEPPED BACK, SILENT.

"You're their child," Gabriel said. "The child of the Father of Fear. What else would have been sufficient to bring the men of Taprobane on a voyage halfway around the world? No ordinary treasure would, no mere prize, no artifact. But a sphinx cub, unlawfully bred, the unlawful child of an illicit union—that they could not let alone. They came for you, they found you, and they brought you back here. *You* were the treasure—your father's divine treasure, your mother's holy treasure. And then they… what? Punished them? By turning them to stone?"

"They gave her a choice." The sphinx's head was bowed, its eyes downcast. "I was tiny then, a newborn practically, no more than a century and a half; but I remember it as if it were this morning. She could die, or I could.

"They told her my father had already chosen, that they'd left his body deep within his temple, at eternal rest. That he'd gone with her name on his lips. And they showed her a coin, I remember, from his land…"

Gabriel reached into his pocket and drew out the pair of coins. He held them out on his palm. The female sphinx and the amphora on one, the male profile on the other, the two facing one another in his hand.

The sphinx's cheeks trembled as it looked from one

to the other. It threw back its head and howled, tears running down its face.

"And this place," Gabriel said, "became your cradle, this dark and terrible mountain. Have you never left it? For two thousand years?"

"Longer," the sphinx said. "Even longer."

"But you must leave it sometimes," Gabriel said, "if just to hunt for food—"

"I am old," the sphinx whispered. "I hardly hunt anymore. I hardly eat anymore."

There was a tone of despair in its voice, a sound of finality.

"We can *get* you food," Gabriel said. "I can arrange for supplies to be flow in, I can—"

"And face men each day? No. No." It stepped back, toward the shadow. "You have given me all I need. You have shown me my mother's face again."

"Please, let me do something to help—"

"Gabriel," Sheba said.

He turned to her. "What?"

"Look," she said, and pointed.

Turning back, he saw the gray of the sphinx's fur deepening, darkening; then he saw the skin of its face turning stiff, blank, saw the liquid surface of its eyes harden. The change crept across its body gradually, but rapidly. In seconds it was over.

Gabriel stepped forward, touched its shoulder. The stone was still slightly warm. But as he felt it, it cooled beneath his hand.

He took the two coins, stacked them, and gently slid them into the statue's open mouth, beneath its tongue.

27

THEY FOUND A STAIRWAY, CARVED INTO THE ROCK, that led up to the top. The climb was torment—by the end, Gabriel's legs were burning with pain and Sheba could barely walk.

They came out into a clear night sky. The storm had passed. The stone surface glistened wetly, but the air was warm and dry.

At the far end of the rock, near where DeGroet's body lay, a familiar helicopter stood, its door open. The pilot was by the door, talking into a microphone, and when he spotted them walking toward him, he shouted.

"Hold on—yes, hold on! I found them!"

They staggered forward.

"How did you...?" Gabriel began, but for the moment he couldn't get any more words out.

"Talk to your brother," the pilot said, and handed over the microphone, then stepped around Gabriel to help Sheba up into the cabin.

"Gabriel? Are you okay?" It was Michael's voice.

"I've been better," Gabriel said.

"I want you back here *now*."

"Not half as much as I do," Gabriel said. "How did you find me?"

"We tracked your signal," Michael said.

"What… what signal? I don't have a cell phone, I don't have…"

"That guy, Cipher," Michael said. "He sent me e-mail saying he'd given you a device to track someone else, right? Well, he had the good sense to slip in a transmitter going the other way so we could track you, too. Clever, right? And we didn't even ask him to do it, he just thought of it on his own."

Gabriel found himself smiling. He saw his leather jacket lying ten feet away, a wet and crumpled heap on the stone. Somewhere in the heap was a pocket, and in the pocket Lucy's box was silently sending out a signal. "Very clever."

"I wish I could thank him properly," Michael said. "But he refused to take any money. It's strange, dealing with someone this way. I've never even met the man. I don't even know what he looks like."

"Oh, he's… uh…"

"What?" Michael said.

"Big," Gabriel said, and wiped a tear out of his eye with the back of one thumb. "A big, big man. My size. Mean-looking." He took a deep breath. "Lots of tattoos. Not your kind of guy, Michael. I think it's better if you don't meet him in person."

"Well… maybe you're right," Michael said. "But I'm still grateful to him."

"Me, too," Gabriel said, climbing into the cabin. "Me, too."

ABOUT THE AUTHOR

Charles Ardai is a writer, editor and television producer. He founded the Hard Case Crime imprint in 2004, publishing pulp-style novels by the likes of Stephen King, Lawrence Block, James M. Cain and Mickey Spillane. He is the author of several novels, and has won both the Edgar and Shamus awards. He lives in Manhattan.

Read on for a novelette by Charles Ardai

NOR IDOLATRY BLIND THE EYE

I

THE HEEL OF THE BOTTLE CRACKED AGAINST THE BAR ON the first swing and then shattered on the second. The few conversations in the room died. In the silence Malcolm could hear glass crunching under his feet. He felt his legs shake and put out his other hand to steady himself.

There were three of them, and a broken bottle wouldn't hold them off long enough for him to get to the door. Assuming he could even make it to the door without falling on his face. There was a time when he could have made it in a dead sprint, turning over tables as he went to slow them down, but then there was a time when he wouldn't have had to run from a fight in the first place, not if it were a whole regiment facing him. A time when he'd been able to hold his liquor, too. But that was all part of the past—the dead past, buried three winters ago in a cold Glasnevin grave.

He shook his head, but it didn't get any clearer. He

remembered coming to the pub, he remembered taking his first few drinks, and he remembered the three men taking up positions around him, reaching over his shoulder to collect their pints from the barman. Was that how the argument had started? Or had one of them said something? That he couldn't remember. He supposed it didn't matter.

The one in the middle was younger than the other two—just a kid, really. He was wearing a navy peajacket, probably his brother's or father's since he looked too young to have served himself. The others were dressed in denim windbreakers and dungarees, like they'd just stepped off a construction site. Which maybe they had—there was still plenty of rebuilding going on. The one on the left had the crumpled features of a boxer who'd taken too many trips to the mat. The one on the right looked almost delicate, his thin nose and long chin giving him the appearance of a society lad slumming in a tough neighborhood. Malcolm knew which one he'd prefer to face in a fight. Unfortunately, it didn't look like he'd get to choose.

All three had their hands up, palms out, but it was a gesture of mocking deference, not fear. Malcolm swung the bottle by the neck and they didn't even bother to step back.

"Go on, old man," the one in the middle said. "Just try it."

"Leave me alone," Malcolm said, or tried to—the words sounded strange to his ears, like he was talking through cotton. He forced himself to enunciate. "I don't want to fight you."

"Bugger that," the society boy said. "You're bloody well going to."

Malcolm feinted toward the boy's face with the

jagged edge of the bottle, then dodged around him. The door was open and the way before him was clear, but he felt himself stagger as he ran, felt his head spin and the floor lurch up to meet him. He fought to catch his balance and then lost it again. He fell to one knee and the bottle spilled out of his hand.

The first kick caught him in the side as he was standing up, and it laid him out flat on the floor. After that, Malcolm couldn't say who was kicking him or even what direction the blows came from. He covered his head with one arm and tried to back up against the bar.

One boot heel caught him in the chest. By some old reflex, he snaked an arm out and pinched the foot in the crook of his elbow. He twisted violently and its owner came crashing to the floor.

"That's it," one of them said. Malcolm felt a fist bunched in the fabric of his shirtfront, felt himself lifted bodily from the floor and pressed back against the bar. It was the boxer's meaty fist at his throat, the boy in the peajacket looking on angrily over his shoulder. So the society lad must be the one laid out on the floor, groaning curses into the sawdust. Well, he had taken one down, anyway.

"You're going to wish you hadn't done that," the boxer said.

Malcolm swung a fist at him, but it was hardly a punch at all, and the man holding him deflected it lightly with his forearm. In return, he threw a right cross that snapped Malcolm's head violently to the side. Malcolm felt blood on his cheek where the man's ring had scraped a ragged groove, and he tasted bile when he swallowed. He tried to raise a knee toward the man's groin, but he couldn't—they were standing too close together, and anyway his legs felt like lead. He groped behind him on the bar, hoping his fingers would find something—a glass, an ashtray, anything— but all they found was another hand that pinned his firmly against the wood.

"Teach him a lesson," the boy in the peajacket said. He pressed down, grinding Malcolm's knuckles into the wood. "Teach him good."

He felt a thumb and forefinger at his chin, positioning his head, saw the man's fist cock back, saw it snap forward. After that, he didn't see anything, just felt the punches landing from the darkness.

One punch split his lip against his front teeth and he gagged from the taste of blood. He felt the night's liquor coming up and he made no effort to stop it. Vomit poured out of him, a day's worth of food and drink expelled in foul batches. The men holding him yanked their hands away and Malcolm slid to the floor.

"*Goddamn narrowback lush—*" Another kick dug deep into his belly. From somewhere off to one side, Malcolm heard the click of a switchblade opening.

"Cut the sorry bastard—"

He forced his eyes open, rolled out of the way as the blade descended. It was the boy in the peajacket holding it. He swung again, and Malcolm lifted an arm to block it. He felt the blade slice through the sleeve and streak across the flesh beneath it.

"*Stop that!*"

It was a woman's voice. Malcolm hugged his bleeding arm to his chest and looked for the source of the voice. A pair of legs approached, clad in nylons, a tan skirt ending just below the knee. The shoes were brown leather and scuffed, with low heels, the sort a certain type of girl would call 'sensible.' On either side, a pair of paint-smeared dungarees turned in her direction.

"Leave him alone, or I'll bring the police."

"Stay out of this, love. It's not your fight."

"Oh, yes? And what do you call it when my husband is getting himself mauled by the likes of you?"

"You're married to... this?"

"He may not be much," she said, "but I'd just as soon not have him skewered over some tiff in a pub. Now would you be kind enough to help him up so I can bring him home?"

A tense moment passed, the blade still shining under the room's lights. Then a pair of rough hands folded the switchblade shut. It disappeared into the long slash pocket of the peajacket. "He's your problem, love. Help him yourself."

"Jaysus," one of the others said, "bird like you and an old harp like him. No bleeding justice, is there?"

"Bastard." One of them got in a final kick, wiped the sole of his work boot on Malcolm's shirt. Then the men's legs went away. The woman's stayed.

Malcolm wanted to raise his eyes, to look at the woman's face, but his arm had started to throb and he found himself slipping in and out of consciousness.

The stockings took two steps forward, skirting the smear of filth beside him. The woman lowered herself to a crouch. The light was behind her and Malcolm could only faintly make out her features. She had a sharp widow's peak and fair skin, and the largest, saddest eyes he could remember seeing.

"You're Malcolm Stewart?" she said.

He nodded. She looked as though she'd been hoping he'd say no.

"Look at you," she said. "I can't take you to him like this."

"To whom?" he said. He felt dizzy. "Do I know you?"

"My employer. He asked me to bring you to him. He has—" She paused to look him over again, and the disappointment in her voice was undisguised when she spoke. "He has an assignment for you, Mr. Stewart."

"...an assignment?"

"I told him it wasn't a good idea. I told him the reports he had were years old. But Mr. Burke's not one to be put off." She took him by his undamaged arm, pulled him not too gently to his knees. "Come along, Mr. Stewart. Let's get you bandaged up and bathed, what do you say?"

"I say," he mumbled, trying to think of the words. "I say 'thank you'?"

"Well," she said, "it's a start."

THE IODINE STUNG AND THE BANDAGE SMARTED. HE'D burned his tongue on the coffee she'd given him, and his chest was erupting with colorful bruises. His head was still ringing. But he'd showered (carefully, leaning against the wall) and he could feel sobriety returning to him, timidly, like a husband tiptoeing back into the house after an evening's debauch.

"Have you got a name?" he said. "Or would you rather I just thought of you as an anonymous benefactor?"

She was watching him from one of the bedroom chairs, legs crossed primly at the ankles, hands laced in her lap. She had an admirable figure and a face just this side of beautiful. And she was young, too—still in her early twenties, Malcolm guessed, which would make her less than half his age. He could understand why the lads in the bar might have had a hard time picturing them as man and wife.

"My name is Margaret Stiles. But that's not important. Only Mr. Burke is, and what he wants to talk to you about."

"And what is that?"

"He'll want to tell you himself."

"I see."

"Please choose a shirt and get dressed," she said. "We shouldn't keep Mr. Burke waiting."

There were three shirts laid out on the bed. Malcolm selected the softest of them, a red flannel, and drew it on over his bandaged arm. He winced as he buttoned it.

He was still wearing his own pants—they hadn't been spattered as badly. And the boots were his as well. A quick dunk under the tap had restored them to whatever prior vitality they might have claimed. His shirt had been ruined. He imagined it was now being incinerated in some hidden chamber of this house.

"Your Mr. Burke knows I'm here?"

"I spoke to him while you were in the shower."

"And he wants to see me now?"

"In a manner of speaking."

"Why 'in a manner of speaking'?"

"Come on," she said, standing up. "We've lost enough time."

"I want to know what you meant. He doesn't want to see me?"

"I imagine," she said, "that he would like to see you more than anything. But that's hardly an option."

"Any why is that?"

"His eyes, Mr. Stewart. He was blinded in North Africa."

North Africa. The words brought a rush of painful

memories. The press toward Libya, the desert winds in his throat, the baking heat, and in the middle of it all, between spells of tortured boredom, the moments of utter chaos: the mortar rounds tearing great gouts out of the sand, and out of the men who sped across it. So Burke had been an 8th Army man? And had paid for it dearly, though not so dearly as some.

"I'm sorry," Malcolm said. "I was in that campaign myself."

"I know you were," she said. "It's one of the reasons he selected you, though perhaps he'll think better of it once he meets you."

"That's rather harsh, my dear."

"Harsh? Look at you. And what he'll ask of you, Mr. Stewart... it's ever so much worse than dealing with those three in the pub."

"I've dealt with worse."

"Yes, but recently?" She waited, but he had no answer for her. "Now will you please follow me?"

He stepped out into the hall. She led him down to the main floor on a staircase wide enough to hold four men abreast. The building was deceptive: From the front as they'd come in it hadn't looked nearly as big as it turned out to be once you were inside. There was money behind this Burke, generations of it. It didn't show in ostentatious ways—no chandeliers dripping with crystal or gold leaf on the picture frames. But the pictures themselves looked like they'd fetch a pretty sum at auction, and the carpeting was the sort that costs as much as most people spend to furnish their entire homes.

They passed from the entry hall into a library, and on through a short connecting corridor into the kitchen, where a woman in a cook's smock stood cutting potatoes into a copper kettle. She looked up as they passed. He thought he spied a look of pity in her eyes.

"Another, Miss Stiles?"

Margaret moved them along without slowing.

Malcolm looked back over his shoulder. The woman was still watching, knife at the ready, supper temporarily forgotten.

Malcolm didn't say anything till they were out of earshot. "What did she mean, 'another'?"

"Never mind her." Margaret stopped at a closed door. She tugged on a brass pull set into the doorframe at eye level. He could hear a bell ring within and, moments later, a man's voice called out. "Miss Stiles?"

"Yes."

"Have you got Mr. Stewart with you?"

"Yes."

"Bring him in." It was a deep voice, muffled by the door, but strong, Malcolm thought, and self-confident. He was put in mind of his commanding officers from the army—it was the sort of voice you were trained to use when marshalling troops for a charge across a no-man's zone. Some men didn't need to be trained, of course. They'd learned it in the nursery or had it bred into them from birth.

Margaret swung the door open. He was surprised to see no light behind it. She made no move to turn one on.

"Come in, Mr. Stewart," the voice intoned. "Don't let the darkness bother you. Miss Stiles will show you to a chair." She took him by the arm and steered him through the room, navigating obstacles he could see only dimly. It was oddly damp in the room, as though a window had been left open, but the only windows he could make out appeared to be shut and heavily curtained.

"It's for my eyes, you understand," Burke said.

"Dark, cool, moist—I'm afraid it's the only way for me to be comfortable any longer."

"I'm sorry," Malcolm said.

"Come," Burke said. "Sit by me, and Miss Stiles will join us."

She put his hand on the arm of a chair, and he sat. Now that his eyes had begun to adjust, Malcolm could make out the outlines of Burke's face where he sat two feet away. He wore a beard, and his hair curved up from his forehead in uneven curls. The man leaned forward with his left hand out. Malcolm took it. Burke's grip was firm.

"What happened?" Malcolm said. "To your eyes, I mean. Shrapnel? Or fire?"

For a moment, Burke didn't say anything, and Malcolm thought perhaps he'd crossed a line. But for Christ's sake, the man had brought the subject up himself. And after all, hadn't Malcolm served in the same campaign, hadn't he seen plenty of friends lose eyes and worse—?

"No," Burke said. "Not shrapnel, nor fire, nor any of the other causes you'd imagine. I'll tell you what happened, Mr. Stewart, but that is the end of the story, not the beginning. Miss Stiles, could you turn up the fan? Thank you."

Malcolm heard Margaret's footsteps retreat and return. A mechanical hum he hadn't noticed before got louder, and he felt the air stir.

Burke leaned forward with his forearms on his knees. Malcolm could see he wasn't wearing anything over his eyes—no dark glasses, no patch. He didn't seem to blink, either. Of course, perhaps he had glass eyes... but no, that wouldn't explain the need to sit in the dark and keep things as damp and cool as a cellar.

"Mr. Stewart, I want to thank you for hearing me out. I need your help. Or to put it another way, I need the help of someone who knows his way around a part of the world I understand we have in common. Someone who's not easily frightened or put off the scent. I've asked around and people think highly of you."

"You must not have asked anyone in town," Malcolm said. "You'd have gotten a different picture."

"Yes, Miss Stiles told me about the scene in the pub. Most regrettable. You drink too much, Mr. Stewart."

"Or not enough."

"More and you'd be dead of it, and no use to me. Let's not fence with each other, shall we? You were a good man once. I heard it from men I trust. Until your wife died, I gather, and since then it's been one long bender, hasn't it?"

Malcolm flinched. "Not so long."

"Three years, man. And you once a good soldier. Where's your backbone?"

"I left it behind in the sand," Malcolm said, "where you left your eyes."

"Nonsense. You've still got a spine, man, you've just let it soften in that embalming fluid you insist on pouring into yourself. If you're to work for me, you'll do it dry, you understand?"

The voice of command—Malcolm almost felt himself sitting up straighter in response, against his will. "And am I to work for you?"

"I hope to god you are—I've exhausted everyone else."

"What is it you want done? I don't see you as the type to raise a private army, and I'm out of the soldiering business anyway."

"No. I've never been a soldier myself. What I have

been—what I am, Mr. Stewart—is a student of history. When I went to North Africa it was not because of the war but in spite of it. I wasn't part of the military action, I was there on my own, pursuing of one of the greatest mysteries of the ancient world."

'Greatest mysteries of the ancient world'? The man sounded like a radio programme. But he had a job to offer, apparently, and such offers were not plentiful these days.

"I understand," Malcolm said. "You were in Africa hunting something, but instead of finding it, you came across the military action instead?"

"No, Mr. Stewart. I found what I was looking for. I found it exactly where I thought it would be. I saw it with my own eyes. I'd searched for a decade and more, and by god, I found it." He fell silent.

"What happened?" Malcolm said.

"Some antiquities, Mr. Stewart, are hidden by time alone—a cave's entrance is covered in a sandstorm and forgotten, and no one sees its contents again for a thousand years. But others are kept hidden deliberately, passed from generation to generation in secret. The price for learning the secret is a vow to preserve it, and the penalty for revealing it is death. It is antiquities of this sort that are the harder to find. They aren't lost, you see, and the people who know where they are have an interest in keeping them from you."

"But you did find… whatever it was."

"I did, and I did it the hard way. You wouldn't know it to look at me know, but I was a stronger man than you, and faster, and better with a gun. I knew what I was after. I hunted it and the men who kept it, I hunted it through nine countries on three continents, and I found it, Mr. Stewart." His voice broke. "I found it. But I couldn't keep it. They caught me, and for several days they held me while they discussed what to do with me. Then they cut off my right hand—I'd touched it with that hand, you see. And of course I'd seen it, Mr. Stewart. I'd seen it."

Burke leaned over the side of the chair and pressed a switch on the desk beside him. A shaded light went on—low wattage, but enough to illuminate one side of Burke's face. The other side remained in shadow until he turned to face Malcolm full-on. Burke's eyes were wide open and leached of all color, only the faintest outline of concentric circles to hint where pupil and iris had once shown.

"They cut off my eyelids, Mr. Stewart. With the sharpest of knives, and gently, so gently, holding my head so I couldn't scream or injure myself. They wiped the blood from my eyes with silk. With silk, Mr. Stewart—I'll never forget the touch. Then they carried me out into the desert west of the Gattara Depression, left me in the Great Sand Sea, completely naked, left me to go blind and mad and then die— and I would have, surely, if I hadn't been found by a pair of soldiers from a British regiment who had wandered off course. They saved me from madness and death, Mr. Stewart. But it was too late to save me from blindness."

He switched off the light, but the image of the lidless, sun-bleached eyes hung between them. "The touch of light is quite painful still," he said. "But I wanted you to see. There should be no mystery between us."

It took a moment for Malcolm to find his voice. "What is it that you want me to do?"

"I've found it again," Burke said. "It has taken me

years, and more money than you can imagine. It's cost several good men their lives. But I've found it, and this time it won't get away from me. Not with your help."

"And why should I help you?"

"There will be money, of course—quite a lot. But I know what you're going to say: Of what use is money if you're not around to spend it? And that's so. But there's more. This is your chance to be a part of something much greater than yourself, greater than me, greater than all of us. You will play a role in unraveling one of the greatest unsolved riddles of all time."

"Is that what you told the other men? The ones who died helping you?"

"Yes, Mr. Stewart, it is. It was the truth."

"And they took the job."

"I pay extremely well. And the men I chose had something in common with you."

"What's that?"

"Nothing to lose," Burke said.

It stung, but only because it was true. He had no family and no employment. His army pension kept his glass full as long as his tastes were cheap, and occasional under-the-table assignments paid the rest of his bills. He'd fetched and carried for some of London's worst, had ridden shotgun for questionable deliveries, had taken part in labor actions on whichever side cared to have him. It was a life, but only in the barest sense. Even when he'd had reason to, he'd never shrunk from risking it. Why would this be the assignment to make him put his foot down at last? And yet the image of Burke's lidless eyes was a hard one to rid himself of.

"Tell me, Mr. Burke, what it is that I'd be collecting for you, and how much you would pay me for it."

"I'd pay enough that you'd never need work again," Burke said.

"If you please, I'd prefer a number."

"Fifty thousand pounds, or its equivalent in any currency you choose. Gold, if you like."

Malcolm's mouth went dry. "You can't be serious. What are you asking me to do, steal the crown jewels?"

"Oh, something much more valuable than that. Do you remember your Bible, Mr. Stewart?"

"Not too well."

"There's a story in it about a man called Moses," Burke said. "You may recall he went up into the mountains for forty days, leaving his people behind. We're told they grew restless, that when he didn't return as promised, they called on his brother, Aaron, to make them an idol to protect them. A figure of a calf fashioned from the melted-down gold of their earrings and wristlets and such. When Moses returned and saw them worshipping this golden calf, the bible says his anger was terrible. He smashed the tablets he was carrying, ordered the calf destroyed—ground to powder—and then mixed the powder with water and made his people drink it."

"And?"

"Like most of what's in the Bible, there are elements of historical truth to this story, but there is also much that's unreliable. Moses existed, surely, and so did the golden calf, and when he saw the thing being venerated at the foot of Sinai, it's very likely he did order it destroyed. Perhaps he even thought it had been, that the powder he was forcing down his people's throats was the residue of its destruction. But he was just a man, after all, and easily deceived.

"The golden calf was not destroyed, Mr. Stewart.

I've *seen* it. I've touched it, I've held it in my hand. For three thousand years, it's been hidden, preserved by a priestly sect that moves it from place to place at two-year intervals. They'll kill any outsider who gets close to it. They tried to kill me, and they'll try to kill you. But they won't succeed—not if you're as good as people say."

"I was once," Malcolm said.

"And you shall be again. No more wine, man. You have a job to do." Burke extended his hand again, his left hand, and Malcolm watched it hang in the darkness, drawing him into a covenant that could cost him his life or worse.

Lydia, he thought, *if you were here, I'd spurn the offer and not think twice. But you're gone, my darling, in heaven or in sod, and I'm left behind to end my days alone. What harm if they end quickly?*

He took Burke's hand, felt it tighten around his own.

From the darkness, he heard Margaret's breath catch and felt a flicker of anger. She was the one who'd brought him here. What had she expected him to do?

MALCOLM STRODE PURPOSEFULLY THROUGH THE rooms, retracing their steps to the entry hall. Margaret had to run to keep pace.

"So, how many of us have there been?"

"Four. Unless you count the ambassador. He refused the offer."

"Probably the only time anyone has refused that man anything."

"He's a great man, and he's suffered greatly," Margaret said.

"And made others suffer."

"He's not made anyone do anything. He's offered the opportunity—"

"Four men have died chasing his opportunity."

"Then why did you say yes?" She wheeled on him and grabbed his arm. "No one forced you to."

"Maybe I just want the money."

She held his eyes, searched in them for something.

"I don't think so," she said. "I don't think you expect to see the money."

"Well, then, maybe I just need something to do, something that will get me out of this town."

She shook her head.

"So tell me, Miss Stiles, why am I doing it?"

"I don't know. I'd like to think it's because you recognize the importance of what he's discovered. But I don't think that's it at all. I think maybe it's the danger that attracts you. I think maybe you want to die."

"You're wrong," Malcolm said. "If that's what I wanted, this city's got no shortage of roofs to jump from."

"And pubs, where you can get yourself stuck by a boy with a knife."

"I didn't start that fight," Malcolm said.

"None of you ever starts a fight. But somehow you end up in so many. And eventually one of them's the death of you."

"Eventually. But not today."

"Only because I was there."

"And I've thanked you for it," Malcolm said.

"Who will you thank in North Africa, Mr. Stewart? When you're crossing the Jebel Akhdar, who will you lean on for support?"

"Maybe you'll come with me," he said, with a small smile. "And watch my back for me on the Jebel Akhdar."

She released his arm and he started toward the front door. She called out after him.

"You know what the difference is between you and the other four?"

He looked back. "What."

"They had a chance," Margaret said.

II

HE NEEDED A DRINK IN THE WORST WAY. IT WASN'T
just the heat, nor the deprivation—he'd gone without
for longer when he'd had to. It was the touch of the
familiar he yearned for. A bit of the house red might
have dimmed the sun and cooled the air; most of all, it
would have made the place feel less alien.

Six years had gone unnoticed here. The flags of the
Reich were gone, but no new standard had taken their
place—the few flagpoles still standing were bare. The
harbor hadn't been enlarged: two ships of modest size
still filled it to capacity. And bullet holes of various
vintages scarred the walls of every building, silent
reminders of the place's violent history.

Malcolm carried his bag into the center of town,
waved off the attempts of two locals to take it off his
hands for a couple of dirham. The papers Margaret
had given him directed him to the hostel by the
souq, and Malcolm picked his way to it through

the crowded, listless streets. There were tradesmen bargaining, displaying their wares from hooks driven into the walls a century earlier. Reed baskets and hammered metal copils, cloth woven with traditional arab motifs hanging side by side with war booty, bits of parachute silk and laceless boots, bayonet blades brown with rust and blood. Who would buy these things, Malcolm wondered, and with what money? But the merchants were there, and they didn't look like they were starving.

He palmed some folded dinars to the man behind the front desk at the hostel and was taken to a third-floor suite. The bed was low to the ground, and other than a mat and a basin the room had no furnishings, but it would do. It would have to. At least the elevation put it off limits to all but the more adventurous burglars—there was no balcony outside the window, and a thirty foot fall to the cobblestones would end a man's career even if it were not fatal.

The call of the muezzin sang out and Malcolm closed the shutters of the window to muffle it. He'd have to get used to it—he'd be hearing it five times every day. But he was still tired from his trip, his healing arm was still sore, and he figured he could start getting used to it tomorrow.

He unpacked his revolver, wiped it down, sighted along the barrel and practiced firing a few times before loading it and sliding it into the holster on his hip. With his jacket on, all but the bottom of the holster was covered. Anyone looking for it would spot it, but a casual passer-by might not.

He folded Margaret's tidy pages of notes and tucked them into one of his shirt's breast pockets. He'd committed the information to memory during the crossing, but these names—he couldn't always remember which was the person's, which the street's.

The currency Burke had supplied went into his other breast pocket. Malcolm buttoned this one closed.

The rest? His clothing could stay here. It would be pawed through by the management, but as long as they expected another night's stay from him, they'd be unlikely actually to take any of it. He slung a small leather satchel over his shoulder and around his neck. The two paperbacks he'd brought as shipboard reading he wrapped in one of his shirts and shoved to the bottom of the bag. One was the new James M. Cain, the other a copy of the Bible, and both would excite comment if left lying around.

Finally, he unfolded the crushed Borsalino he'd bought just before leaving, patted it back into shape. Every soldier knew you couldn't get by in the desert without a decent hat. It didn't have to be a Borsalino, but for god's sake, it was Burke's money he was spending, this might well be the last hat he'd ever own, and damn it, he'd bought the Borsalino.

He put it on and headed down to the street. He didn't bother to lock the door.

DR. ETTOUATI'S ROOMS WERE IN THE OLD QUARTER, where the buildings were smaller and the streets tighter. Standing with your arms out, you could almost touch the walls on either side. Malcolm consulted the notes, tucked them back into his pocket, and made his way to the building Burke had named.

It was a low, terraced building done in the Andalusian style, with rounded arches supported on the backs of narrow columns. There were fewer bullet holes here, and fewer people. One old woman watched from a nearby corner, leaning on a whiskbroom she'd been using to stir the dust between the cobblestones. He felt her eyes on him as he climbed the exposed staircase to the building's second story.

The doctor came to the door wiping his hands, and wiped them again after closing it behind them. He was a short man, no more than shoulder height to Malcolm, but solid, as though he'd be awfully hard to tip over. Malcolm was reminded of the statues he'd seen in Derna's museum when he'd passed through in '43, the heavy-featured stone guardians and gods, carved and unmovable.

"Burke wired me to expect you. You are the American, eh?"

"Hardly," Malcolm said.

"British?"

"That depends who you ask."

"Well. Which of us is not a citizen of the world, yes?" He waited for a response, got none, and went on. "Burke indicated that he wanted me to give you certain information I have collected for him about the Ammonites and their descendents. He seemed to think there was a modern sect carrying on their practices. This is, of course, highly unlikely.

"But there are ruins. Aren't there always? And there are records, and you're welcome to my notes on both." He pushed a notebook across the table between them. Malcolm thumbed through it briefly.

"Mr. Burke said you'd be able to point me toward a particular temple," Malcolm said. "North of Mechili."

"The Mechili find? Oh, I wouldn't call that a temple—really just a way station for travelers. And it's in poor condition. But if you want to see it..."

He took the notebook back, paged through it, found what he was looking for and handed it back, tapping a forefinger on an illustration. The pencil sketch showed a stone altar, crudely carved with figures that might have been animals or people, or perhaps a bit of both.

"The Ammonites were a sacrificing people, and they missed no opportunity to provide their gods with a tribute. See this surface here?" He pointed to a flat rock protruding from the wall in the illustration. "That's where they would slaughter the lamb, or goat, or bullock, or what have you, and then burn it as an offering. There are channels here and here for the blood to run. You'll have to forgive the drawing, I am a poor draftsman…"

Malcolm thought the drawing was quite clear, actually. A grooved stone surface just large enough to hold a small animal, posts on either side to bind the struggling creature, channels to catch its blood.

Dr. Ettouati went on. "Young infants were also sometimes sacrificed, in times of—"

"Infants?"

"Yes," Ettouati said. "Is that the wrong word? I mean to say children, boy children. In times of crisis. Is this not what the word means, 'infant'? How do you say a boy child in English?"

"You say infant," Malcolm said. "Nothing wrong with your English."

"Good. Good. They would sometimes sacrifice an infant, although this was rare."

"It would more or less have to be, wouldn't it?"

"Well, a woman had more children then, but yes, they were not so plentiful as goats."

Malcolm turned the page. A hand-drawn map

showed the approach to the temple—the way station, whatever it was—through a mountain pass. It was on the other side of the great Green Mountain, the Jebel Akhdar, with its sheer rock faces and endless twisting paths. Getting there wouldn't be an easy journey for a fully equipped party, much less a man traveling alone. But according to Burke, that's where he had to go.

"Tell me," Dr. Ettouati said, "has Burke told you what you are looking for?" He was wiping his hands again, Malcolm noticed, perhaps unconsciously but quite eagerly.

"No," Malcolm said. "Did he tell you?"

"Not a word. I don't imagine Burke as the type to root around in ancient sites for purely scholarly purposes, but he's said nothing about what he hopes to find. Ah, well. 'Ours not to reason why,' as your poet had it. Do you mean to go to Mechili?"

Malcolm nodded.

"I can come with you if you like," Ettouati said.

What would Burke say? He hadn't brought Ettouati into his confidence, and presumably he wouldn't want Malcolm to do so either. On the other hand, having a local to guide him through the mountains would make the journey easier.

"I'd appreciate it," Malcolm started to say—but before he could get the words out, a spray of blood covered his hands.

Everything seemed to happen in an instant, and in reverse: first the blood, streaking across his hands, then Ettouati's face crumpling as a bullet passed through it, and finally Malcolm became conscious of the sound, the thundercrack of gunfire echoing from wall to wall inside the small room. It took him longer than it should have to react: a bullet clipped his shoulder as he tipped over his chair and fell to the floor in front of the desk.

Where? How? He fought to call the layout of the room to mind as he jammed the bloody notebook into his pocket and fumbled his gun out of its holster. There had been two windows behind Ettouati, both shut. And beyond them a balcony? Probably—he'd seen a door in the other room.

He heard the rapid slap of running footsteps, chanced a look up over the top of the desk. The shutters of one window had been blown away, and through it he caught a glimpse of the shooter's arm, his back, as he sprinted for the door. Malcolm raced to the window, stuck first his gun and then his head through, but the man was already off the balcony, in the other room. Malcolm slid along the wall to the corner by the door with his gun raised in both hands. His hands were shaking, damn it, and it wasn't the shoulder wound doing it—the bullet had only grazed him. It was the shock of seeing a man killed just inches from his face. You thought you'd put it behind you, and in an instant it all comes back: the blood, the smell of a body suddenly opened to the air, the sick feeling in the pit of your stomach, the helplessness—

Damn it, pull yourself together. He gripped the gun tighter, swung around to face the door and kicked it open. He was firing before his foot touched the floor. There were two men, one in a sand-colored jalabaya, one in western-style khakis. A pair of red stains bloomed on the jalabaya and the man fell backwards, the gun tumbling from his hand. Malcolm swung to face the other man, saw a curved blade flashing as the man raced toward him. He pulled the trigger twice.

The first shot went wide, took a chunk out of the far wall and ricocheted off. The second caught the man in the gut. The dagger clattered to the floor as the man doubled over.

The front door was open, and through it he saw the old woman, now at the top of the stairs, the broom still in one hand, the doorknob in the other. She let the broom fall and took off, screaming for help.

Malcolm stepped around a low table to where the second man lay, gasping, struggling for breath. The knife was within the man's reach, and he saw the man go for it. Malcolm kicked it away, placed the sole of his boot on the man's hand, and leveled his gun at the man's face. "Who sent you?" Malcolm said.

The man was going into shock: his skin was grey and his face was shaking. The look of rage on his face was replaced by one of despair as the pain intensified. He spoke in a child's singsong whisper, the same words over and over: "*Molekh sh'ar liyot bein tekhem.*"

"Who sent you?" Malcolm put more pressure on the man's hand. "Were you after Ettouati or me?"

"*...sh'ar liyot bein tekhem,*" the man whispered. "*Molekh sh'ar...*"

There wasn't time for this. The woman's screams had faded, but she'd be back any minute, together with whatever passed for the authorities in this town. They'd find him with a half empty revolver in an apartment where three men had just been shot. He'd didn't want to find out what the inside of a Libyan prison was like.

He returned the gun to his holster and stepped off the man's hand. It wasn't mercy: the man would die of his gut wound, probably quite painfully as his stomach acids leaked out to poison his body. Shooting him now might have been more merciful. But Malcolm couldn't spare the bullet.

He took the stairs two at a time. In the alley behind the building, he found the transportation the men had used: a BMW R12, left over from the Wermacht. The sidecar was dented, the kickstand missing, the carriage streaked with rust. The glass cover of the headlamp was smashed in and one of the rubber handle grips had been torn off. But the engine was purring softly and when he gunned it, it responded instantly.

He pushed off against the wall with one leg and drove along the narrow alley as quickly as he dared, taking a sharp right when it became clear that continuing straight would take him to a dead end.

There was no time to return to the hostel, even assuming he could find it again. Between buildings, he could see the mountain in the distance and he used that to orient himself. He prayed the motorcycle's saddlebags held some water. It would be a short expedition if they didn't.

From behind him, he heard the roar of another motorcycle engine, and further back the throatier growl of a truck. He shot a look back over his shoulder and after a second saw the other cycle round a corner. The man driving it held a machine gun in one hand, the barrel resting on the handlebars. He shouted something in Arabic, raised the gun.

Malcolm took another corner, skirting the stone wall of the building by inches. The whine of his pursuer's engine grew higher pitched as he accelerated. Malcolm turned his handgrip to match and felt the cobblestones streak by beneath him, jolting him, forcing him to hold on tighter than his wounds would allow. His sleeve was wet where his shoulder had bled, and his forearm still ached from the slash he'd received in the pub. He struggled to keep the machine upright, to find the end of this maze of alleys, to keep at least one turn between him and the men behind him.

Was this how the others had died, shot from behind or smashed against a wall? He tried not to think about it, forced himself to concentrate on steering.

He was glad now that he hadn't taken a drink. His heart was racing and his reflexes, he knew, weren't what they once had been, but his hands were relatively steady and his vision clear. He heard Margaret's voice again—*The other four… they had a chance*—and gunned the engine.

They shot out from the old quarter, first Malcolm, then, some distance back, the man on the cycle, and finally what looked, at the edge of the circular mirror mounted on his handlebar, like an American jeep. There were no more turns to make: just the city's wide southern gate and, past it, the open desert. A spray of bullets shot in his direction, missing him narrowly. He grabbed the gun out of his holster. Only two shots left and no way to reload while driving, but it was still better than facing a machine gun unarmed. He sped through the gate, then took a hard left and braked to a stop behind the city wall. He turned back, lay low against the chassis, and waited for the other cycle to burst past.

But it didn't. The other cycle braked just inside the gate, idled as the jeep pulled up. He couldn't see them from where he was hidden, but he could hear their voices, the old woman and several men, all speaking in a tongue of which he understood only a few words. Among the words he recognized were "desert" and "death." It sounded as though they were deciding whether it was worth pursuing him. Why bother? One man alone in the desert would get all the justice he deserved. The night was coming; it was growing dark and cold. Let the man enjoy his victory—it would be brief.

Only don't allow him to seek refuge by sneaking back in. With alarm, Malcolm saw the heavy doors draw shut and heard the wooden bolt slide into place. Derna was off-limits to him now.

THE FOOTHILLS OF THE JEBEL AKHDAR WERE DISTANT, and who knew how long his petrol would last—but that was the only direction open to him.

Could he make it? He'd have to; there was no choice.

He drove off. Within minutes it was dark. Fortunately, the headlamp still worked, shattered glass or no, and he used it to cut a narrow path through the night. The light illuminated a trail of hard-packed sand and scrub, just a few feet at a time. He couldn't see the mountains any longer, but he took it on faith that he was still pointed in the right direction. In the morning he would check Ettouati's map, would correct his course. For now, all he had to do was drive—that, and stay awake.

The strange silence lulled him. Rarely, he would hear the cry of a distant bird, some nocturnal hunter calling to others of its kind; otherwise, the only sounds were those of his tires scouring the sand and his engine tearing through the night.

In his mind, he saw Burke's face, the naked eyes bulging in the half-light. He heard Margaret's voice: *Why did you say yes? No one forced you to.*

And he saw Lydia's face, too, remembered her as

he'd seen her last, breathing shallow breaths in the hospital bed, delirious from the pain but clinging tightly to his hand, until all at once she wasn't any longer, all at once her face was still and her suffering was over. It had only been four months since he'd returned from the army. Four years he'd spent away, always a sea or an ocean or a continent between them, and then when he'd been able to return home at last, she'd been just a few months away from death.

When he'd been here last, in the desert, with tanks and munitions and men eager to kill for their masters, she'd kept him alive. He'd see her face when his eyes were closed, would whisper her name at night, would kiss the one snapshot he had of her when other men kissed crucifixes. He used to imagine that she'd protect him in battle, keep bullets from his path. He'd prayed to her: *Darling, let me come home to you, safe and sound, let no man take me from you.* And no man had.

But the reverse—that he had never considered, that she might be taken from him. In the prime of life, in peacetime, in a clean, quiet room overlooking a shaded yard, she'd died holding his hand, and he'd been able to do nothing to prevent it.

He found the road before him blurred and realized he was weeping. He wiped the tears away on the back of his sleeve and didn't slacken his pace. His only hope was to reach the mountains before the heat of day, and he found himself praying to her again. *Darling, stay with me now. The drive ahead is long; I need your help.*

Why had he said yes to Burke? He couldn't have answered Margaret honestly at the time; he hadn't known. But now he knew. Here in the desert again, more alone than he'd ever been, rocketing through the night with nothing but carrion birds for company, he felt closer to her than he had at any time since she'd died. She was there in the night, wrapping her arms about him and whispering softly in his ear. There was nothing left of her back home, nothing but a headstone and fading memories, but here he felt her presence as he hadn't in a very long time.

He wiped his eyes once more and bent low over the handlebars.

THE DAWN, WHEN IT CAME, BROKE SUDDENLY. Malcolm saw the first shadings of gray light against the rocks and within minutes the light had turned from the cool of early morning into the harsh, hostile glare it would remain for the rest of the day. Malcolm pulled over into the shadow of a boulder to rest the overheated engine.

He took his bearings. Somehow he'd managed not to stray too far from the path he'd meant to follow. The mountain was still some distance away, looming lush and green like a mirage. The Jebel Akhdar got its name from the trees and vegetation it supported, and he imagined he could find water once he got there. But until then, he was limited to whatever he had with him.

He searched through the saddlebags hanging on either side of the rear wheel. There was a goatskin canteen in one, half-full. He sniffed its contents and took a careful sip. It tasted stale, but it was water. He allowed himself two swallows before he recapped the canteen and put it back.

He stripped off his jacket and shirt, looked sideways at the trail of dried blood that ran across his left shoulder and disappeared down his back. He flexed his shoulder, stretched his arm, massaged the muscle. It wasn't a deep wound, and he didn't think it had gotten infected, but good god, he'd forgotten how much it hurt to get shot.

He put his shirt back on, folded the jacket and laid it in the bottom of the sidecar. From his shoulder pouch he took his ammunition case and reloaded his revolver. Then he got back on the cycle.

The fuel gauge showed the tank as nearly empty. It wouldn't last all the way to the mountain, that was certain, but it would take him a few more miles, and then he'd walk. He glanced at the map from Ettouati's notebook—the sketch wasn't as clear as he'd have liked, but it looked like he wanted to be west of where he was. He oriented himself against the sun, kicked the engine to life and settled in for the ride.

The heat grew, and his fatigue grew with it, till at midday he found himself drifting, felt his head jerk as he caught himself on the verge of sleep. It was tempting: Pull off, take a few hours to recuperate. But there was no shade here, and lying down in the open sun was suicide. He took another swig from the canteen, and drove on.

The foothills were in sight when the engine finally coughed and died. Malcolm took his jacket, slung the canteen across his chest, and started out on foot. The sand was hot, and soon the soles of his boots were, too. But there was nothing to be done for it. The hat kept the worst of the glare out of his eyes; and if it was hot, well, this was the desert, what did you expect? He bulled forward, keeping the base of the mountain in sight.

By the time he reached it, the canteen was empty, his throat was parched, his legs ached, and his head swam. He kept moving forward mechanically, putting one foot in front of the other, hardly feeling the soreness in his shins, his shoulder, his sunburned neck. The hours in the sun had turned him into a desert creature, shambling forward without a thought other than the desire to get out of the heat. When he reached the first tree, he sank to his knees in its shade.

He didn't intend to sleep, and wasn't conscious of having done so, but when he next opened his eyes, the sun had shifted. He dug out the map. It showed a stream nearby and after searching for a bit, he found it. The water level was low, but it was fresh water and clean. He drank and refilled the canteen, then did the best job he could of washing his wound.

There were perhaps two hours of daylight left. The last thing Malcolm felt like doing was beginning the climb, but it had to be done. He set off. At first, the paths were nearly flat, but they grew steeper as he climbed, and the sparse vegetation of the mountain's base turned into something more like a forest as he rose, with ample undergrowth to trap his feet and make progress difficult. When the sun went down, what had been merely difficult became impossible, and finally Malcolm allowed himself to stop. He was hungry, but since he didn't know what around him was edible, he didn't take any chances. He wedged himself between a tree and the rock wall against which it had grown, tipped the hat forward over his face, and slept.

The next day's climb was easier, as the mountain leveled out for a stretch. To either side, he saw the curving paths along the rock walls slope upward alarmingly, but he stuck to Ettouati's map and followed the shallower course of the pass. He found a

tree that resembled a date palm and took a chance on
its fruit. He filled his pouch and when, several hours
later, he still felt no ill effects from the first piece, he
allowed himself a few more. Only a few—even edible
fruit could give you the runs if you ate too much of it.
But at least he wasn't ravenous any more, just hungry.

The path meandered, and he ached to cut across it,
to attempt to find a shorter route, but he didn't dare.
The mountains were treacherous here, famous for
sudden drop-offs into gorges five hundred feet deep.
If Ettouati had been there, he'd probably have known
some better paths, but he wasn't, except in the form of
his map. Malcolm had no choice but to treat the map
as scripture.

He thought about Ettouati as he climbed, thought
about the men who'd killed him. They'd looked more
Egyptian than Libyan. Broader features, for one thing,
and then there was the knife with its scalloped blade,
the sort you'd find in Cairo sooner than in Tripoli.
But he wasn't sure they'd been Egyptian, either. The
language the second one had been speaking certainly
hadn't sounded like Arabic.

He thought, too, of Burke and the assignment he'd
accepted from him. Even if Malcolm made it to the
Mechili temple, what was he supposed to do when
he got there? Burke hadn't said, and Margaret's notes
held no clues. There were dangerous men about, that
much was clear—the ones who'd caught and mutilated
Burke were presumably also the ones who'd sent the
assassins to Ettouati's home. They'd seen to it that the
other men Burke had put on their trail hadn't returned
home, and they'd do what they could to add Malcolm
to the list. So his first priority was staying out of their
hands. But supposing he succeeded at that, how was

he to find the bloody statue he was being paid to recover? He could hardly expect the thing to be sitting out in the open.

All Burke had said was that the statue was protected by a sect that moved it from place to place. The last word he'd had suggested it was at the Mechili site: Margaret had shown him the telegram. The man who'd sent it had been killed the next morning, strongly suggesting that he'd been on the right track. But that didn't mean he'd actually found the thing. And if he had, wouldn't they have moved it since?

No, Burke had insisted, they only moved it once every two lunar years. It's a practice they'd observed since biblical times, and they wouldn't deviate from it just because someone located the site. They might not even know Lambert had sent a telegram—they might think they'd silenced him before he could tell anyone what he knew. And even if not, they'd have confidence in their ability to silence anyone else who came looking. In addition to the four men he'd sent, Burke had turned up stories of a dozen other men over the past century who'd gone looking for the calf and never returned.

Hearing that, Malcolm had very nearly backed out. A dozen other men—why think he'd fare better? The only man who'd made it out alive was Burke himself, and look what had happened to him.

But he'd already bought the fucking hat. And he'd shaken hands on the deal. And what was the alternative, drinking himself to death slowly in a succession of West London pubs? Burke had been right: what did he have to lose?

Malcolm spent the second night between the roots of a giant acacia and woke with water on his face. It didn't rain often in this part of the world, and you took advantage of it when it did. He stripped off his clothing, put his gun under his jacket to keep it dry, and stood with his head tilted back. It was a brief shower, not even enough to wash all the dust off him, but its touch invigorated him. The morning sun dried him rapidly and he climbed back into his clothes before he could burn. He ate the last of his dates and started downhill.

He could see the way off the mountain by noon and set foot on level ground before nightfall. The southern desert stretched out before him, flat and featureless. Near the coast there had been frequent patches of vegetation and signs of animal life; here there was nothing except for the occasional jird scuttling ratlike across the sand. And the sand itself—it wasn't the rolling dunes you saw in Foreign Legion pictures, just a parched surface that had been bleached the color of bone and packed so hard it barely took footprints. He remembered a line from a poem they'd made him recite in grade school: *Boundless and bare, the lone and level sands stretch far away.* He'd had a mental image of the desert, he remembered, as a sort of giant beach. The reality, of course, drove such images out of your mind forever. You couldn't imagine the size of it, the emptiness, till you were standing inside it.

He started walking, setting a roughly southwesterly course. Traveling by night would be less arduous than trying to cross to Mechili with the sun beating down. He had a full canteen and he'd packed his pouch with whatever bits of fruit he'd been able to find on the way down the final slope. He could do the seven miles before dawn if he pushed himself. He'd be tired when he got there, which was not the best condition in which to face whoever might be waiting for him at the temple, and worst of all, if the landscape didn't change along the way, they'd be able to see him coming for the better part of a mile, but that was just all the more reason to approach at night. He pocketed the hat, shifted the strap of his bag so it cut into a different part of his back, and pushed forward.

At a certain point, the dusk gave way to total darkness. He had a tin of matches in his bag, but it wasn't worth using them up for the few instants of light they'd provide. His eyes adjusted, though it hardly mattered: there was nothing to see by day, less still at night. There was a hot wind that blew past from time to time, stirring the sand around him. He listened to his footsteps landing rhythmically. There was nothing else to do.

Was this what it was like to be blind? He couldn't imagine what Burke must have gone through, wandering the desert with the sun searing his unprotected eyes until at last they were burnt out like useless candle stumps. How he must have treasured the night! Until all he had was night.

It was strange, Malcolm thought, how the man burned to recover the least of what he'd lost—not his sight, not his hand, not the normal life he'd had, but that thing, that useless, useless thing he'd lost his sight pursuing. Oh, it was valuable, no doubt—priceless even—and Malcolm imagined that archaeologists and museum docents could jabber about it for a thousand years, but what good could it possibly do Burke? A three thousand-year-old statue—was this worth a dozen men's lives? Or even one man's? There would be a certain satisfaction for Burke in recovering it, Malcolm supposed, in victoriously closing a chapter that had opened in bloody defeat. But in the clear light of day, what was that really worth?

In the clear light of day. Look at me, Malcolm thought, walking through the night at the arse end of nowhere, talking about the clear light of day. Who am I to take potshots at Burke for chasing some relic out of his past, when at least he has the good sense to do it from his armchair at home, with his fan blowing cool breezes on his brow? I'm the one on a trek through a desert I never thought I'd come back to. How's that for useless?

Fifty thousand pounds. That's not useless.

It is when you're wandering in the desert, Malcolm reminded himself. Nothing more useless then.

He drank a bit of his water, recapped the canteen, and kept going.

ETTOUATI'S MAP HAD SHOWN THE TEMPLE AS HIDDEN inside the curve of a rocky outcropping, and in the half-light preceding sunrise Malcolm caught sight of a craggy shape in the distance, listing at an angle like a ship run aground. He was perhaps forty meters off to one side, but that was just as well: he'd be able to approach it from the side instead of straight on.

He crept up to the rocks slowly, revolver in hand, circled around the long way. He saw no one. There was an opening in the rocks where Ettouati had indicated, and he stepped in with his gun raised, but no one seemed to be inside either.

It was cool inside, and dark—stepping in from the desert was not unlike entering Burke's room back home, only less damp, and with the whirring of the electric fan replaced by the skittering of rodent feet.

Malcolm lit a match, saw the carvings on the walls jump in the flickers of orange light. Animal-headed men in rows, some kneeling, some upright—the Egyptian influence was clear. But there was also an unfamiliar quality. These weren't ordinary hieroglyphs.

The images converged on the altar, which was larger than he'd thought it would be. You could fit a fairly large animal between the posts, and the drainage channels ran deep enough to catch quite a lot of blood without spilling over.

The match went out, and Malcolm decided not to light another. It wasn't bright in here, but enough light leaked in from outside that he could see what he needed to. He ran his hand along the surface of the altar and its underside, bent low to look closely at the wall. The carvings continued all the way around the altar and were framed by a rectangular groove extending from the ground on either side and meeting across the top. Malcolm felt along this groove, tried to fit the tips of his fingers inside it. It looked almost like the outline of a doorway, but when he pushed against the wall, it felt like pushing against solid rock.

He ran his index fingers along the length of the channels on the altar and at the far end of each, near the wall, he felt a pea-sized hole. This surprised him—it put him in mind of drainage and implied that the altar itself was hollow. He leaned forward and blew into one of the holes. A puff of dust rose and slowly settled.

He looked around. There had to be more here. Lambert's telegram had referred to a temple—an altar in a cave was not a temple. If there was a temple in this cave, it was somewhere deeper inside, but how were you supposed to get there from here? He tried to put himself in the place of the men who had built and used this place. If there was another area, what would they have done to gain access to it?

What, indeed. Ettouati's words came back to him. *The Ammonites were a sacrificing people. They missed no opportunity to provide their gods with a tribute.*

He lit another match, watched the ground as a handful of jirds scattered. They were not large animals, about the size of rats, but—

Three or four, he imagined, might be equal in size to a small kid. Goat, that is. A small goat.

He dug through his shoulder pouch until he found his pocketknife and unfolded the longer of its blades. Then he took a few pieces of fruit—two dates, a wild fig—and cut them each in half. He pocketed the knife, placed half a fig on the ground and stood as close to perfectly still as he could. After a few seconds, he saw the dim shape of a jird nosing up to it.

He dropped his hat over the animal and scooped it up, pinning the sides of the brim between his fingers to trap it. It struggled violently and he almost lost his grip, but with his other fist he bunched the hat closed and smashed it twice against the cave wall. The jird went limp inside the hat.

He poured the body out onto the altar. It wasn't dead, he didn't think, but it was out cold and would stay where he left it. He put the other half of the fig on the ground and stepped back to wait.

In all, he managed to catch four. After that, though he still heard tiny claws clattering in the shadows, he wasn't able to lure any more into the trap. He looked over the bodies arranged in a row on the altar. They were smaller than he'd thought. Would four be enough?

There was only one way to know. He picked up one

of the animals, held it firmly by its hindquarters above the left channel, and with one stroke of his knife sliced its head off. Its blood flowed freely, if not for long. He held it upside down directly over the hole at the end of the channel, watched as the flow drained off into the body of the altar. He pushed against the wall, but there was no movement. He tried using the posts for leverage, gripping one in each fist and straining. Nothing.

He decapitated the second jird, holding this one over the right-hand channel. Then he did the third and fourth. His hands were greasy from their fur and sticky with their blood. He wiped his hands roughly against the seat of his pants and took hold of the posts again. This time he thought he could feel something as he strained, some small shifting of the stone. But no more than that.

He cast about for something else he could use. Could he catch more jirds? It didn't seem likely, and even if he could, the blood from the first four would have dried up by the time he did, so he'd be starting over from scratch. There had to be another way.

He hefted the canteen. It was better than half full. He hated the idea of using any of his water this way, but—

He uncapped the canteen and carefully poured a thin stream into each channel. This time, when he pushed, he could hear the stones shift, some heavy internal counterweight slowly turning. He poured in some more, closed the canteen, took hold of the posts and pushed with all his strength.

The wall moved—slowly, with a grinding of stone against stone, but it moved, the altar and the section of the wall behind it both turning on some invisible, freshly lubricated axis.

There was light behind the wall, first a narrow orange crack and then an expanding glow like the flames of a thousand candles. And as the wall continued to turn, more smoothly now, more easily, Malcolm saw that there was also a man there, a man in a gold skullcap and patterned robe, standing with one arm crossed over his chest. The other arm was extended toward Malcolm, and held a gun.

III

MALCOLM NOW REGRETTED HAVING HOLSTERED HIS
own revolver, but there was nothing to be done for it.
His couldn't outdraw a man who already had the drop
on him, never mind doing so when his hands were
sticky with blood.

His mind raced. The man hadn't pulled the trigger
yet, but neither had he lowered the gun. He seemed to
be weighing which would be more appropriate.

Malcolm dropped to his knees, held his bloody
palms out. *"Molekh sh'ar liyot bein tekhem,"* he said.

Slowly, the gun lowered. *"Molekh sh'ar,"* the man
said.

THE ROOM BEHIND THE ALTAR STRETCHED ON FOR
some distance and the ground sloped steeply
downward. By the time Malcolm had followed the
man to the far end, he suspected they were past the

edge of the outcropping entirely and standing beneath the desert floor. The man slipped the gun inside the pocket of his robe and took out a ring of keys, one of which fit the lock set into the wrought-iron gate that barred their way. He swung the gate open and passed through without speaking a word.

Which was just as well, since Malcolm had used up all the words he knew in the man's language. If he'd tried to start a conversation, Malcolm would have had to make an attempt for the gun, however hopeless it might have been.

The room on the other side of the gate was several times the size of the entryway, a hollowed-out octagon with shallow alcoves carved into the walls, each containing a dish of tallow and a dancing flame. The center of the room held a freestanding stone altar in the shape of a giant hand, palm pointing toward the ceiling, fingers slightly curled.

There was one man kneeling in front of the altar and one standing behind it; on the altar itself was a pile of stones that looked as if they might have been chipped from the walls, only glowing, like the embers of a fire. It wasn't clear what the source of heat was, if indeed there was one—maybe it was just a source of light. The man behind the altar was short and wore the same sort of robe and skullcap the other man had on, while the one on his knees wore only a breechclout, a twisted strip of cloth knotted around his waist and between his legs. He swayed from side to side in time with a wordless chant, sometimes bowing forward to touch his head to the ground.

The robed men stood in silence, waiting, and Malcolm stood silently as well, but he used the time to steal glances around the room. There were openings in several of the walls leading off to dark corridors. Was the idol down one of them? If so, which one? And for how much longer could he maintain the charade of being a fellow worshipper? If he hadn't walked in on a ceremony in progress, surely they would have spoken to him already, and would instantly have found him out.

The kneeling man was swaying faster now as his chant grew louder. He reached out toward the altar, toward the stones, and jammed his hands in among them. Malcolm recoiled as the air filled with the stink of burning flesh. The man was howling now, screaming, in transports of pain and ecstasy.

Perhaps there would be a better opportunity later—perhaps. But it didn't seem likely.

Malcolm stepped up close to the man who had let him in, darted his hand into the pocket of the robe and grabbed the pistol. It was a German gun, heavy and cold to the touch. He whipped an arm around the man's neck and held the gun to his temple. The other robed man started forward.

"Take one more step and he dies," Malcolm said. "Do you understand me?"

The kneeling man rose to his feet. Malcolm saw that he still held a hot stone in each of his hands. His cheeks were covered with tears. His chest was scarred, long welts running haphazardly across his breastbone and along his ribs. Even barefoot as he was, he stood well over six feet tall, and his frame was formidable. But when he spoke, his voice was soft, calm.

"No, he doesn't understand you. Neither of them speaks English."

Malcolm found the man's voice unnerving. It was the furthest thing imaginable from the wordless howl it had been just moments before.

"He understands this," Malcolm said, gesturing with the pistol.

"You may shoot him if you want," he said. "It is what he deserves for letting you in."

Malcolm unwound his arm from around the robed man's throat and shoved him away. He reoriented the Luger's sight so that it pointed squarely at the giant's naked chest. "And what about you, brother? Are you as ready to throw your own life away?"

Slowly and with a casual stride he came forward. "I am not afraid of pain. If it is Molekh's will that I die, I shall die."

"It's *my* will you need to be concerned about right now," Malcolm said. "The good news is I'm just here to do a job and leave—"

"You will never leave."

"We'll see. Why don't you back up against the wall, and tell the other two to do the same thing." The man paid no attention. Malcolm cocked the gun. "Now, or I swear to god I'll shoot you where you stand."

A voice spoke from behind him, a reverberant voice that rang from the stones. *"You swear to god?"*

Malcolm spun to find its source, but there was no one there.

"And which god is it that you swear to? When you are in my temple, do you swear to me?"

Malcolm saw movement in the corner of his eye and turned back, but the giant was suddenly beside him, and then the stones, still hot, were pressed against his gun hand, one on either side. He strained to pull the trigger, but the man had his hand firmly pinned. He felt his skin starting to sear.

Malcolm reached under his jacket left-handed, drew his own gun from its holster, jammed it into the man's gut and fired. The force of the gunshot sent the man stumbling back, freeing Malcolm's hand. He leveled the Luger at the man's head and pulled the trigger. A bloody spray stained the chamber floor.

The other two men were fleeing awkwardly in their cumbersome robes, heading for corridors on opposite sides of the room. To raise an alarm? To get reinforcements? He couldn't take the chance. One bullet apiece—left hand, right hand—and they were down.

Malcolm's heart was hammering, his head reeling. He heard the sound of laughter all around him, echoing louder as the thunder of gunfire died down. *"Blood!"* The voice was exultant. *"You do swear to me—you swear in blood, the blessed offering."*

"Who's talking?" Malcolm said, turning in a circle, scanning the shadows, a gun in each fist. "Where are you?"

"I am the Lord of this place and this people. I am brothergod to the Lord you worship, and have been since men first spoke of gods. I am many-named: men call me Melech, and Molekh, and Moloch; I have been called Legion, and Horror, and Beast, in fifty tongues and fifty times fifty, but men also call me Father, and Master, and Beloved. There is no end to the names men have given me."

"Enough," Malcolm said. "Save the booga-booga for the natives. Come out and face me."

"No man may look upon me and live."

Malcolm worked his way along one wall of the room, scanning the rock for a concealed loudspeaker, or some other mechanism that might explain where the voice was coming from. "Let's get one thing straight, Charley," he said. "I'm not here for the sermon. I'm not here for your fifty tongues or any of the rest of it. A man sent me here to collect a statue—either you have it or you don't. You leave me in peace and I'll leave you in peace."

"Peace!" The laughter was explosive. *"You talk of peace? Look about you. The blood of my servants stains my altar and you speak to me of peace?"*

Malcolm completed his circuit of the room. There was nothing—just rock and flame and the voice, shouting in his ear. The entrance to one of the dark corridors was next to him, and he stepped into it, but the voice followed him, chasing him along its length until he came out into a room much like the first. Only this one's altar was shaped like a pedestal, and where the other had held stones, this one held—

He couldn't see clearly what it held. There was a shape, but Malcolm could only see it through a haze, as though of smoke. Could it be the outline of a calf? It could be anything, he realized. And as he watched, the smoke closed up around the altar, obscuring the figure.

"You say you seek a statue. If so, your quest is doomed, for the statue you mean was destroyed a hundred generations ago."

"But—"

"But a man told you he saw it. You are not the first he has sent to me, this blind man. And you, so quick to believe, you take the word of a blind man over that of your own scripture?"

"He wasn't blind when he saw it."

"You are all blind." The voice was now a guttural whisper, cold and insinuating. *"You see only what you wish to see. Each man who faces my altar sees that which he most desires and, addressing it with impure heart, gains only what he most dreads."*

The smoke began to thin, as though blown by a breeze.

"Your blind man spent a lifetime searching for my mount,

the figure they made for me at the foot of Sinai, so when he came before me, that is what he saw.

"Look closely, child. What do you see? Like your ancestors before you, you have wandered in the desert and climbed the mountain's slopes. You did not bear this burden in pursuit of another man's quest."

Malcolm could make out the altar again, and upon it he saw a form, a human shape, but it was still indistinct.

"Do you even know what you are searching for?"

And the smoke vanished, in an instant, leaving the figure behind it bare. She was naked and pale and trembling, and Malcolm fell to his knees before her.

"Each man worships at the idol of his choosing."

"No," Malcolm said, shaking his head. "She's dead. I buried her." He turned to the woman seated on the altar. "You're dead, three years dead."

Lydia stepped down, came toward him, one arm outstretched. "My love, my poor love," she said.

He shrank from her. "It's impossible," he said. He shouted it: "It's impossible! This is a lie!"

"Why impossible? Do you doubt my power?" From the corridor, Malcolm heard the echo of footsteps approaching, and then one by one the men he'd killed entered the room, the two in robes and the third in his loincloth, his bloody trunk and head still bearing their horrible, fatal wounds. *"Over certain among the living I have influence, but over the dead—over the dead, I have utter command."*

"No," Malcolm said. But he couldn't deny the evidence of his eyes. These men—they had died, he had struck them down himself, had seen them fall. Yet here they were. And here she was, looking exactly as he remembered. His mind recoiled at the thought. And yet—

She reached out for him again, but the dead men in priestly robes each took one of her arms and between them they pulled her back toward the altar. The third man followed, his naked back gleaming in the candlelight, bloody and torn where the first bullet had emerged above his hip.

Malcolm launched himself to his feet, threw himself at the three men, but while the priests secured Lydia to the altar, the giant swatted him away, sent him reeling to the floor with one swipe of his scarred palm. Malcolm drew his gun and fired, twice, three times, till the chambers were all empty, but this time the bullets had no effect.

The priests stood back, and he saw that they had shackled Lydia to the stone, ankles and wrists encircled with iron bands. From the folds of his robe, one of them drew a knife with a curved and scalloped blade and handed it to the third man, the barebacked giant who had so casually fended off Malcolm's charge. The second priest positioned himself behind Lydia's head and placed one hand firmly on either side of her face.

"Close your eyes," the giant said. His voice was soft and calm and Malcolm's blood froze at the sound of it.

"Malcolm!" Lydia's cry took him back in an instant to her bedside at the hospital. "Help me."

"It's not real," Malcolm said. He shouted it to the ceiling of the cavernous room. "It's not real!"

"*Your arrogance is awesome,*" the voice intoned, "*if you presume to state what is and is not real.*"

"My wife is dead. You cannot change that. No one can."

"*Perhaps. But can the dead not also suffer?*"

And from the altar came a shriek of purest terror, of anguish beyond measure. He saw only the giant's broad back, stooped over the bound figure, saw the hugely muscled arms, streaked with sweat, rock as he gently worked the knife.

"Stop it," Malcolm said. "Please stop."

"Why, if it is not real?"

Malcolm had to struggle to keep his voice under control. "Why are you doing this?"

"Because I can, child, and because it is my pleasure. It is my pleasure that my power be revealed, that men may know a god of might still walks among them, that they may bend their knees in supplication."

"You want me to kneel?" He dropped to his knees, spread his arms out. "Please."

"Kneeling is more than a matter of being on your knees. I will spare her for you—and then you will kneel to me in earnest, you will bow to me and do my bidding, as your blind man does in spite of himself. And in time you will speak my name with true reverence rather than with deceit in your heart."

The men surrounding the altar stepped away, and Malcolm saw that Lydia was still bound to it, her face smeared with blood. He ran to the altar. She was shaking and pale, her torso covered with sweat, and he took her hand gently. One of the priests held a square of silk out to him. He took it and carefully wiped the blood around her eyes.

"My darling," she whispered. "Don't leave me."

So, Burke, he thought, here's your golden calf. I understand now. There's a thing you love and crave, and you had it once, too briefly, and now you ache to have it back. Yes, I know how you ache. There is no way you could leave it behind in the desert: you're bound to it for life, you are its slave. Even if it no longer exists outside your imagination.

I crave, too, Malcolm thought. You're not the only one; my imagination is no less troubled. But I am not blind, Burke, and I have not your capacity for blind faith.

"I left my wife in Glasnevin," he said softly, "and I'm going back to her there."

He let go of her hand, stepped back from the altar, and walked as rapidly as he could toward the corridor through which he'd entered. Behind him, the voice thundered.

"If you go, you will never see her again."

He kept walking.

"You will never speak to her, touch her, hear her voice."

He bit back tears.

"She will suffer torments you cannot conceive!"

And then she screamed, a shattering, curdled scream that seemed to contain more pain in it than any body could bear. Malcolm ran from it, tore through the first chamber and the iron gate and the entry hall, pursued by the sound of it. The flames of the candles lining the walls all at once were snuffed out, and at the far end of the corridor he saw the stone wall slowly swinging closed.

"Coward! You will curse the day you abandoned her to me."

The hall seemed endless, the band of light beyond the wall shrinking as he ran toward it. He bent forward and strained for extra speed, for the last desperate dregs of energy that would carry him through, and he reached the wall at last when only inches remained. He squeezed through sideways, scraping against the rock on either side. From inside, a final angry whisper came, one he could only barely make out.

And then the wall slammed shut.

He leaned against it, breathing heavily, sobbing freely. What have I done, he thought. What have I done?

* * *

IT WAS TWILIGHT OUTSIDE AND DRY AND HOT. HE HAD
little water and less food, and seven miles between him
and the nearest source of either. There was nothing for
it. He started walking.

I'll make it, he told himself. I'll make it home. I'll tell
Burke nothing—let him think I died, let him send other
men after me, I don't care. Just let me make it back.

An image came unbidden into his mind: the
shackles, the altar, the woman writhing upon it.

It wasn't her, he told himself. It wasn't. The dead
don't walk, or speak, or feel pain, or beg you not to leave.

But it looked—her touch, her voice, it was all—

Rubbish. It was an illusion, a dream, a bit of desert
madness.

In his jacket pocket, where he'd crammed it as he
ran, he felt the crumpled square of silk, still damp. He
took it out, turned it this way and that in the fading
light. It was real, and the blood on it was real—not
a dream, not an illusion. But what did that mean?
Something had happened in the temple, something
terrible; but not to Lydia. That wasn't possible.

Are you certain? a voice in the back of his mind
whispered.

Yes, damn it. I am certain.

Then why are you so frightened?

Because—because—

Because you saw her with your own eyes, you held
her in your hand, and now you've gone and left her
behind…

It wasn't her. It couldn't have been.

No, no, of course not. It couldn't. But you'll never
know that for sure, will you?

And he remembered Molekh's final, whispered imprecation, the words hissed out at him just before the stone walls ground together. *You may leave this place*, the voice had said, *but you will never escape it.*

The Jebel Akhdar was barely visible at the horizon. He marched on, and the night closed in around him.

Read on for an extract from the next

GABRIEL HUNT ADVENTURE

HUNT AT WORLD'S END

1

GABRIEL HUNT HAD TAKEN A LOT OF PUNCHES TO THE face over the years. He'd come to think of it as an occupational hazard, dealing as he often did with criminals, pirates, gangsters, brawlers and all kinds of thugs who let their fists do the talking, and he usually gave as good as he got. But this time was different. This was the first time the guy throwing the punches was wearing a big, sharp silver ring in the shape of a horned stag's head.

The punch stunned him, knocked him back into one of the large elephant tusks flanking the fireplace of the Discoverers League lounge. The tusk wobbled on its base, and Gabriel, feeling wobbly himself, dropped to his knees. Blood trickled along his cheek where the stag's horns had cut him. He looked up at the slender blond man standing over him in a gray houndstooth blazer and gray slacks. He was wearing a crooked sneer. Glancing at his hand, he wiped a spot of blood off his ring.

"We can continue this as long as you wish, Mr. Hunt," he said. "I have nowhere else I need to be. But you see my friends back there? They don't have as much patience as I do."

Behind the blond man, three men clad all in black stood with guns in their hands. One revolver was trained on Wade Boland, the weekend bartender, where he stood behind the bar. The second was pointed at Clyde Harris, a retired cartographer in his seventies who came to the League every Saturday to partake of his two favorite pastimes, drinking and swapping tall tales. He sat on his usual barstool at the end of the counter and stared at the gun unblinking. Neither Wade nor Clyde looked particular frightened by this turn of events, though they kept their hands dutifully raised above their heads.

But the third revolver was leveled at Katherine Dunlap, and she was a different story. The willowy redhead sat trembling at the table she'd been sharing with Gabriel before the blond man and his cohorts had stormed in and started waving their guns around. Her fingernails dug into the plush arms of the red leather chair, and her pale green eyes were as wide as soup bowls. It was obvious she'd never had a gun pointed at her before. Gabriel had only met her that morning, on his flight back from Brazil to New York City. Seated next to her in first class, he'd passed the hours answering her questions about his just-completed expedition along the banks of the Amazon, and once they'd landed he'd invited her back to the Discoverers League for a drink. She clearly hadn't expected their date to end in violence. Of course, neither had he.

The blond man reached into the inside pocket of his blazer, pulled out a large, well-polished chrome handgun and leveled it at Gabriel. Gabriel eyed the gun unhappily. The three bouncer types he figured he could take even though they were armed. But this man was another matter. Compared to the other three he looked almost scrawny, but he punched like someone had taught him how, and he was holding his gun with a professional's grip.

"I don't have what you're looking for," Gabriel said, rubbing his jaw.

"I want you to think very carefully about what you do next, Mr. Hunt. I'd hate to have to tell my men to start shooting." The man gestured around the lounge at the bookshelves filled with antique volumes and the display cases of artifacts, many of them fragile, all of them irreplaceable. "These beautiful things might get damaged. Bloodstains, you know. So difficult to wash off."

"Gabriel," Katherine pleaded, her voice shaking.

The man smiled. "You see? Your friend has a good head on her shoulders. I'm sure she would like it to remain there."

Gabriel rose slowly to his feet.

"No more heroics, Mr. Hunt," the man cautioned. "And no more lies. I know you were in the Amazon until this morning, and I know you brought the Death's Head Key back with you. Just hand it over and we'll go quietly." He smiled slightly. "Its name notwithstanding, no one has to die over the thing."

"Why should I give it to you?" Gabriel asked.

The blond man cocked his head and knit his brow. "Why? Because I am the man with the gun, Mr. Hunt."

"Why do you *want* it?" Gabriel said. "It's not that valuable. It'll fetch maybe five, six grand on the black market, if you're lucky. It hardly seems worth your time."

The blond man stepped nearer. This close, Gabriel got a good look at the man's eyes and could see the brutality he concealed beneath his veneer of civility. The man opened his mouth to answer, then changed his mind and swung his Magnum, slamming the heavy butt into Gabriel's jaw. Gabriel's head snapped back. At least this time he managed to stay on his feet.

"The key," the blond man repeated.

Gabriel narrowed his eyes. He tasted blood and spat red-tinged saliva onto the carpet. "You better hope I never see you again."

The man cocked the Magnum. "You will never see *anyone* again, Mr. Hunt, if you don't hand over the key." And when Gabriel failed to do so: "For heaven's sake, Hunt, what difference does it make to you? What were you planning to do with it, stick it in one of these cases? Photograph it for *National Geographic*? Give it to the Metropolitan? What a colossal waste. You don't even know what the key unlocks."

"And you do?"

The blond man leveled the barrel of the Magnum at Gabriel's forehead and said, "Five."

"Tell me," Gabriel said. "Tell me what the key opens."

"Four."

"Gabriel, for God's sake," Clyde muttered from his barstool. "My ice is melting. Just give the man whatever he's looking for, and I'll buy you and the lady a round."

"Three."

The blond man swung the gun to point it at Katherine. Her hands shot up as though they might be able to deflect a bullet. "Two."

"*Gabriel!*"

"One—"

"All right," Gabriel said. "All right. Just… put that thing away."

The blond man took the gun off of Katherine and swung it to face Gabriel instead.

Gabriel unbuttoned his shirt. The Death's Head Key hung on a leather strap around his neck. He lifted it over his head. The blond man snatched the heavy bronze key with his free hand and held it up, eyeing it with satisfaction.

No one knew how old the Death's Head Key was. It had been given its name in 1581 when the explorer Vincenzo de Montoya found it on a trip through Asia and noticed its bow was shaped like a skull, with concavities where the eye sockets might have been and a diamond-shaped groove between them. No one, not even de Montoya, knew what it unlocked—but whatever it was, Gabriel could guess from the look of the thing that it was no simple door. Most keys had a single blade that fit into the keyway of a lock, but the Death's Head Key had three, one straight and the other two flanking it at forty-five degree angles. De Montoya had reportedly worn it around his neck as a good luck charm, but it hadn't kept up its end of the bargain. His luck ran out when he disappeared during an Amazon expedition a few years later, and the Death's Head Key had been lost with him.

Lost, until Gabriel found it, still dangling from the broken neck of de Montoya's skeleton at the bottom of a deep pit in the rain forest.

Now, watching the blond man stuff the Death's Head Key in his pocket, Gabriel couldn't help feeling it was about to become lost once again.

"Very thoughtful, Mr. Hunt," the blond man said.

"You've saved the custodians of this establishment quite a bit of mopping." He backed slowly toward the lounge door, keeping his gun leveled at Gabriel. "Let's go," he said, and the three thugs holstered their revolvers and exited before him. The blond man gave Gabriel a final nod and disappeared through the doorway.

When he heard the front door open, Gabriel followed at a run, passing Hank, the League's elderly doorman where he lay slumped unconscious on the floor.

In the street outside, a pair of doors slammed on a gunmetal gray Cadillac and it peeled off, tires squealing against the asphalt. Gabriel raced out into the street and ran half a block after them, but they shot through a red light and vanished in the distance.

Gabriel walked back to the League building and into the lounge, where Wade was already dialing the police from the phone behind the bar. "Button up, young man," he said, aiming a finger at Gabriel's chest. "There are women pres—oh, hello, yes, I'd like to report an incident."

There was only one woman present, and Gabriel lowered himself into the chair beside her, fuming. For weeks he'd meticulously traced de Montoya's path through the Amazon, sweating through the jungle heat and all the days of false starts and backtracking, and for what? So the artifact he'd worked so hard to recover could be stolen by some skinny blond thug with bad taste in jewelry?

He looked up and noticed Katherine was still trembling. "Are you okay?" he asked her.

She stood slowly and walked to the bar, grabbed the scotch glass out of Clyde's hand and downed it in a single gulp. Then she returned to the table where Gabriel sat. She put a hand on his arm.

"So," she said, and Gabriel could tell she was trying to keep her voice steady. "Does this happen every time you take a girl out for drinks?"

Gabriel touched the cut on his cheek and winced. "Not every time."

Katherine patted his arm. "Don't call me," she said. Then she turned and walked out. A moment later they all heard the front door shut.

"The police are on their way," Wade said, handing Clyde another scotch. Then he reached into his pocket, pulled out two twenty-dollar bills and handed them to Clyde as well. When he saw Gabriel watching the transaction, he said, "We had a bet."

Gabriel frowned. "What kind of bet?"

"I bet Clyde twenty bucks you never lose a fight."

"I could have told you otherwise," Gabriel said. "What's the other twenty for?"

"I also bet him that you always get the girl." Gabriel rubbed his sore jaw. "Sorry to disappoint," he said. "And sorry about…" He waved his hand in a circle, indicating the room's two overturned chairs, the painting that had been knocked askew, the shattered decanter still in fragments on the floor.

"How long have we known you, Gabriel?" Clyde asked, sipping his scotch. "We're used to it by now."

2

GABRIEL SAT ON THE TABLE IN AN EXAMINING ROOM
at Lenox Hill Hospital with the noise from the
emergency room seeping in through the closed door.
He fidgeted, the stiff paper that covered the table
crinkling under his weight. The police officer standing
by the door fidgeted too. He tapped his pencil against
his notepad like he was marking time.

"This is ridiculous," Gabriel said. "I told you I'm
fine."

"It's standard procedure following an assault," the
officer said. He was a few inches shorter than Gabriel,
maybe five-nine, with curly, close-cropped hair and a thin
mustache. The nametag above his badge read JACKSON.
"Most people appreciate being taken to the hospital after
they've been beaten, slashed and pistol-whipped."

Gabriel hated hospitals, especially the strong,
antiseptic smell of ammonia that seemed to permeate
every square inch of them. It was the same smell he

remembered from the hospital in Gibraltar when he'd gone there in the early weeks of 2000 in the hopes of identifying his parents' remains. Ambrose and Cordelia Hunt had been on a millennium-themed speaking tour of the Mediterranean when their ship disappeared. No visuals, nothing on the radar, just gone. Three days later it had appeared again out of nowhere, not a living soul on board, only the dead bodies of three crew members. Soon after, more bodies began washing ashore—crewmen, passengers, more than three hundred in all—but a dozen or so never did. It had been a bad few weeks, looking at corpse after corpse and not knowing each time whether to hope he wouldn't recognize it or that he would. In any event, he never did. And nearly a decade later, the smell still got to him, still gave him an uncomfortable feeling of bad news and unfinished business.

"So this man," Officer Jackson said, looking at his notes. "About your height, six feet, blond hair, slim build, gray blazer and slacks. And you say he was in charge of the others, the three other men?"

"That's right. He gave the orders. The others didn't talk at all."

"Have you ever seen him before?"

Gabriel shook his head. "No. Never."

"Are you sure? It's easy to forget a face."

"I tend to remember the men who hit me."

"Have there been a lot?"

Gabriel rubbed his sore jaw. "One or two."

"Well, you say this one knew your name, knew where to find you and knew you were in possession of this… this *key* he took from you."

"That's right."

"So you think he's been following you, or what?"

"I've been out of the country for the past several weeks. I doubt he could have followed me where I was. But someone must have gotten word to him about what I brought back—one of the locals, possibly, or someone on the expedition."

Jackson nodded and scribbled in his notepad, though that answer put it well out of his jurisdiction. "There anybody you can think of who might have it in for you?"

Gabriel sighed. "How much time do you have?"

The officer flipped his book shut, capped his pen. "Not enough," he said. "You ever think of changing professions, Mr. Hunt? Maybe something a little safer, like firefighter or undercover narcotics officer?"

"I'd miss the flexible hours," Gabriel said.

The door opened then, and a woman in green scrubs stepped in. She had straight black hair tied back in a ponytail, deep brown eyes and smooth skin the color of caramel. She clutched a clipboard to her chest and nodded at Officer Jackson. "Can you give us some privacy?"

Jackson said, "All right. Mr. Hunt, we're going to put your assailant's description out there and try to get a lead on him." He didn't sound too optimistic. "If you think of anything that might help, call the precinct, okay?"

"Of course," Gabriel said.

Officer Jackson left, closing the door behind him. "I'm Dr. Barrow." The woman scanned the papers on her clipboard. "Gabriel Hunt, is it? Okay, Mr. Hunt, let's take a look at you. Would you mind taking off your shirt?"

Gabriel frowned. "Really, doc, I'm fine. This isn't necessary."

"That's what they all say. Then one day they collapse in a grocery store and it's our fault. So. Your shirt."

Gabriel unbuttoned his shirt, pulled it off and tossed it onto the empty chair by the door. "I got hit in the face, nowhere else," he said.

"You think that can't put stress on your neck, your windpipe, your heart?" Dr. Barrow took the stethoscope from around her neck, put the buds in her ears and placed the metal disk against his chest. "Breathe for me."

Gabriel breathed.

"Again." She moved to his other side and he felt the cold metal press against his back. "Once more."

He kept breathing and she kept shifting the stethoscope around. Then the metal went away and he felt her finger tracing a line along his shoulder blade. "This looks like a scar from a knife wound," she said.

"Yes, well, there's a reason for that," Gabriel said.

"And is this—" she probed a little lower "—from a bullet?"

"Grapeshot."

"And this?" Her finger pressed lightly at the base of his spine.

"Spear," Gabriel said.

"Good lord," Dr. Barrow said. "I'd say the cut on your cheek is the least of your worries."

"You should see the mark a saw-toothed Aztec dagger left on my thigh. It's a beauty."

"Maybe some other time," she said.

"Yeah," Gabriel sighed. "I'm getting a lot of that today."

WHEN GABRIEL LEFT THE HOSPITAL, HIS BROTHER Michael was waiting for him outside, pacing on the sidewalk, his straight, sandy hair blowing in the breeze. He pushed his round, wire-rimmed glasses up his nose. "Well, well, well. I guess I am my brother's keeper after all."

"You didn't have to pick me up," Gabriel said. He touched the bandage on his cheek. It protected the four stitches Dr. Barrow had given him. She'd told him he was lucky his jaw hadn't fractured. Then she'd recommended rest, aspirin for the soreness and, if possible, significantly fewer gun butts to the face.

"Come on," Michael said. He put a hand on Gabriel's back and led him to the shiny black town car waiting at the curb. He opened the door for Gabriel, then slid into the back seat next to him.

Up front, an older man with a salt and pepper mustache looked at Michael in the rearview mirror and asked, "Home?"

"Yes. Thanks, Stefan." The driver nodded and pulled out into traffic. "I hope you don't mind coming back with me," Michael said, turning to Gabriel. "It's just that I feel better about our security at the Foundation than what they've got at the Discoverers League. Those men might come back for you."

"They already have what they came for," Gabriel said. "I'm sure they're long gone by now. Back to whatever hole they crawled out of."

"Maybe you're right," Michael said, "but better safe than sorry." He looked out the window. "You know I really wish you'd stop all this and just come work with me at the Foundation."

"Doing what?" Gabriel asked. "Answering mail? Reading grant applications? I'd go stir crazy within a week."

"You'd get fewer guns pointed at you. Not the worst tradeoff, Gabriel."

"That's a matter of opinion," Gabriel said.

The car pulled up in front of the marble entryway of the Hunt Foundation's five-story brownstone on 55th Street and York Avenue, in the heart of Sutton Place. They got out, and as Stefan drove the car off, Michael fished his keys out of the pocket of his tweed jacket and opened the door. Inside, he pressed a code into an alarm panel on the wall, which beeped in response. Satisfied, he led the way up the stairs, past the offices on the first two floors of the building and up to his triplex apartment.

He turned on the lights, big hanging chandeliers that illuminated an enormous library lined with bookcase after bookcase. Beginning with the numerous volumes their parents had amassed, Michael had compiled the largest collection of obscure and ancient texts since the Library of Alexandria, a collection Gabriel himself had made use of many times. A red leather couch sat in the middle of the room, with a wrought iron, granite-topped coffee table in front of it and a long polished oak desk off to one side. The pages of a manuscript lay stacked on the table: the *Oedipodea* of Homer, translated by Sheba McCoy. *Good for her*, Gabriel thought, remembering how close they'd both come to getting themselves killed after discovering the lost epic in Greece. *Have to read it one of these days, find out how it ends.*

At the far end of the library, an enormous stuffed polar bear, rearing with its mouth open and its teeth bared, towered above a small breakfront bar. "Would you like a drink?" Michael asked, opening the breakfront and pulling out a bottle of Glenfiddich.

"Definitely."

Gabriel sat on the couch. Beside Sheba's manuscript,

there was an open cardboard box with the Hunt Foundation's address written on one of the flaps in black marker. He reached inside and dug through shredded paper until he felt something dry and brittle. He pulled the object out. It was a shrunken, mummified human hand. With six fingers.

"Gloves, gloves, gloves!" Michael yelled. He nodded anxiously toward the box of disposable latex gloves sitting on his desk. "You know better."

Gabriel dropped the hand back in the box. "Sorry."

Michael carried over a glass, handed it to him.

"None for you?" Gabriel said, sipping.

"In a moment." Michael went over to his desk and opened his laptop. "I just need to check on something." He clicked the mouse a few times, and then a cloud of disappointment darkened his features.

"What is it?"

Michael slumped in his chair and rubbed his face with both hands. "I was hoping I'd have an email from Joyce Wingard. We gave her a grant for a research trip to Borneo and she's been there since August. She was checking in with me every day, and then three days ago the emails stopped."

"How well do you know her? Maybe she just ran off with the grant money."

Michael stared at him. "You don't recognize the name? Joyce Wingard. Gabriel, she's Daniel Wingard's niece."

Daniel Wingard. There was a name he hadn't heard in years. Wingard had been a professor of archeology and cultural anthropology at the University of Maryland and a good friend of their parents. And Joyce Wingard... now it came back to him. The last time he'd seen Joyce he'd been fifteen, and she'd been, what, seven? Their parents had taken them to spend the weekend with the professor and his niece at Wingard's home on the shore of the Potomac. Gabriel remembered an impatient little girl with blonde pigtails. During dinner, she'd called him stupid and dumped a bowl of potato salad in his lap.

"Joyce Wingard," Gabriel said. "What the hell is that little girl doing in Borneo?"

"Working toward her Ph.D., Gabriel. She's thirty years old."

"I guess she would be, at that," he said. *Thirty years old and probably still a terror.* "Does she have any field experience?"

"She didn't need any. This was just supposed to be a research trip."

"What was she researching?"

Michael got up and walked to a bookcase. He scanned the spines, pulled a weathered tome off the shelf, and brought it back to the couch. He sat next to Gabriel and opened the book. The title page said ANATOLIAN RELIGION AND CULTURE.

"Have you heard of the Three Eyes of Teshub?" Michael asked.

"I've heard of Teshub. Storm god of the Hittites, right?"

Michael turned the pages until he found the photograph he was looking for: a stone carving of a bearded man with a conical headdress standing on an ox's back. Beneath the photo was the caption TESHUB IDOL, 15TH–13TH CENTURY B.C.E. "According to legend, Teshub gave the Hittites a powerful weapon called the Spearhead to protect them from their enemies. But the Spearhead was so powerful that Teshub had second thoughts. He came to believe that even his beloved

Hittites lacked the wisdom to use such a weapon responsibly, so he took it away from them and hid it until some unspecified future date when three armies would meet in battle to decide its fate." He flipped the page and handed the book to Gabriel.

On the next page was an illustration of three enormous jewels. "Looks like an ad for DeBeers," Gabriel said.

Michael shook his head. "Those are the Three Eyes of Teshub. Supposedly, they were three gemstones that together were the key to using the Spearhead—or possibly to locating it, or perhaps to retrieving it from where it was hidden, the stories varied."

"Don't they always," Gabriel said. He downed the rest of his scotch.

"Documents from the period say that when Teshub hid the Spearhead away, he called up three winds to blow the gemstones in three different directions, scattering them as far apart as possible, so that they would never be found. People have looked for them, of course. No one has found any evidence that the Three Eyes of Teshub actually existed."

"But Joyce...?"

"Joyce discovered incomplete rubbings from a pair of tablets she thought might shed some light on the legend. The original tablets are buried away in the archives of Borneo University. She applied to us for a grant to cover the cost of her trip." Michael returned the book to its spot on the shelf. "Her application might not have leapt to the top of the stack otherwise, but..." He went back to his desk, checked for new e-mail once more. Nothing. "But how could I say no to Daniel Wingard's niece? And it wasn't much money. I figured no harm could come of it, a trip to

NICHOLAS KAUFMANN

a university library." He dropped into his chair. "And now she's missing. I've tried calling her, I've called our man down there, I've asked people at the university if they've seen her—nothing. Who knows what sort of trouble she might have gotten herself into? I couldn't live with myself if I thought anything had happened to her because of me."

Gabriel set his glass down on the table, pushed the box containing the mummy's hand to one side. "If you're really worried about her, Michael, I can go down there and look around a bit. Shouldn't be too hard to find her."

Michael shook his head firmly. "No. Bad enough that she's missing, think how I'd feel putting you in danger as well."

"Putting me in danger? You're kidding, right?" Gabriel said. "I don't think a week's gone by since Joyce Wingard was in pigtails when I wasn't in danger. It's what I do."

"And you know I've never been comfortable with it," Michael said. "I certainly wouldn't want to be the cause of it."

"You wouldn't be the cause," Gabriel said. "Joyce Wingard would. Besides, I haven't been to Borneo in ages. About time for a trip back."

"You might not recognize it," Michael said in a quiet voice. "Half the rainforest's gone."

"All the more reason to go now, before they cut down the other half."

"Gabriel…"

"She's probably fine, Michael. I'll probably find her in the museum archives, elbow deep in notes and files, with her phone turned off and no idea how long it's been since she last e-mailed you."

"But what if you don't?" Michael said.

Gabriel thought of the headstrong, impish, pigtailed girl chasing him around her uncle's picnic table, squealing with laughter as she tried to catch him. He remembered her showing him her toys, how she took special pride in one in particular, a Barbie dressed in safari gear and an explorer's pith helmet. He remembered her playing tag in the woods with Michael, who'd been only a couple years older than her. Joyce had fallen, skinned her knee on a rock, and wouldn't let anyone pick her up and carry her back to the house. She'd insisted on walking, even with blood trickling down her leg, and shouting that she could do it herself, didn't need anyone's help.

But this time maybe she did.

"Then you'll be glad I went," Gabriel said. "How soon can you have the plane ready?"

**DON'T MISS THE NEXT EXCITING
ADVENTURE OF GABRIEL HUNT!**

THE GABRIEL HUNT ADVENTURES

"A pulp adventure series with classic style and modern sensibilities... Escapism at its best."
Publishers Weekly

From the towers of Manhattan to the jungles of South America, from the sands of the Sahara to the frozen crags of Antarctica, one man finds adventure everywhere he goes: Gabriel Hunt.

Backed by the resources of the $100 million Hunt Foundation and armed with his trusty Colt revolver, Gabriel Hunt has always been ready for anything—but is he prepared for the adventures that lie in wait for him?

HUNT AT THE WELL OF ETERNITY
James Reasoner

The woman carrying the bloodstained flag seemed desperate for help—and the attack that followed convinced Gabriel she had something men would kill for. And that was before he knew about the legendary secret hidden in the rain forest of Guatemala...

HUNT AT WORLD'S END
(May 2014)
Nicholas Kaufmann

Three jewels, lost for centuries and scattered across the globe, hold the secret to a device of power, and only Gabriel can prevent them from falling into the hands of a Hittite cult—or of a rival bent on world domination...

TITANBOOKS.COM

HUNT BEYOND THE FROZEN FIRE
(June 2014)
Christa Faust

Dr. Lawrence Silver vanished while researching a mysterious phenomenon near the South Pole. His beautiful daughter wants to know where and why—and it's up to Gabriel Hunt to find out. But what they'll discover at the heart of nature's most brutal climate could change the world forever…

HUNT AMONG THE KILLERS OF MEN
(July 2014)
David J. Schow

The warlord's men came to New York to preserve a terrible secret—and left a dead body in their wake.
Now Gabriel Hunt is on their trail, a path that will take him to the treacherous alleyways and rooftops of Shanghai and a showdown with a madman out to resurrect a deadly figure from China's past…

HUNT THROUGH NAPOLEON'S WEB
(August 2014)
Raymond Benson

Of all the priceless treasures Gabriel Hunt has sought, none means more to him than the one drawing him to the rugged terrain of Corsica and the exotic streets of Marrakesh: his own sister's life. To save her, Hunt will have to challenge the mind of a tyrant two centuries dead—the calculating, ingenious Napoleon Bonaparte…

ALSO AVAILABLE FROM TITAN BOOKS

THE MATT HELM SERIES
Donald Hamilton

DEATH OF A CITIZEN
THE WRECKING CREW
THE REMOVERS
THE SILENCERS
MURDERERS' ROW
THE AMBUSHERS
THE SHADOWERS
THE RAVAGERS

Praise for Donald Hamilton

"Donald Hamilton has brought to the spy novel the authentic hard realism of Dashiell Hammett; and his stories are as compelling, and probably as close to the sordid truth of espionage, as any now being told."
Anthony Boucher, *The New York Times*

"This series by Donald Hamilton is the top-ranking American secret agent fare, with its intelligent protagonist and an author who consistently writes in high style. Good writing, slick plotting and stimulating characters, all tartly flavored with wit."
Book Week

"Matt Helm is as credible a man of violence as has ever figured in the fiction of intrigue."
The New York Sunday Times

"Fast, tightly written, brutal, and very good…"
Milwaukee Journal

TITANBOOKS.COM

HARD CASE CRIME
From Mickey Spillane & Max Allan Collins

THE CONSUMMATA
Mickey Spillane & Max Allan Collins

Compared to the $40 million the cops think he stole, $75,000 may not sound like much. But it's all the money in the world to the Cuban exiles who rescued Morgan the Raider. So when it's stolen, Morgan sets out to get it back.

DEAD STREET
Mickey Spillane

For 20 years, former NYPD cop Jack Stang has lived with the memory of his girlfriend's death. But what if she weren't actually dead? Now Jack has a second chance to save the only woman he ever loved—or to lose her for good…

DEADLY BELOVED
Max Allan Collins

Marcy Addwatter killed her husband—there's no question about that. But where the cops might see an open-and-shut case, private eye Michael Tree—*Ms.* Michael Tree—sees a conspiracy. Digging into it could mean digging her own grave… and digging up her own murdered husband's…

SEDUCTION OF THE INNOCENT
Max Allan Collins

Comics are corrupting America's youth. Or so Dr. Werner Frederick would have people believe. When the crusade provokes a murder, Jack Starr—comics syndicate troubleshooter—has no shortage of suspects.